The Peace of Sleep Was Denied Her.

As dawn painted the horizon a deep gold, Meryl was still trying to force sleep to take over her weary body. By the time the sun poured its rays through the blinds, she gave up and made her exhausted limbs move. Trying to ignore the perspiration that drenched her body, and her pounding head, she perched on the side of the bed.

How much longer could this go on? she lamented to herself as she cradled her head in her hands. It had been two years. An eternity. Dreams of Reese's mouth and hands as they had once caressed her body continued to haunt her nights. She drew a deep, shuddering breath.

If only . . .

Dear Reader:

There is an electricity between two people in love that makes everything they do magic, larger than life. This is what we bring you in SILHOUETTE INTIMATE MOMENTS.

SILHOUETTE INTIMATE MOMENTS are longer, more sensuous romance novels filled with adventure, suspense, glamor or melodrama. These books have an element no one else has tapped: excitement.

We are proud to present the very best romance has to offer from the very best romance writers. In the coming months look for some of your favorite authors such as Elizabeth Lowell, Nora Roberts, Erin St. Claire and Brooke Hastings.

SILHOUETTE INTIMATE MOMENTS are for the woman who wants more than she has ever had before. These books are for you.

Karen Solem
Editor-in-Chief
Silhouette Books

Memories
That Linger

Mary Lynn Baxter

Silhouette Intimate Moments
Published by Silhouette Books New York
America's Publisher of Contemporary Romance

To Mary Clare Susen
This one's yours! With love and gratitude.

SILHOUETTE BOOKS, a Division of Simon & Schuster, Inc.
1230 Avenue of the Americas, New York, N.Y. 10020

Copyright © 1984 by Mary Lynn Baxter

Distributed by Pocket Books

ISBN: 0-671-49673-5

First Silhouette Books printing May, 1984

10 9 8 7 6 5 4 3 2 1

America's Publisher of Contemporary Romance

Printed in the U.S.A.

Books by Mary Lynn Baxter

Silhouette Special Edition

Silhouette Desire

Silhouette Intimate Moments

Chapter 1

Galveston, Texas: Winter, 1982

AS THE DAMP COLD AIR ASSAULTED HIS SENSES, REESE CORBETT
breathed deeply into his already expanded lungs and upped
his pace, stretching his calf muscles to their limit. The
turbulent thoughts that had kept him awake most of the night
vanished, leaving him feeling refreshed and at peace with
himself. But his inner calm was short-lived. Against his will,
his thoughts once again shifted to the pain and bitterness in
his life.

If only Kathy had let him bring Jason with him . . . No! He
wouldn't allow himself to think about either of them now. He
simply could not handle it.

Instead, the words of his longtime friend and chief of staff
at the hospital came to mind: "Reese, the pressure's getting
to you. I haven't said anything before now, because I didn't
think it necessary. But when your problems start to interfere
with your capabilities as a surgeon, it's my duty to step in."

"Please, Emory," he had pleaded, "I just need a little
more time. Kathy's so close . . ."

"No, Reese. My mind's made up. I want you to take a
couple of weeks off, go back to that cabin on the beach and
do nothing but sleep, fish and exercise. What I'm telling you,
man, is that you have to pull yourself together. A lot of
people depend on your expertise, so you really have no
choice."

Again Reese increased his pace, positive he could outrun
his troubles. He savored the taste of the salty air as it slapped

7

him in the face, bringing with it another reprieve. He raised his head and gazed into the huge expanse of overcast sky, savoring yet another stolen moment of blessed tranquillity.

She was upon him before he realized it. In fact, if he had continued on his present course, they would have collided. He stepped aside automatically, letting his eyes rove over the refreshing loveliness of the girl now in his direct line of vision. But before he could fasten his eyes on her face, he was mesmerized by her rounded breasts that rose and fell in time with the graceful movement of her body.

Suddenly it dawned upon Reese what he was doing. He jerked his head back in an effort to right his senses, and their eyes met for only a moment. But in that moment Reese found himself drowning in a pair of liquid brown eyes that were a perfect backdrop for the delicate lines of her cheekbones and the sad, sultry shape of her lips.

She seemed embarrassed, trapped and agitated at having to acknowledge his presence. Her pace had slowed considerably, as had his, making it impossible for them to ignore each other. She gave him the slightest of nods as she glided by him, her dark curls tumbling in the breeze.

"Good morning," Reese said, a half-smile tilting the corners of his mouth. But he too made it a point to move past her as quickly and unobtrusively as possible. Gut instinct told him that even his polite greeting had been an unwelcome intrusion. He craned his neck over his left shoulder and watched her retreating figure continue its lonely vigil down the deserted beach. She seemed so lost. . . .

As his own feet continued to splatter the soft earth, his thoughts dwelt on the woman. There was something about her that both piqued his curiosity and pulled at his heartstrings. Was it perhaps the way she tightened up when she realized she couldn't completely ignore him? Or was it the seemingly defeated air about her? Or, closer to the truth, was it the fact that she had *wanted* to ignore him? He wasn't used to that kind of treatment from women.

Hell, man! Have you lost your friggin' mind? That kind of

thinking was not only crazy, it was totally absurd. Here he was feeling miffed because a total stranger failed to notice him, but worse than that, he was feeling sorry for someone who probably didn't even need his sympathy, much less want it. He gave a disdainful laugh. She was more than likely a happily married woman with a burly husband and two pink-cheeked children waiting for her back at their cabin.

Anyway, didn't he have more on his plate than he could take care of? He certainly didn't need to speculate about someone else's possible misfortunes, even if that someone was one of the loveliest creatures he had ever seen.

With a harsh sigh he forced his legs to come to an abrupt halt and, totally ignoring the loud beating of his heart and the tingling in his calf muscles, he turned and made his way back toward his silent and empty cabin, his shoulders folded in dejection.

The blustery salt air whipped across Meryl's face as she stepped out of the cabin just as dawn was peeping over the bay. She shivered, tightening the drawstrings around the neck of her jogging suit to ward off the dampening chill.

This was the first time she had come to the cabin since Elliot's death a year ago. She should do something with this place, she thought. But for some reason she was loath to do so; maybe it was because it was her only hiding place. Here she could nurse her loneliness and insecurities without being under the watchful eye of her twin sister, Morgana, and other well-meaning friends.

Another sharp chill made her shiver. Quickly wrapping her arms tightly around her slender frame, she sat down on the edge of the step. She retied a loose shoelace and then for a moment raised her knees and hugged them close to her chest. These days, nothing seemed to penetrate her clouded senses. No matter how hard she tried, she could not shake the feeling of despondency that dogged her every footstep. It went hand in hand with her barren and indecisive life.

She was on her own, she might as well face it. Why couldn't

she pick up the pieces and go on? She wasn't the only woman to lose her husband to the dreadful hands of lung cancer. But lately she had felt that the wall she had built around herself was beginning to crumble. She knew it was time to get on with her life, to make a stand, to make decisions. But how?

Even at thirty-three, she felt there had to be something productive she could still do with her life. If only she weren't so alone. If only she'd been able to have the child Elliot wanted so desperately. She knew he had never forgiven her, not once during their fifteen years of marriage. And she had never forgiven herself.

The day before she left for the beach, hadn't Morgana raked her over the coals, body and soul, for her continued obsession about this very thing?

"Dammit, Meryl," she had said, "why do you punish yourself like this? Elliot's gone and there's nothing you or anyone else can do to bring him back. My God, you gave him the best years of your life as it was. You were nothing but a slave—"

"Stop it, Morgana!" she had cried. "I won't let you talk about Elliot this way. Have you no shame, saying vile things about the dead?" She sniffed back the tears. "After all, he was my husband, and I owed it to him."

"Garbage!" Morgana hissed brutally. "That's Aunt Sophia talking, and you know it. Thank God one of us had enough sense to ignore those words she preached to us daily: 'A woman's place is always in the home, beside her husband, doing his bidding,'" she mimicked. "God forbid!"

"What on earth am I going to do?" Meryl wailed, and wrapped her arms tightly around her slender body. "I'm so lost. . . ."

"I can tell you what you're going to do, sister dear, you're going to let go of the past and concentrate on the future. Have you looked in the mirror lately? You are wasting away to nothing, and you're pale as a zombie." She crossed the room and hugged Meryl close against her, all the while brushing the tear-dampened curls off her face. "Don't you think you've tortured yourself long enough for not giving him a child?"

"Oh, Morgana," Meryl cried, "if only I'd loved him, I mean really loved him, things might have been different."

"Be realistic. It wasn't your fault he had cancer. For two years you waited on him and took care of him. You did your best, Meryl, and that's all a person can do."

"How can you be so insensitive?"

Morgana's eyes turned into chips of ice. "By God, someone needs to make you see the light, before it's too late!"

Suddenly tired of her dreary thoughts, Meryl jumped up and got in position to do her morning warm-ups. As she began bending from side to side, forcing her stiff limbs to loosen up, an ironic smile crossed her lips. She must be crazy, she thought, to get out of her snug bed in forty-degree weather in order to run a mile, but lately these long exercise sessions had been her salvation.

Meryl dipped down and began touching the tips of alternate shoes with her fingers, purposely emptying her mind of all thoughts. Feeling the kinks slowly fade from her body, she turned and began the long trek down the deserted stretch of beach.

Then she saw him. He was headed toward her. This time he would pass her and she would be forced to speak to him. Damn! Meryl closed her eyes briefly, hoping he would disappear. But when her eyes flew back open, nothing had changed. The gloomy overcast morning was still with her, and the handsome stranger was still making his way toward her.

The second Meryl dragged her body into the suffocating warmth of the snug three-room cabin, she pitched her earmuffs on the nearest chair and collapsed on the couch. She ignored the stiffness and bluish tint of her fingers, having forgotten her gloves, as her thoughts drifted back to the man on the beach. She was still trying to recover from the tremor of excitement that had shot through her body when he had spoken to her. Such a deep and pleasant voice, too, she thought.

Today was not the first time she had seen him. When she had arrived three days ago, his tall strapping figure had caught her attention as he swept past her, obviously out for a morning run. She had been unloading the trunk of the car and had paused and watched him for several seconds.

Although she had not been privy to a close-up view of him, she was nevertheless aware that he could be labeled a rare specimen of manhood. From afar she had admired the whipcord leanness of his frame, clothed in a pair of navy sweat pants and hooded jacket as his feet pounded the wet sand in perfect time to the swishing of the surf and the mane of dark hair, battered about his head by the wind.

She had wondered what he was doing here on the beach this time of the year. Alone. She had been positive he was alone. There had been something about the man, about his early-morning run, that had made him seem too vulnerable, too solitary, too alone. Her plight exactly, she had thought.

Realizing what a ridiculous turn her thoughts had taken, she had abruptly slammed down the trunk and with it had banished further thoughts of the stranger from her mind.

But now here he was again uppermost in her mind. Seeing him at close range and being forced to acknowledge his presence had strangely upset her.

She wanted to be alone with no outside interference of any kind, which meant that she wanted to avoid any casual acquaintances. Just knowing he was staying three cabins down from her was unsettling. She rubbed her aching temple, feeling another bout of depression wash over her.

And it was all *his* fault! She couldn't seem to delete from her mind the loneliness he represented, leaving her feeling curious and fascinated at the same time. Suddenly irritated with herself for these useless musings, she hurled herself off the couch and stomped toward the bedroom, stripping her clothes from her body as she went.

What the hell! She couldn't care less if he was lonely or not. But somehow that wasn't quite the truth. It was just sex rearing its head, she argued. It was that simple. She had been without a man too long. *That's all it is!*

Meryl gave in to the stinging spray of the water as it pelted her sensitive skin with undue force, desperate for any remedy that would revive her falling spirits. Fifteen minutes later she emerged from the bedroom fully dressed in a pair of faded jeans and a V-neck velour sweater. Her chocolate-auburn curls clung in soft tendrils to her heart-shaped face, giving her natural beauty an added freshness.

She was determined to salvage the remainder of the day, and a loud hum parted her soft lips as she strode into the kitchen with the sole intention of satisfying the hunger pangs that gnawed at her insides. She had just cracked an egg in the skillet and stood watching it sizzle in butter when a subdued knock on the door diverted her attention.

With a frown marring her features, she turned the burner on simmer and scurried to the door. She knew before she opened it who would be standing there. Her pulse quickened as she placed her hand on the doorknob and slowly drew it toward her.

He was leaning nonchalantly against the doorjamb, an apologetic expression on his face. "Hope you don't mind the intrusion, but . . ." His voice trailed off as his eyes fell to the object dangling from his right hand. It was a measuring cup.

For a moment Meryl looked completely baffled. Then a dimpled smile broke across her lips. "Milk or sugar, which is it?" she asked.

His smoke-velvet eyes were dazzling and so was his sheepish grin. "An omelet doesn't taste worth a damn without milk," he admitted apologetically, his facial expression that of a lost little boy.

In spite of her efforts to remain aloof and unresponsive, Meryl's eyes came alive with an answering twinkle. She stepped aside. "By all means, come in. Never let it be said that I stood in the way of a man trying to cook."

He stepped inside and laughed, the sound of it cutting through Meryl like a knife. It was a deep, uninhibited laughter that she could listen to forever and never get tired of. *God, what rubbish!* she thought, before turning to meet his quizzical gaze.

Then the bottom dropped out of her stomach. They just stood and stared at each other; a strange fluid passion seemed to flow from his eyes into her.

Meryl tried to swallow and relieve the tight band that had formed around her throat, but she couldn't. She was held powerless by the smoldering intensity of his gaze. Up close, he was startlingly handsome. But older than she had first guessed. Silver threads were interwoven throughout his chestnut-colored hair, giving him a distinguished look, far above his actual age, she knew. (She judged him to be in his early to middle forties.)

His maturity was reinforced by the faint lines that fanned out from his eyes. But there was more than just the experience of years in the velvet gray eyes. In their depths one could almost capture a sense of suffering and something else. Was it sadness?

She studied his thin but beautifully shaped lips, the aquiline nose, the hard squareness of his jawline and the faint suggestion of a cleft in his chin. Yes indeed, he was a fine specimen of manhood.

"Are you intimating that the men in your life aren't adept in the culinary arts?" he asked, his teasing grin helping to smooth the lines of tension in his face and shatter the breathless silence that surrounded them.

Meryl bit her lip and purposely shifted her eyes. The man had completely unnerved her. The intensity of her attraction to him was overwhelming and so unreal that she was at a total loss as to how to handle it. She felt herself unraveling.

She struggled for something to say. "I've . . . never known too many men who even bothered to try to cook," she muttered inanely. Now, why had she said something stupid like that? Who cared if this stranger could cook or not? Damn! She must indeed be slipping.

"Well, this one at least tries, but that's about as far as it goes. I'm like a bull in a china shop when it comes to the kitchen." A smile twitched at the corners of his mouth.

She smiled in return, and he realized suddenly just how lovely she was when she smiled and how attracted he was to the sound of her voice. It was low and husky, different, but somehow it suited her.

He cleared his throat as he reluctantly pulled his eyes away from her and looked around him. God! What must she be thinking of him, staring at her like some starry-eyed teenager? *Fool!* he chastised himself. *Don't make the mistake of getting to know this woman, Corbett. So you're lonely. So what? You can survive—others have. Think of Jason. He's the top priority in your life, the only thing you should be concerned with.*

He stood gazing at the surprisingly high beamed ceiling and the skylight under which were several plants hanging suspended. Instead of adding clutter to the small room, the greenery seemed to give it added dimension. The only furniture consisted of a brightly cushioned love seat and matching chair, with a solid oak coffee table. Across the room a small Franklin stove occupied a corner. A hanging Tiffany lamp graced the opposite one and was glowing softly. The floor was covered by a woven rug. It had an air of hominess about it that had a settling effect on his jangled nerves.

"This place is great, a far cry from mine." He rammed his hands down into his pockets. "From the looks of things, I take it you're not a first-timer here?" Refusing to heed his own warning, he wanted to know everything about her.

"No . . . but actually it has been over a year since I've been here," she answered from the kitchen, trying to curb the jittery restlessness she felt.

Reese followed the sound of her voice into the adjacent room, where she stood by the counter filling his cup with milk. His eyes then strayed to the stove and saw the half-done egg in the pan.

"Why didn't you tell me I was interrupting your breakfast?" His tone was mildly chastising.

"You didn't." She wet her lips. "Well, you did, but it doesn't matter," she added hurriedly, feeling like an idiot with her adolescent stammering.

She hadn't convinced him. There was a moment of awkward silence as Reese shifted his weight to one foot and then the other. "Well, I'll just take the milk and get out of your way."

There was another short silence.

She smiled, and then, surprising even herself, said, "But we haven't introduced ourselves." Her good sense seemed to have completely deserted her. "I'm Meryl Stevens." She held out her hand to him and it became immediately lost in his firm grasp. The contact created a loud thumping in her chest.

He was reluctant to let it go. "I'm Reese Corbett. Dr. Reese Corbett." The moment he said those words he was sorry. God, he sounded like a pompous ass! But he had worked long and hard, not to mention overcoming insurmountable odds, for the right to call himself "doctor," and he was proud of it. But he couldn't voice those feelings aloud. It would only make him look worse in her eyes.

But she seemed to be able to read those hidden thoughts. Her next words proved this as she carefully disengaged her hand. "I don't blame you, Dr. Corbett. If I had 'doctor' in front of my name, I'd be proud of it too."

He blinked, feeling more like a jerk by the minute. Without even knowing the reason why, he wanted to impress Meryl Stevens, dangerous though it was, and the harder he tried, the more asinine he sounded.

He reached for the cup of milk on the countertop, moving closer to her. This sudden motion caused her eyes to fly upward. She stared at his strong neck, where the muscles tensed and the blue veins showed faintly under his tanned skin.

"I'm not in the habit of tooting my own horn, if you know what I mean," he said softly, his minty breath whispering against her cheek.

She didn't dare move, afraid it would be visibly rude if she did. But his proximity was somehow threatening. He was so real, so overpowering; he dwarfed the kitchen.

"I understand," she said simply. And somehow he knew she did. There was something about this quiet woman that inspired confidence and radiated understanding. And God knows that was an ingredient that had been missing from his life for a long time.

Still he did not move. He was so near she could smell the freshness of his shirt, the aftereffects of his morning spray of cologne. He smelled very good, very male.

"Is your practice in Houston?" she asked, desperately trying to keep her mind on track. She turned and poured herself a hot cup of coffee and automatically reached in the cabinet for an extra cup.

"That's right." He smiled, looking down at her again. "On Fannin, in the Medical Center. You are familiar with Houston, aren't you?" She had such clear, smooth skin.

It was obvious he was fishing for information about her. She was flattered. And she saw no reason to keep where she lived a secret. What a curious effect this stranger had on her, she thought. She knew instantly that he was a man she was going to like, and yet also . . . fear. She was not ready to become involved with another man, not really. Maybe sexually she was—she'd admit that—but not emotionally. And with this man, she knew she could not have one without the other.

"Actually, I live in Houston too," she answered a trifle shakily, handing him a cup of coffee at the same time.

"What part?"

"Memorial."

"Nice area. There was a noticeable pause. "I almost built a house there once."

This time he made no effort to hide the grimace of pain that flickered across his strong features. It was there for the whole world to see. Meryl turned away and unconsciously headed for the family room. She couldn't bear to witness his suffering. It was suddenly like seeing a mirror of her own soul. She shuddered.

In reality it was only a moment before he followed her, the mask carefully back in place. "Sorry," he apologized, before an engaging grin relaxed his mouth and eased the lines around his eyes. "It seems no matter how hard we try, we can't always run from our past, can we?"

"I thought I was the only one with that problem." She laughed, but the laughter failed to reach her eyes. Then, deciding this conversation was headed in the wrong direction, she quickly changed the subject.

"How about yourself, do you come here often?" she asked.

Reese thought for a moment. "Unfortunately, no. This is only my second time. Actually I'm just borrowing the cabin for a few weeks from a buddy of mine." A note of grimness had again infiltrated his voice, making it low and raspy. "And not because I wanted to, either. It was all under duress."

Meryl waited for him to explain further, but he didn't. Instead he smiled suddenly, a sweet, beguiling smile that caused her heart to flutter. His eyes spoke volumes.

"But now I'm glad I came," he said softly. "I need a friend, Meryl Stevens. Are you willing to be that friend?"

A wave of sexual warmth touched her as she stared at him for a moment, pondering her unease. She was attracted to him, alarmingly so. But despite his easy banter, she sensed a tension in him, a brooding unhappiness that festered deep within.

The warning bells clanged loud and clear inside her head, but for some reason she pushed them aside, determined to ignore them. She realized with a shock that she was feeling sorry for this stranger. If she were smart, though, she would steer clear of him. Judging from what he had just said on top of his other comments, he had more problems than she. And she'd bet it had to do with a woman, too. Suddenly a ripple of jealousy coursed through her veins. God! What was happening to her?

She picked at the cover on the decorator pillow on which she leaned an elbow. She was trying to collect her scattered thoughts. "Exactly what did you have in mind?" Her voice sounded foreign even to her own ears. It, too, was low and husky. And her eyes seemed to devour him, staring, half-wild, half-afraid.

Excitement rose in his blood, only to recede just as quickly. What could he say? he thought. Don't be afraid of me? Because it's not true. *Be afraid of me!* He was as dangerous as a man dying of thirst who had stumbled upon water in a dry desert. His gaze traveled unobtrusively from her face to her breasts. No bra. The nipples were large, the hard shape of them visible under her sweater.

Reese forced his breathing to become normal, although his mouth felt like it was full of sawdust. "For starters, how about a few minutes of friendly conversation?" Although his eyes were serious, Meryl couldn't help but notice the grin that flirted with the corner of his lips.

Meryl sensed something was wrong. He seemed tight as a violin string, but she played along with him. "I've no objection to that," she said coolly.

"Are you here on vacation?" He leaned over for his coffee, which was in easy reach of his fingertips.

Meryl couldn't help but notice his hands. They were a surgeon's dream: broad hands with long narrow fingers and clean nails. And they appeared so capable, yet gentle and sensitive. She'd be willing to bet they knew how to bring a woman to the ultimate heights of pleasure.

Feeling a dot of crimson stain each cheek, she forced herself to curb her errant musings. "You might call it that. Actually I'm here for both business and pleasure."

He smiled. "I thought I was the only crazy one for choosing to come to the beach in the middle of winter. But now that I'm actually here, I find the wind, the sea gulls, and the deserted beach a welcome relief from the pressures of my job." He failed to add that it was more than a welcome relief from his personal problems as well.

Meryl's eyes widened. "Funny, but that's how I feel too. I love the outdoors—jogging, fishing, swimming." She wrinkled up her nose. "I guess I'd rather be exercising than eating."

"I can tell."

Be careful. Play it cool. She forced herself to sip slowly on her coffee, forbidding her hands to waver. "Oh, really?" she said with feigned disinterest.

"Don't worry, you're perfect the way you are."

His words put her immediately on the defensive. She frowned. "I wasn't worried in the least."

Dammit, he couldn't seem to do anything right, he thought contritely. Knowing he had made her uncomfortable as well as himself, he quickly switched the conversation. "Do you work?" he asked, concentrating on how gracefully she moved as she tucked her feet up under her.

A sigh escaped her lips. "No . . . no, I don't. However, I hope to change that in the near future."

"How's that?" he pressed.

She laughed, but it had a hollow ring to it even to her own ears. "I'm not sure . . . yet."

He looked confused. "Care to explain?"

"I'm a widow," she said bluntly. She heard his sharp intake of breath before she plunged on. "It was a year ago this week . . . that my husband died, and so far I haven't been able to piece my life back together."

"Did you love him?" The words tumbled out of his mouth before he could stop them. Immediately he wished he could recall them, but too late; the damage was done. He watched as the color receded from her face, leaving it tissue-paper white.

Meryl was taken aback at his bluntness. She groped for words to answer him. "Not . . . not like I should have," she admitted truthfully. "We . . . we married young." She struggled to keep her voice even. "Over the years we seemed to grow apart; then he became ill . . ." She couldn't go on. God, what was she doing? she asked herself. For one thing, she was doing all the talking, baring her soul to this man. She couldn't believe it. Time to reverse the questions.

Reese said nothing. He was feeling more like an ass by the second. She must think him an insensitive fool. But how the hell was he to know? *You should have known,* an inner voice taunted. *You* should have known something out of the ordinary had happened. No woman that's a cross between Farah Fawcett and Jaclyn Smith would be alone on a deserted beach unless *something* was wrong. *Dammit, Corbett, you're treading on dangerous ground, asking for trouble. Back off!*

"Your turn."

Her quietly spoken words brought him back to reality. "I beg your pardon?"

"What about yourself?" *Why are you here alone?* she wanted to add, but didn't. *Go ahead, find out what you want to know,* she urged herself. *Satisfy your curiosity, then tell him to get the hell out and leave you alone.*

Meryl saw him stiffen, although he tried to disguise it. "It's a long story, dull and very boring," he said. This time he made no effort to curtail the bitterness in his voice. "I won't burden you with the details." Then he smiled, transforming his features. "But this midwinter vacation is just what the doctor ordered—no pun intended—and I aim to make the most of it."

So much for his deep, dark secrets, she thought, turning abruptly and reaching for the small coffeepot. She then picked up their cups and refilled them with the hot liquid, trying not to look at him. She was convinced now that a woman had done a number on him. Wife? Ex-wife? It sounded like he'd just been through a nasty divorce, she thought. The signs were there. The same ones that Morgana had sported when she went through her divorce.

Even though she had shifted her gaze, Reese knew her eyes would be soft and round and troubled. She had naked eyes.

An unusual dark brown color, almost black, surrounded by long thick lashes that often served as a screen to hide her pain and vulnerability. Suddenly he ached to hold her.

Having sat back down, Meryl tried to relax, drinking her coffee. But her eyes migrated back to his face. He had a masculine nose, strong and well-defined, though not perfect. An added curve made her think of a possible football injury. That would go hand in hand with the long-limbed looseness he seemed to possess naturally. Her mind played a terrible trick on her, suddenly creating a heavily detailed image of the two of them naked together. Naked and prone. *Stop it!*

"Do you run every morning?" she asked. Anything to vanish that image. "I've only been doing it faithfully for about six months, but now I can't imagine not getting up every morning and hitting the jogging trail." She paused and smiled mischievously. "After I got rid of my shin splints, that is." She knew she was rattling, but she couldn't stop talking any more than she could stop staring at him.

He laughed, the sound instantly putting her at ease. "It's been many a year since I suffered that malady, but nothing, and I mean nothing, will ever erase the memory of it from my mind, either." He tried to determine the shape of her breasts under the sweater, but couldn't get a definite impression, nor could he control the color that rose into his face at not being able to halt his profound curiosity about a woman's body.

"I've often thought I'd like to teach other women the proper way to exercise and take care of their bodies." A self-conscious smile crossed her lips. "I know that sounds absurd to you," she said soberly, "but I'd really like to try it." Her eyes sparkled with excitement. Then the excitement disappeared just as quickly as it had appeared. She felt like a fool, voicing aloud her idiotic dreams and fantasies.

"I think that's a great idea!"

Meryl shook her head. "Please . . . don't. I could never . . ." She spread her hands. "I'm just talking—it means nothing . . ."

"Hey, don't talk like that," he commanded, inching closer

in his effort to build her confidence. "Why not try it? With your lissome figure, you could certainly be an example to the ones that are less fortunate than you."

"Well"—she cleared her throat, still uncomfortable at blurting out her dreams to this man—"we'll see."

His eyes grew serious. "Don't ever lose sight of your dreams," he said, studying the expression in her solemn eyes. "Promise me you'll give it serious thought."

Meryl swallowed the lump in her throat and then threw him a watery smile. "Maybe I will at that."

"Atta girl," he said, reaching over and briefly squeezing her hand before getting up. "I'd better be getting back," he added. "I've monopolized too much of your time already."

"Oh, wait," she said rather breathlessly, her hand still tingling from where he touched her, "don't forget your milk." She all but ran into the kitchen, relief easing her muscles. She was glad he was going. He knew too much, saw too much.

"Thanks," he said, looking uncomfortable at once, glancing toward the door.

She swept past him to open the door, then stood looking up at him. "Come again," she said, a thread of uncertainty running through her voice. If she had any sense, she'd make it a point to stay away from him. He was dangerous, big and dangerous. And definitely not for her.

"You can count on it," he said softly. By sheer force of will he kept his eyes from peering once again at the pointed outline of her nipples as they pushed against the soft fabric. Instead he wondered how it would be to kiss her mouth, those soft-looking full lips. Oh, God! A treacherous combination. "You make great coffee."

"Thank you."

There was a moment of awkward silence; then he went out the door. She stood leaning against the doorjamb, watching him.

At the end of the steps, he stopped and turned around. "Maybe you'd like to go sailing with me sometime," he offered.

"I'd like that," she answered politely. But the bad part about it was that she would. But he'd never ask. They were both just being polite.

He squinted his eyes and stared at her for what seemed like an eternity and then turned and walked away. "See you."

Meryl stood and watched him, biting down on her lip and using every ounce of willpower she possessed not to call him back.

Chapter 2

SHE WAS MISERABLE. FOR THE REMAINDER OF THE MORNING AND the three days that followed, nothing she did appeased her. She tried dabbling in her oil painting, she even hand-laundered several articles of clothing, she exercised for hours, she jogged, she walked longer hours, always keeping her eyes peeled for the sight of his hard-toned body; he never appeared. Yet nothing could undermine the fact that she wanted to be with *him*.

Instead of forming concrete plans for her future, what was she doing? She was mooning over a total stranger, that's what! A stranger, she sensed, who wouldn't seek her out again, no matter how much he wanted to.

The electricity was undeniable. But he would hold back, not give in to it. It was there, in his eyes, the uncertainty, the caution, the fright. Or were those just glossed-over terms for the word *rejection?* she wondered.

"Damn!" she vented aloud, jerking the needle of the stereo, oblivious of the horrendous scraping sound that followed. Her chest suddenly tightened with anger. Why was she doing this to herself? She'd had ample opportunities to go out with men since Elliot's death, but she hadn't had the slightest inclination to do so. Until now. God! What was so special about this man? She didn't know. She honestly didn't know.

And why the hell was she fighting this sudden attraction so violently? Why not give in to it? Was it because *she* was still afraid? Beads of perspiration dotted her forehead. She had never denied that Elliot's taunting remarks had gotten to her. But obviously they had done much more damage to her self-image than she'd ever imagined.

"That's a cop-out and you know it," she raged aloud, the harsh words ricocheting off the walls with the force of a bullet. *Your problem, Meryl Stevens, is physical. Just the unmistakable urge to feel a warm, muscular body drape over yours. Ignore it. It'll go away.*

But it didn't. She felt trapped at every turn. Every time his face and body swam before her eyes, she became slightly more pliant inside with needing and wanting, only then to feel torn into two individual parts by her body's betrayal and her mind's determination to keep her distance at all costs.

Finally at wits' end as to how to regain control of her body and soul, she decided the next best thing was to feed it. A cup of tea and a salad sounded good, she thought, reminding herself that she couldn't ignore the needs of her body just because her mind was in shambles. Then maybe she would be able to run two, maybe three miles. When all else failed, she could always count on that to soothe and unclutter her mind. It had to work. It just had to.

Reese Corbett paced back and forth across the room until he was certain he had worn a trail in the already damaged carpet. Damn! But he hadn't wanted to leave her. And for the past three days he'd had to physically restrain himself from going to her cabin. He had confined himself to this one room and shuffled through mounds of paperwork that he'd stuffed into his briefcase almost as an afterthought, never intending to open it, until he was nearly stark raving mad. He was absolutely fixated on the idea of seeing her again. Why? He couldn't figure it out.

Today was no different. He stalked to the window, shoving the curtains aside, and stared out into another overcast and gloomy day. He recalled the mysterious darkness of her eyes, her daintiness, the haunting perfection of her mouth. It was alluring, though not intentionally. He couldn't figure her out. He was intrigued, bemused.

What harm could there be in seeing her again? he asked himself logically. As a friend, nothing more. Then a cold sobering note shook him to the core. *Just who in the bloody hell do you think you're kidding?* He had no business whatsoever having anything to do with this woman. She was off limits. His shoulders sagged against the glass. But deep down he knew this quiet, unassuming woman would be a balm to his battered heart. *But only if you keep friendly,* he cautioned himself again. If for no other reason, just being with her would keep his mind free of his own tangled problems. Today. Just for today, he promised himself. He wouldn't allow himself to think beyond that.

His mind made up, he took a quick shower, threw on a pair of faded jeans, a sweatshirt and a windbreaker. As he slammed the door behind him, he paused and drew a long, shuddering breath before walking in the direction of her cabin.

Unconsciously his steps faltered. If he had half a brain, he'd turn around and scratch this plan, he thought. Already he was letting things get out of perspective. Visions of her hands, long and tapered, the vulnerability of her exposed throat, the allure of her rounded breasts, teasingly full and free beneath her clothing, drew him steadily forward.

She answered the door, a startled look on her face. She blinked her eyes as if to bring him into focus. Had she been sleeping? he wondered, taking in the disarray of her curls and the long lounging robe that concealed everything, yet allowed his imagination free rein.

"Were you asleep?" he asked, feeling overheated.

"No, no I wasn't." A flush crept up her neck and into her cheeks as she realized she was naked beneath her robe. She smiled at him tentatively to try to cover up her embarrassment.

Reese stood motionless and watched as her smile faded.

They just stared at each other, not saying anything, just staring, both their thoughts splintering in the same direction: It was almost as if they had known each other forever, and questions were asked not because they didn't know the answers but because it was so good to hear the other's voice, one soft and the other strong like the wind whipping across the sea.

"Would you like to go sailing with me . . . now?" he blurted out before he lost his courage.

Seeing the confusion settle across her features, he persisted. "You *do* like to sail, don't you?" he asked in what he hoped was a nonchalant tone, while conscious of the perspiration that had popped out on his upper lip. He had never in his life been so blatantly aroused by a woman, not even Kathy, never Kathy, as he was by this one. And God knows he'd had his share of women in his span of forty-one years.

She looked at him with uncertainty, her mouth slightly open, her eyes big and round. "Would you believe it if I told you I'd never been in a sailboat?"

"I'd believe it." His smile almost stopped her heart. "Care to rectify that?"

"Are you serious?" she asked breathlessly.

"You bet."

She sighed. "I don't know . . ."

"Come on, you don't really have anything better to do, do you?" he asked, stopping short of pleading. His eyes were bright, intense.

Meryl stood speechless and gave in to the warm aching tightness that twisted in her belly as his deep penetrating stare sent a charge of electricity crackling between them.

Dare she do something frivolous for a change and spend the remainder of the day in this man's company? Well, why not? she asked herself. Wasn't this what she'd been wanting? It would be absurd now to deny she found him utterly fascinating, especially after she had carried on like a lovesick teenager for three days. And furthermore, what harm could she come to by merely exchanging nonsensical chatter with him? He was merely being personable. *No big deal.*

"All right," she murmured, "I'll go." The nonchalance of her comment was marred slightly by the flags of color that rose to her cheeks.

"Great." He grinned, his eyes dancing now with excitement. "Grab a warm coat, gloves, the works, and meet me in front of my cabin. It'll take me a minute to get things together."

Meryl's head was reeling. She was suddenly frightened. Things were moving much too rapidly to suit her. "What . . . what about food?" Not giving him time to answer, she went on, stalling for time. "At least let me fix us a bit of something before we go."

"Good idea. Why don't you just pack a couple of bacon-and-tomato sandwiches." He grinned and patted his flat stomach. "They'll taste mighty yummy after we set sail." Velvet gray eyes held hers an instant longer; then he waved and strolled out the door with leisurely assurance, whistling cheerfully.

Meryl sat motionless for a moment after the door swung shut on squeaky hinges behind him. She couldn't believe the sudden turn of events. Earlier she had been frightfully alone, bemoaning the fact that she would probably never see him again, only to have him seek her out and ask her to spend the day with him—or practically the whole day, she amended quickly.

She was strangely excited, yet there was an underlying uneasiness associated with the venture. But she couldn't quite put her finger on what it was. What difference could it possibly make? she scolded herself severely. She would most likely never cross paths with him after today, except on the jogging path. *For heaven's sake, Meryl, don't go borrowing trouble.*

It took her exactly twenty minutes to hustle herself into a

pair of jeans and a sweater, prepare the bacon sandwiches, which she immediately wrapped in foil to keep warm, fill a thermos with freshly perked coffee, and grab her coat, earmuffs and gloves. She dashed out the front door and slammed it behind her.

He met her halfway, a frown on his face. "I've been thinking, why don't we scratch the sailing idea and instead walk awhile on the beach, then build a fire and have our picnic?" He paused and looked around him. "I don't like the looks of this weather. I figure though by midafternoon the wind will have quieted and perhaps we'll even see the sun." He shook his head. "But right now I don't much like the idea of taking you out in the sailboat."

Her eyes were apprehensive as they looked up at him and then at the sky. "That's fine with me." She grinned. "I guess we can eat our soggy sandwiches on the beach as well as in the boat."

He was like an eager boy. "Let's get started. I know a perfect place to have our picnic."

"Would . . . would you mind if I stopped every so often and looked for unusual shells?" she asked, determined to have something to occupy her hands and her mind. Again she was shy and uneasy of this big man at her side who had the power to make her forget everything except his presence.

Reese flashed her a bright easy smile, hoping to put her at ease. "Don't tell me you're one of 'those' collectors?"

She laughed delightfully and cut her eyes sideways at him. "Well, as a matter of fact, I am. I have about three or four boxes full, stashed under my bed at home, not counting the dozens I have on a whatnot shelf." She shrugged softly. "I think I must have scavenger blood in me from somewhere."

"I bet you're also a pack rat . . . never wanting to throw anything away for fear you may need or want it ten years from now." Laughter was spilling from his eyes. He felt wonderful.

"Unfortunately, and as much as I hate to admit it, you're right," she answered saucily.

"Well, then, let's get to work. Never let it be said I stood in the way of you cornering the market on shells."

"Lead on," she said with a grin.

They walked in silence, each enjoying and soaking up the sights of the barren Texas coastline along with smelling the odor of fish, pungent in the early-morning air.

Although it was an unconscious movement on both their parts, it seemed the most natural thing in the world for their hands to become entwined as they continued to amble wordlessly along the beach with the rough surf pounding in their ears.

Reese's fingers were callused and strong as he gently swung Meryl's hand in time with their slow, even strides. When he had first folded her small hand within his, she felt as if she had been plugged into a live socket. Sparks shot up her arm straight through her breasts and into her heart. But she made no move to pull away. She had no intention of breaking this sudden threat of heady excitement that bound them so tenuously together. This whole feeling was not only crazy but temporary, and she intended to savor each one of these stolen moments.

"Hey, here's a real beauty!" Reese announced excitedly as he bent down suddenly and began digging a partially embedded shell out of the sand.

This sudden action on Reese's part caught Meryl off guard. "Damn!" she groaned as she stumbled, making an all-out effort to dodge his crouched form, but instead she plowed into the muscled hardness of his upper thigh and completely lost her balance. Her hand gripped the front of his jacket for added support to keep herself from groveling in the wet sand.

At the sudden contact of their bodies, she heard Reese's terse expletive before he turned and looked up at her with a dangerous glint in his eyes. Suddenly time had no meaning. Then, leisurely, as if in slow motion, he reached up and pulled her gently down beside him, his eyes drinking in the lovely curves of her face. Then, without hesitation or provocation, he kissed her eyelids and the tip of her cold nose and her cheeks and the round smoothness of her chin and her throat, kissing her over and over, going over the same places.

"Oh, God, Meryl." His voice was vibrant with emotion. "What have you done to me?"

The sweet agony in his voice turned Meryl's bones to warm butter. She felt her legs threaten to snap beneath her, both from his exquisite touch and the awkwardness of her position. Still in a hypnotic daze, she leaned heavily against him as they rose together.

She peered up at him from under silky eyelashes, her breathing shallow as she tried to control her disturbed feelings. She reached up and brushed the taut column of his throat with her hand. He flinched then, almost as though her touch had burned his skin.

"*Meryl!*" he exclaimed with sudden violence, shoving her away from him. "Don't look at me like that! I can just stand so much and no more." He ran his hand through his hair, not bothering to mask his agitation.

She shivered before turning away. She, too, was at a loss as to how to handle this situation.

After that, there was no more holding hands. In fact, Meryl was positive Reese went out of his way not to touch her. It was best that way, she thought. She feared it would take only one more passionate look, one more tender touch, to spark the flame of passion that simmered just beneath the surface. She didn't know if she was ready for that. It remained an enigma to her how this man could cause her heart to beat wildly with as little as a look.

"Do you think you've collected enough?" Reese asked after both their jackets were bulging with all types of shells. "I'm starving, how about you?" he added, striving like hell to lighten the mood of the moment. But from past experience he knew he was fighting a losing battle. The ache within him had resumed its insistent clamor, and the tight rein on his control was slipping.

"Me too," she said, trying to keep her teeth from chattering. "And I'm freezing as well." But she had an idea that her immediate problem was an attack of nerves more than the weather.

Reese stopped suddenly and looked down at her, his eyes dark with concern and something else. "What do you say we scrap this idea for a picnic and go back to your cabin and build a fire and eat our victuals in comfort?" He shivered. "I agree, it's too damned cold out here."

Meryl's mind began to churn. She could almost taste the tension in the air, it was so strong. If they went back to the cabin, she knew what would happen. It was inevitable; they could barely keep their hands off each other as it was. Was that what she wanted, had been aching for—sex with this man?

Would letting him make love to her be the panacea she needed to calm the upheaval in her life and make a dent in the loneliness she wallowed in daily? No. It wasn't just sex, she avidly assured herself. Her attraction to Reese Corbett was more than that; it went much deeper. If she were willing to face the truth, she would have to admit she was falling in love with him. Oh, God, surely not, she moaned silently. Suddenly she felt as if she were on a fast-moving elevator, only to have it stop abruptly, knocking the bottom out of her stomach.

"Meryl?"

The desperate note underlying the quiet use of her name jarred her out of her reverie.

She raised her face to meet his, oblivious of the wind that was whipping locks of hair in her face and mouth. She was no longer able to squelch the desire that rippled through her like hot wax. She could only nod, but that was enough.

There was a hint of something hanging in the air between them, a sense of waiting, a kind of breathless awareness. Suddenly her world went into a slow spin.

"Let's go," he whispered urgently, but his eyes were hooded and his expression unreadable as they fell in step and began the long walk back toward the cabin. *Why had he kissed her?* he questioned himself brutally. Why couldn't he control the physical needs of his body? Why had he let them get the better of his common sense?

Meryl sensed that once again he had wanted to pull back, to deny himself what she knew he wanted. She could feel his uptightness; his arm was like a steel band around her shoulders. Although they moved together in perfect harmony, silence hung heavy between them.

By the time they reached their destination, Meryl's eyes strayed to the watch that circled her slender wrist. Surprisingly, she noted it was already midafternoon. And the sun showed no promise of shining. If anything, the sky looked more ominous than ever, Meryl thought, giving it a cursory glance. The dampening chill had penetrated both her windbreaker and sweater. It was all she could do to keep her teeth from chattering.

"You're freezing, aren't you?" Reese asked as they conquered the few remaining yards to the cabin door. Knowing he was hammering yet another nail in his coffin, he nevertheless pulled her closer against the hard warmth of his body, feasting his eyes on her pink cheeks, colored by the wind, and the screen of thick lashes that shielded the liquid darkness of her eyes.

Nor could he help but watch in total fascination as she knocked the wet sand from her shoes; she inclined her head downward so that her hair swung outward, exposing a small pink ear.

Reese groaned inwardly, crushing the urge to dip his tongue into the center of the opening before nibbling on the tiny earlobe. He felt himself grow hard, excruciatingly and painfully hard.

Once they were entombed in the warmth of her cabin, his thoughts continued to click. He had dreaded this day for a long time. And it had finally come. His best friend and lawyer had warned him this would happen, but he, Reese, had scoffed at the idea. No way, he had vowed to his friend. After the battles he had fought with Kathy, he was convinced there would never be another woman who could ever again make him feel warm and tender on the inside, as though he were melting.

But then, as sneaky as a thief in the night, it had happened. He had found a woman who had caught hold of his heart and had refused to let it go. But any type of relationship with her was dangerous. An affair? Impossible. He could not allow himself to throw a cog into the wheels of justice now. The whole goddamned mess was too close to being settled.

"Will you throw some logs in the stove while I pour us some coffee?" she asked hesitantly, her eyes darting back and forth across his features. He hadn't said a word since following her into the cabin. His mood seemed to have taken a forty-degree turn.

"Huh?" he asked absently. And then quickly refuted his own statement by rubbing the back of his neck and saying tightly, "That's fine. You go ahead."

Determined to appear calm and unaffected by his sudden change of attitude, she sidestepped into her bedroom, where she kicked off her sneakers and slipped into a pair of woolen house shoes. A quick brushing restored the natural fall of curls that clustered around her head.

When she returned to the family room, a fire crackled in the stove, removing all traces of the lingering chill.

He was on bended knees poking the hot coals with a long forked tool. He smiled lopsidedly, an apology flashing from his eyes. "It's a shame we have to scratch our outing altogether now." His expression, however, belied his comment.

Meryl raised her eyebrows. "Oh, why is that?"

"You mean you haven't heard the pitter-patter of tiny raindrops on the rooftop?" he asked with a teasing grin.

"You've got to be kidding," she replied, agilely covering the short distance to the window. She whisked aside the drapes and took in the dark sky and the heavy rain. "And all in a matter of minutes, too," she added, her heartbeat accelerating at the sudden intimacy of the situation. "I don't think the sun is ever going to shine again," she added, a jittery edge to her voice.

He smiled easily, sensing her nervousness and taking great precautions to dispel it. "While you get the coffee, I'll prepare the picnic. I'm famished, and I know you are too."

She laughed. "My stomach gave up a long time ago on getting anything to eat." She turned to go and then paused. "Would you like a shot of amaretto in your coffee? If you've never tried it, it's delicious." She grinned impishly, deepening her dimples. "Guaranteed to give it a little pizzazz."

He chuckled, displaying even white teeth, reinforcing his startling attractiveness. "By all means, give me a hearty dose of the stuff. It sounds like what I need to relax my weary old bones."

"Pooh! That's the last thing you are . . . is old, I mean." She made no effort to hide the fact that she was enjoying looking at the hard sinewy strength of his body. Then she realized what she was doing. She took a deep breath and let it out slowly, wondering what sort of madness held her in its grip.

"Hurry," he demanded softly, though his tone was slightly strained. "Unless you want me to pass out at your feet from hunger." But his gnawing hunger was not from lack of food and drink, he added silently. God help him, he wanted her so much he could taste it, as though it were something tangible.

It didn't take Meryl long to prepare the coffee, laced generously with amaretto. She noticed just as she was about to set the tray on the coffee table that it was already occupied. Reese had spread the contents of their sack lunch on top of it and had placed a scented candle in the center, its glow adding a mellow brightness to the shadowed room.

Meryl's heart swelled with pleasure at this unexpected thoughtfulness, even though she knew he meant it as a playful joke.

"Would your highness care to be seated?" he asked in a most regal and formal voice, patting the carpeted floor with a hand, but the grin that flirted with his lips was itching to break through.

She played along, enjoying this absurd playacting to the hilt. "Why, of course, I'd be delighted." She strove to keep a straight face. "Never let it be said that I passed up a chance to dine on soggy sandwiches straight from the delicatessen."

Suddenly they looked at each other and then burst into laughter, neither able to contain it a moment longer.

That siege of laughter set the precedent for the remainder of the afternoon. They talked, they laughed. As far as they were concerned, they were alone in the world. The rain continued to splatter against the windowpane, at times coming down in torrential sheets. But they couldn't have cared less. They were immersed in each other.

Meryl found herself forgetting her own identity, who she was as well as where she was. She even forgot to wonder who *he* was, the man underneath the armor of charm . . . it was easy. They discussed their likes and dislikes pertaining to books, music, movies. Food. Nothing highly personal, nothing controversial.

Stomachs no longer rumbling, coffee cups emptied, they had journeyed from the floor to the soft comfort of the couch. Almost against his volition, his arm went around her. She didn't protest the movement, and in time it was only natural that she began to touch his fingers, idly running her own along them, still so excitingly stimulated. She loved being exactly where she was, harbored in his shoulder, leaning against his strength, idly talking and inhaling his deliciously masculine scent. It was like a potent drug.

Finally their voices quieted, and it was all Meryl could do to keep her eyes open. His warm husky body, the sizzling fire, the effects of the spiked coffee were too much.

"Mmmm," she murmured. Throwing inhibitions to the wind, she nestled closer against him and began rubbing her cheek up and down his chest. "I don't remember the last time I've been this relaxed or felt this good." She laughed softly. "It's all I can do to keep my eyes open."

"Me too," he whispered as he buried his face into her sweet-smelling hair. It was like a fragrant cocoon where a man could hide his fears and manufacture dreams of delights untold. But not him. Never him. Somehow he'd found the strength to deny himself the final temptation of her delectable body, and through this sacrifice he'd miraculously been able to restrain his passion.

"I guess I'd better mosey on back toward my cabin and let you go to sleep," he added, his tone both regretful and once again noticeably strained.

Meryl's eyes flew open beneath heavy lids, yet she didn't move, though every muscle in her body tensed. She couldn't believe he was going to leave her just like that. Yet he hadn't moved his arm; it still circled her tightly. But he had made no attempt to kiss her again, either, much less make love to her.

And that was the whole crux of the matter. In spite of her convictions to the contrary, she wanted him to make love to her. Her body yearned for his. Why was he holding back? What secrets did he harbor? She was positive he wanted to kiss her again and, yes, to make love to her too. Still he continued to hold back with that leashed control. *Why?* The question rose to haunt her.

For a prolonged interlude, neither one spoke.

Then Meryl reluctantly inched away from his enveloping security and ran her eyes over his chiseled face, the tangled hair, the troubled intensity of his eyes.

Without realizing it, she was looking at him from her heart. Her tongue circled her lips, unaware that her own yearning for something as yet unfulfilled was clearly visible in her face. She was so enchantingly innocent, yet so tempting.

A groan escaped, its roots deep within him. It shattered the lingering silence into a thousand pieces.

"Meryl . . . please . . . don't do this . . . I . . ." He

couldn't say anything else, a wealth of pain suffocating his words.

"Reese?" She knew this was what she wanted, what she had wanted from the first day she met him on the beach. She gave him a look of such unrestrained trust, filtered with unconditional longing, that he felt like a giant pair of tweezers were squeezing his heart, knowing himself to be totally unworthy of it.

"No . . . we shouldn't . . ." Again his tone bespoke silent agony. This was not a woman with whom to satisfy a craving of the flesh. He was certain that to go a step with her would be to go a long way. He could not take the chance, he told himself. It was too risky.

He didn't want to hurt her, nor let her hurt him. *Okay, Corbett, you have no other alternative. Haul yourself up and go back to your cabin; pack your bags and get the hell out of here!* No damage had been done—yet. Leave it at that.

The flickering candlelight allowed her to see the conflicting emotions that played across his face. She didn't understand what was going on inside of him, and the bad part about it was, she didn't care. All she could think about was that if she couldn't have him, she would die.

Not stopping to consider the consequences, Meryl reached for his hand and placed it on a breast. "Now, tell me we can't," she whispered boldly. *What are you doing?* she demanded of herself. *Are you completely mad? You're actually inviting him to make love to you. Have you no shame!* She had never done anything so irrational in all of her thirty-three years. What must he think of her?

At that precise moment, Reese couldn't move, couldn't think; he could only feel. He stared down at his hand, mesmerized by the sensation of having it filled with her round breast, full and firm. And the nipple. Ah, the nipple. It tormented his palm as it hardened. He groped to control his body's response. He failed. He'd gone instantly, achingly erect at the feel of her breast.

"Please . . ." she said brokenly, looking up at him, her heart racing, frightened by both her desire and her action.

A muffled curse tore through his lips. Damn, he groaned inwardly. He wasn't a robot that could be programmed. He was a man with an aching need.

He dipped his head and claimed her lips hungrily. His last vestige of control was gone. He touched her hair, the satin finish of her cheek, as his lips became gentle and pliant where before they were greedy and demanding.

He finally released her mouth, only to bury his head at the side of her neck, caressing her there with tiny, darting nips.

"Oh, God, Meryl, you smell so good, taste so good . . ."

Unable to utter a word, Meryl raised her arms and wound them around his neck, her fingers moving into his hair. She laid her lips against his mouth, with her tongue pressed between his lips and searched the interior like an animal searching for food. Removing his hand from her breast, he slowly lifted the bottom of her sweater and placed his hand against her warm flesh, kneading as his hand traveled upward to reclaim a breast.

Meryl reveled in the pleasure his talented fingers were bringing to her. "Oh, yes . . . don't stop . . . please." Nothing had prepared her for such gentle handling of her body. Elliot had never once wooed her like this. It was always a rush to get to the culmination. This man knew how to love. What he was doing to her was exquisite torture.

He squeezed her nipple, his thumbnail scratching reverently across the sensitive area. Soon his hand moved from her breast, and before she realized what was happening, he had removed her sweater, leaving her uptilted breasts and ripe reddish-brown nipples naked to his gaze.

"You're beautiful," he told her intensely. "More perfect than I ever imagined."

His hands once again sought and found her breast and closed tightly about it. It was like a sun-warmed apple in his hand, and the scent of her flesh was in his nostrils, fresh and maddening and—forbidden. His thumb gently traced an invisible circle around the bumpy dark halos. He couldn't remove his eyes from her face.

He bent to kiss each nipple, and a soft moan of pleasure escaped her. He took each in turn into his mouth, sucking and nibbling and using his tongue until they seemed to grow impossibly large, as though trying to fill his mouth.

Meryl shivered within the grip of this new kind of passion. Her hands in turn found their way under his sweater, fingers clutching at the dark graying forest on his chest. Lost. Lost. Wanting. Wanting.

Suddenly, so unexpectedly, Reese drew away from her warm mouth. "Meryl . . ." he gulped, searching for air, "I can't stand much more . . . If we don't . . ."

She reached up and placed a finger across his lips. "Please, I want you to make love to me." Her voice was soft, tremulous; it was lusty, bordering on the sensuous. Yet it sounded just a shade unsure, just a shade frightened. And suddenly so vulnerable, seeking reassurance from him.

Still he hesitated, fighting for strength to deny her. "Maybe . . . maybe we should talk," he insisted, striving to ignore the tremor of desire that was ripping his insides apart.

She shook her head, and he saw that she held back tears. "Just love me, Reese. Please, love me."

"Oh, Meryl," he ground out, his control gone, "you win."

He stood up and scooped her up in his arms and made his way undeterred into the bedroom and set her down on the side of the bed. But he was trembling. His brain was shouting *No! Don't do this,* but his body was betraying him. *It's too late to stop now!*

With a quick graceful motion she shrugged her jeans and slippers off and was about to remove her panties, only to have her hand stilled. She looked up at him, feeling as though her bones were disintegrating.

"Let me," he implored. He knelt down and slowly peeled the wispy garment down the length of her legs and then pitched it aside.

Before lowering her back across the bed, he kissed her

tenderly, and instinctively she opened her mouth, accepting his tongue, responding without knowing why or understanding what there was about this man that captivated her so and made her behave so wantonly. She responded purely to the dictates of her body, unable to think, purely responding to being touched and kissed.

She wanted to touch him. She wanted to bring him to the same heights as he was bringing her. While his mouth continued to devour hers, she reached out and pressed her hand against him. The thick fabric of his jeans was an aggravating protection for his hardness.

"Yes . . . oh, yes!" Reese ground out. "Don't stop . . . feels so good, so right." He thought it would all be over before he could get his clothes off.

As he lay down beside her, he began to touch every inch of her flesh. To him, it was like warm milk. He kissed her face, tasted the sweetness of her skin.

She bit down on his lower lip, sucking it into her mouth so wonderfully that he released his breath in a rushed sigh of delight.

"Meryl," he said, rocking her gently against his chest, the lulling motion overflowing into his voice. "I've never felt this way, ever . . . you've given me a new lease on life."

"Oh, Reese, I feel the same way." She paused and laid her lips against the tender bud that lay hidden within the furry chest. "This . . . is all so sudden, so crazy, but I . . . I want you so."

"And you shall have me, my darling, all of me." *And my heart in the bargain,* he thought. Why couldn't he close out his mind and accept it as a purely physical encounter? Why did he have to think? To *know?*

In that moment, he knew he had fallen in love with this beautiful petite woman who lay so gracefully beside him. *Oh, God,* he cried in silent agony. *How could he have let this happen?*

Because of this startling realization, everything had to be

right, perfectly right between them. He drew her closer into his arms, savoring the fullness of her breasts crushed against his flesh, her long limbs tangling with his.

His hands began a leisurely stroll down her back, her spine, finally to halt at the firm roundness of her buttocks. He massaged the warm flesh until her moans of pleasure could not be contained.

Suddenly he drew back, creating a hairbreadth between them. Then he lowered his head and put his mouth on her honeyed sweetness as simultaneously he worked magic with his fingers.

Meryl's insides were on fire. He thrilled her senses, guiding her on a sensual path she had never imagined possible. He was so knowledgeable of her every aching need. Then his eyes turned toward her and she was held spellbound, until— he made it happen. With a deep moan and shudder, she gave in to the pleasure striking her body.

Then, gently but quickly, he positioned himself above her, and before she realized what was happening, he had penetrated her fully, in one exquisite stroke. "Yes! Oh, please . . ." she whimpered.

Her body underwent a spasm of physical joy. He was a big, a very big man. It was suicide trying to embody him.

"God, Meryl," he moaned. "Don't let me hurt you."

She had never been so totally filled. They seemed to touch everywhere. And ignoring the madness of the encounter itself, she locked her legs around his hips and gave herself up to his skilled possession of her. She had never been made love to in the way he made love to her, evoking responses she should have been reluctant to give. But no matter. She no longer had any control over how much she was willing to give. She could only give, simply give; and continue to receive.

She moaned unknowingly as his mouth latched onto a nipple as he slowly continued to penetrate. His skill, his knowing, far surpassed any previous experience. Her body was lapped by one gasping tide of pleasure after another until he finally spilled into her.

And when he fell sighing, collapsing onto her breasts, she held him, clung to him and sobbed aloud, *"I love you."* And suddenly she knew that she did. She loved this stranger totally, irrevocably, and without shame. And she also knew that if she had to, she could make this day last a lifetime.

Chapter 3

BUT SHE DID NOT HAVE TO. HER COLLECTION OF MEMORIES WAS only beginning. From that day on they were inseparable. If that first day and night they spent together seemed like a waltz through heaven, then the following weeks had all the ingredients of pure magic.

Even the weather cooperated. The sun shone brightly, enabling them to do the things they both enjoyed. They jogged, they sailed, they fished, but more important, they found pleasure in just being alive, which was something Meryl had not been able to do for a long time. Nor, apparently, had Reese; the lines of tension eroded from around his eyes and mouth, leaving him looking relaxed and carefree as a young boy.

The nights spent in each other's arms were never the same. One time their lovemaking would be lazy and sweet, Reese finding and exploring with his hands and mouth all the hidden delights of her supple body, at the same time teaching her to drop the last of her inhibitions and please him, while another time their lovemaking would be just the opposite, hot and torrid.

But through it all, one thing never changed—their insatiable and compulsive need for each other. For three weeks Meryl could barely contain her happiness. It was like nothing she had ever experienced, including her fifteen years of married life. Each day that passed, she found herself falling more and more in love with Reese.

Her only touch with the outside world was a call from

Morgana one morning just after she had gotten out of the shower and after Reese had left to go jogging.

Remembering the conversation always brought a smile to her face.

"My, my, you sound like a cat that just swallowed a canary," Morgana had said, her bright laughter flowing through the line.

Meryl had turned scarlet as she eyed the rumpled bed where she and Reese had been making slow, sweet love since dawn.

"Well . . . er, I am enjoying my . . . vacation," Meryl had finally managed to stammer.

Morgana laughed. "If I didn't know better, I'd think you had a man holed up there somewhere."

Meryl sucked in her breath. "Whatever gave you that idea?" How had Morgana known? She wasn't ready to share her secret.

"Your voice, you sound different somehow." Morgana had laughed again. "Well, anyway, I'm glad you're enjoying yourself," she had added, changing the subject. "I just called to say hi and to check on you."

"I'm glad you did. Take care, and I'll see you before long."

All too soon. Meryl realized with a sinking feeling in the pit of her stomach that their vacation days were reaching an end, and she didn't know any more about the man Reese Corbett than she had in the beginning. Except physically. Physically she knew him intimately, totally. But mentally and personally he was still a closed book.

She couldn't even get him to talk about his work. She assumed from the few remarks he had let slip that he was heavily into some type of research. Respecting his right to privacy, she therefore clamped the lid down on her curiosity and put it out of her mind. Somehow there never seemed time to divulge or dredge through the skeletons in their personal lives. There was too much laughter to share, too many new experiences to share, leaving no room for recriminations.

And so their "love" was experienced and sought after

minute to minute. It hovered on the edge—always out of their grasp. Unconsciously the dividing line had been drawn; there were strict rules to obey. After that first short inquisition, Reese never again delved into her past, nor she his.

Yet as the days clicked off the calendar, Meryl refused to speculate on the demise of their idyllic time together. So far, Reese had made no mention of seeing her once they returned to the "real world." As a result of that oversight, she could no longer ignore or suppress the nagging question that had lain dormant at the base of her conscious mind—*was Reese a married man?*

And at this particular moment, she was having difficulty quashing the question. Her insides quaked. He can't be married, she told herself over and over. *He just can't be.*

It was simply impossible for her not to believe in the strength, the honor, the sincerity that surrounded him like a shield. Yet, when she first met him he had been like a wounded animal searching for a place to hide. And he had admitted there were problems, problems he had no intention of discussing. But that didn't necessarily mean he had a wife and that he cheated on her. No, of course it didn't, she reassured herself. As usual, she was just borrowing trouble. Now all she had to do was get control of her frayed emotions before Reese returned. He had driven the three miles to the nearest grocery store to buy steaks for their evening dinner. "I feel like having a thick chunk of meat. How 'bout you?" he'd asked, planting a delicious kiss on her smiling lips. "And let's have the feast at my place, since I'm the one with the grill," he'd added with a satisfied grin.

She was going about the task of preparing the salad, a vegetable, and the barbecue sauce for the meat when she heard the rattle of the key being inserted into the front door. Hastily she whirled around and gave him a sweet smile.

"Mmmm, something sure smells good," Reese commented as he strode into the kitchen and plopped the sack of groceries down on the table. He turned and scrutinized Meryl closely.

"It's potatoes *au gratin* that's tantalizing your stomach," she teased, her solemn mood vanishing with his return. "I decided we needed something besides steak and salad."

It was all she could do to keep from devouring him with her eyes. He was so good to look at. This evening he was dressed in a pair of tight-fitting jeans that displayed the powerful muscles of his thighs. Thighs that night after night had rubbed sensuously against her silky limbs. He wore no jacket, even though the weather was damp and cold, just a long-sleeved yellow knit shirt that threw the amazing darkness of his coloring into stark relief.

Before she could disguise her perusal of him, their eyes met and held, velvet gray on translucent brown. In those emotionally charged seconds, a static tension rippled between them, bridging them together by a silent exchange that needed no words. It was always like that between them—a staggering physical attraction that one look, one touch, could ignite into a flaming passion.

Meryl lowered her lashes to rip her gaze from his, and hiding trembling fingers, began chopping a tomato for the salad. *Oh, God, how she loved him.*

"Anything I can do to help before I put the steaks on the grill?" he asked softly, his words effectively disrupting the silence.

Meryl smiled at him from the heart. "No . . . no, everything seems to be under control," she replied a trifle shakily.

She felt his eyes bore into her back for what seemed like aeons before she heard his heavy footsteps shuttle him out the door.

The moment Reese stepped outside, an agonized groan ripped through him. How deeply he had grown to love her. In a few weeks this woman, this delicate round-breasted woman, with her haunted eyes, her words of denial, and her deep sexual hunger, had wormed her way into the depth of his very soul, forcing him to love her. Even now in his mind's eye he could see the soft chocolate-colored curls, the rosy cheeks brought on by the heat of the oven, the full yielding breasts as they brushed against her flowing caftan.

He knew that he truly loved her. Loved her more than he had ever loved any woman in the past, or could ever love any woman in the future. She did not belong to him, but he loved her just the same.

But for now it was not meant to be. To admit he loved her would destroy them both. For himself he cared not a whit, but he couldn't take the chance of bringing her into the tangled mess he had made of his life. He would never ask that of her. Not now. He must wait until everything was right. . . .

"Reese?" The sound of her soft voice yanked him back to the present.

He made sure his features showed none of the turmoil churning inside him before he turned around. The corners of his sculptured lips rose in a bright smile. "The steaks are about ready," he said. "Are you hungry?"

"Starved."

"So am I."

"Well, you just stand by one more second while chef Corbett checks his handiwork." Reese then proceeded to cut a tiny slit in the corner of each steak to make sure they were cooked just right. When finished, he looked at Meryl and winked smugly. "Mmmm, cooked to perfection," he said, throwing her a satisfied grin. "Grab a plate, why don't you, and carry the steaks in while I shut off the pit."

"Humility is certainly not one of your strongest points," Meryl retorted, though a tiny smile played around her lips as she reached for the plate and automatically heaped it full of the piping hot, juicy steaks.

The food and the good time they had while sharing it were just another added miracle for Meryl, another in a long succession of many. After they had finished off a bottle of wine, she was floating on cloud nine as she laughed boldly at a joke that Reese had just told her. A touch of magic was everywhere.

Suddenly Meryl stretched contentedly and stifled a yawn. "Well," she said, looking at the empty dishes with lazy eyes, "shall we draw straws to see who's going to do the dishes?"

Reese's eyes narrowed. "Forget the dishes," he murmured huskily. "I can think of more promising and worthwhile things to do with our time—the most important one, making love to you." The tone of his voice had deepened to a gravelly drawl.

She felt as though her heart had turned over. "Well, if you're expecting a protest on this end," she murmured unsteadily, "then you're wrong."

His eyes were warm, colored with passion. "I was hoping you'd say that," he responded huskily.

He then leaned toward her and bracketed her face with his hands, sealing their bargain with a penetrating kiss, a kiss that Meryl knew was only a sneak preview of what was to come.

The star-studded bedroom was luring them, when suddenly, without warning, the shrill sound of the telephone severed the passion-filled silence.

They froze instantly.

"Damn!" Reese swore softly as he dropped his arms from around Meryl, got up and trudged in the direction of the ominous black instrument.

Meryl finally found her voice. "Don't answer it," she implored him suddenly, quailing beneath a nameless fear that clutched at her heart.

He paused for only a moment. And then, without turning around, he said heavily, "I have to."

Suddenly Meryl wanted to let out a blood-curdling scream as she gave in to the raw fear that her make-believe world was about to come tumbling down around her shoulders. She remained motionless as she watched Reese lift the receiver, a knot of uncertainty and dread settling heavy in her belly.

After a moment of listening to the party on the other end of the line, Reese clipped, "Right. I'll be there as soon as I can."

He faced Meryl with tortured eyes, his face devoid of all color as his hand maintained a hold on the phone.

The silence was grinding, oppressive, and it raked along Meryl's taut nerves with a vengeance as she waited for him to speak.

"I . . . I have to go." His eyes were glistening with pain, regret, and an incredible sadness. "It . . . it's my son. . . ."

"Son! Oh, God no," Meryl cried, jumping up from the table and covering her ears with her hands. She was totally oblivious of the chair as it clattered to the floor, so intent was she on placing as much distance between her and Reese as possible.

She was standing on rubbery legs by the window, looking out into the moonlit night. She knew he was behind her; his presence, his smell, permeated the small space of the room.

Dismayed now by her panicked conduct, Meryl refused to glance his way. She wrapped her arms tightly around her trembling body, a purely defensive mechanism against what she knew was to come.

"Meryl . . ." he began.

She turned to face him as the words, tinged with bitter bile, rushed unbidden from her lips. "You're married." It wasn't a question, merely a statement, ripped from the pages of her heart.

She stood in paralyzed silence and let the seconds crawl by like an eternity. Neither dared move. His face was ashen, his breathing heavy and labored. They were acutely aware of each other. Swift raw panic drilled through her, twisting her insides and wringing the life from her. She waited.

Still he hesitated, and then she knew. "Meryl," he repeated, "I . . ."

"Please, Reese," she said with great dignity, "don't say any more. Just go. Go to your . . . wife and . . . son."

He winced but held his ground. "I can explain—"

She turned on him like a wildcat. "Explain!" she screamed at him. "Damn you! You're married. What's there to explain?"

She whirled around and gave her back to him again before

resting her hot forehead against the cold glass. She must not allow her control to slip any further, not for even a second, for she knew if she allowed another crack in her veneer, even a tiny one, her entire world would give way like a bursting dam.

For a moment Reese was at a loss as to how to combat the words she had hurled at him. He prayed for guidance as he forced his tone to stay even, when all the while he felt like crying himself. *But grown men don't cry.* He had to make her listen. It might be his last chance.

He drew a long convulsive breath. "I can't stay and argue with you now," he ground out. "But I'll be back." He took a step toward her but kept his hands to himself.

Meryl tracked his movements like radar, stiffening when he stopped within inches of her. "Reese, don't," she pleaded, trying to scoot past him, but he read her like a book. His hand shot out and grasped the tender part of her upper arm, halting her in motion.

He was hanging on to his patience by a mere thread as it suddenly dawned on him that she wasn't even going to allow him a hearing. "Don't what, defend myself?" he retaliated bitterly. "Or don't come back? Or both?"

"You're hurting my arm. Will you let go of me?"

"No."

"Please."

He began to talk, forcing her to listen, to understand. "Kathy and I haven't lived together as man and wife for over two years now. I won't pretend we weren't happy from the start of our marriage—we were. But somewhere down the line, it fell apart. We began to want different things out of life. I became engrossed in my work; she began drinking, keeping company with a wild crowd." Reese was trembling as he spoke. "Then she got pregnant—"

"Stop it!" Meryl demanded, tears choking her voice. The guilt, the shame of what she had done, was raging through her insides with frightening force. "God! It's bad enough knowing you're married, but to know there's a child involved . . ." She broke off, the tears finally claiming her voice.

Reese's jaw clenched, the muscles in his cheek twisting violently. "That's why I haven't been able to get a divorce; she's using Jason as a pawn to punish me, and he's ill on top of that." He paused and wiped his palms on the leg of his pants. "Goddammit, can't you see why I needed you, why your freshness, your unselfish beauty, was and is a cure-all for the emptiness in my soul?"

Pain oozed from his voice as he continued. "Believe me, I didn't want this to happen; I fought it like hell, but in the end, as you well know, I couldn't stop myself." He paused and took a deep breath. "When this whole sordid mess is over, then I'll . . . Oh, what the hell!" The last words were barely audible as his voice was strained to the breaking point.

Meryl stood transfixed, unable to completely comprehend all he had told her. But she felt as if someone had slammed her in the chest with a block of concrete, leaving her raw and bleeding.

Hurt and remorse were the twin thieves that were determined to rob her of a clear vision enabling her to see past her own guilty conscience and comprehend what he was so desperately trying to tell her. Hence she couldn't squelch the urge to hurt in return.

"Don't you ever come near me again," she hissed, her eyes spearing him with daggers, effectively masking her bleeding insides. "How could I have been so taken in, so . . . so blind and stupid, not to have seen through your silken-tongued words, your lies—"

"Now wait just one goddamned minute," Reese cut in, his voice riddled with steel. "I never lied to you about anything."

"You never told me the truth, either."

They glared at each other.

"I don't recall your asking."

"It was your place to tell me."

"I wasn't sure you'd care . . . if I was married or not."

"What?" It was a shriek, a disbelieving whisper.

Reese was the first to lower his boxing gloves. Suddenly the fight went out of him. He removed his arm and stepped back from her accusing eyes, her scorn. "I'm sorry," he said sadly. "I didn't mean that." He paused and cleared his throat. "The funny thing about all this—but you notice I'm not laughing—is that I don't consider myself married. If it's any consolation to you, I've never so much as touched another woman since Kathy walked out on me and took my son."

"Please . . . please, don't do this to me," Meryl whimpered. "You're not being fair." Damn him for playing on her sympathy. Damn him to hell. A hell he had sentenced them both to. Oh, God, she'd been such a fool. She had instinctively suspected him from the onset. But because she had wanted him, she had pushed her uneasiness to the back of her mind, wanting to believe the best. In doing so, she had gone against the wisdom of her maturity, and it had cost her dearly. But regardless of the circumstances, he was still a married man, with a family. There was no way she could see him or touch him ever again. To do so now would undermine every principle she held near and dear.

"It's my sanity at stake," he was saying now, lifting her out of the vortex of swirling emotions. "I don't know how to play fair," he added toughly, leading with this shield to protect himself from the answer he expected.

"It . . . it would never work," she whispered, wanting to give in to his honeyed words, yet at the same time hating herself for still loving him.

He was leading with his pain now, completely at her mercy. "I'll be back, hopefully in a few days. Please . . . wait for me. We'll talk more." His voice was brittle, controlled.

She would not panic. Instead she would tell him in a firm voice that it was over, finished. *Now, Meryl! Do it now!*

"I'm . . . I'm sorry," she whispered at last, edging toward the door, determined to leave, to shut him out of her life and her heart.

He refused to surrender. "You won't reconsider?" he asked softly, speaking into her shoulder blades.

"No."

That one tiny word nearly killed him. No. No. He knew he had no one else to blame but himself. He had used language their liaison would not sustain. His grief was a thundering explosion inside him, ripping him apart.

He knew he had lost her. Her silence was the surest sign of all.

Meryl barely remembered stumbling out the door of Reese's cabin and covering the short distance to her own. The moment she invaded her lonely sanctuary, time ceased to exist. How long she remained cocooned like a newborn fetus in the middle of the floor, she did not know. Hours? Days? An eternity? No matter. She had simply given in to the aching misery that rose in her like a festering boil, letting it poison her entire system.

It was over; she knew that without a doubt. She had no choice but to purge herself of the poison and pick up the pieces and go on. She had to think she could do it or she would just wither up and die. A person's heart could sustain only so much pounding before it gave out.

Now, as she stretched her kinked limbs and muscles, she marshaled every bit of self-discipline she possessed to keep herself together while she accomplished her tasks.

Exactly one hour later, she was packed, the cabin was spotless, and she was in the car on her way back to civilization. Her silent companions: a shattered heart and memories that would linger. . . .

Chapter 4

Houston, Texas: Spring, 1984

"OKAY, LADIES, PUT UP YOUR MATS," MERYL ANNOUNCED INTO the microphone attached to the narrow belt at her waist, "then get ready to do the warm-up today to Jimmy Dean's 'Little Black Book.'" She paused and watched as the fifty women scrambled to do as she asked. When they were back in position, she went on. "Following the warm-up, we'll go straight into the Charleston with 'Thoroughly Modern Millie' and continue through the remainder of our routines before concluding with the cool-down to 'Amazing Grace.'"

Meryl stared for a brief moment at her attentive and colorful audience, made up of overweight women and thin ones like herself before asking, "Anyone have any questions before we get started?"

Her only feedback was smiles and good-natured grumblings. Laughing herself, she scooted across the floor to the stereo, flipped the needle on the record, and then scampered back to her position in front of a long mirrored wall.

"Remember, ladies, to keep those stomach muscles tight," she called over her left shoulder before the beat of the music drowned her out.

From that moment on it was down to work.

It wasn't until one hour later that the large room was again relatively silent and empty except for the presence of her secretary and assistant, Nelda Jennings.

"Whew!" Meryl exclaimed, whisking the damp tendrils of hair off her neck. "I'm bushed."

Nelda frowned as she joined Meryl in the small but modern kitchenette adjacent to the main room of the studio. "And you look it, too, my friend," Nelda replied, sipping on the glass of iced tea Meryl had set in front of her. "What on earth possessed you to come down here and do this exercise class after just coming in from a three-week tour?"

Meryl smiled even though every cell in her body was fatigued. "Oh, Nelda, don't fuss at me, please." She shook her head. "I know it was foolish, but I did promise those women I'd be here for this five-twenty class, and I try to keep my promises in spite of my hectic schedule."

Nelda looked unconvinced. "Huh, if you ask me, you're overdoing it. You can't keep up this kind of pace much longer or you'll collapse. Just look at you, nothing but skin and bones."

Meryl's mouth curved into a tired smile. "Well, you may be right, but just look what I've accomplished in two years by working practically twenty-four hours a day."

"Huh!" Nelda snorted again, her square jaw locking in a stubborn stance and her green eyes shooting darts at Meryl. "There's more to life than work, you know," she added sarcastically.

"Oh, come on, Nelda, give me a break. Just answer me this: how many other people do you know who have virtually started out with nothing, only to end up the proud owner, along with the bank, that is, of three exercise studios, a book on nutrition and fitness out in the marketplace, and a possible television show in the offing?"

Nelda's frown had deepened into a scowl as she got up from the table and sauntered over to the refrigerator and reached for the pitcher of iced tea.

Meryl eyed her friend closely as she wordlessly refilled their glasses. It was terribly important to her that she have Nelda's approval. They had met in an exercise class at one of the local spas the summer she had returned from the cabin at Galveston. From that moment on, they had become friends. Nelda had been by her side from day one of this venture. She had encouraged her to keep plugging away when Meryl had wanted to give up. But Nelda, with her red hair and freckled face, wouldn't hear of it. This tall, lanky friend had literally pushed Meryl into turning her dreams into a reality.

So after hours, days, months of hard work, a little luck, fierce determination, friends such as Nelda, a nagging twin sister, and the generosity of a banker and friend, she had opened her first health studio, specializing in aerobic exercises.

From that point on, her career had snowballed. In a year's time that one studio had increased to three and her book on the same subject was on its way to becoming a bestseller.

"Meryl," Nelda was saying, "you know I love you or I wouldn't care if you worked yourself into an early grave. You *do* know that, don't you?"

Meryl's lips thinned in anticipation of what was coming. "Of course I do," she answered shortly.

"Well, then, I'm going to tell you one more time: you've got to let go of the past." Nelda's eyes softened. "Don't you think you've been running long enough? You're ruining your chance of being a happy and fulfilled woman." She sighed. "I know Morgana's been on your case about this too, because we've talked about it."

Meryl couldn't ignore the tightening around her chest. "Please . . . Nelda, not now," she pleaded. "Don't preach to me today, of all days. "I'm not up to it. I've got to go home and get some sleep. I don't even feel like calling Morgana until tomorrow." She smiled weakly before getting up and walking around the table and giving Nelda a swift hug. "You're a doll. We'll talk later, I promise."

"All right," Nelda acquiesced, though her eyes were now dark with concern. "But I want you to promise me also that you'll take a few days off and rest."

"I promise," Meryl replied as she slipped her jogging pants and top over her leotards and tights. "Good night, and thanks for everything," she tossed back before stepping out into the warm spring evening.

As dawn painted the horizon a deep gold, Meryl was still counting sheep and trying to force sleep to take over her weary body and put her out of her misery.

But even this small justice was to be denied her. By the time the sunlight poured through the mini-blinds, she gave up and made her exhausted limbs move. Trying to ignore the perspiration that doused her body and her pounding head, she perched on the side of the bed.

How much longer could this go on? she lamented to herself as she leaned over and cradled her head in her hands. Two years. An eternity, she thought. Still, after these two long years, dreams of Reese's mouth and hands as they had once caressed her body with every intention of pleasing continued to haunt her nights. She drew a deep shuddering breath. If only . . .

Suddenly the jarring ring of the telephone reached through the maze of her cluttered thoughts. She brought her head up in a jerking motion and stared at the phone through unfocusing eyes, hoping that if she ignored the awful sound it would go away.

Again she was denied her simple wish. If anything, the yellow instrument seemed to ring with more persistence.

"Damn," she muttered beneath her breath as she stumbled across the room and groped for the receiver. Tomorrow, without fail, she promised herself, she would have the phone company move the phone to the table beside her bed. Or better yet, maybe she should just have them come and take the whole damned thing out of the wall.

"Hello," she said none too graciously.

"Huh," a soft voice purred, "I can see you've gotten out of bed on the wrong side again this morning, sister dear."

"Morgana, for God's sake," Meryl exploded, "I'm going to throttle you if you don't stop calling me at the crack of dawn."

Morgana's laughter trickled through the receiver. "I'm sorry to disappoint you, but it's hardly the crack of dawn. Try twelve o'clock instead." She laughed again. "The way I see it, it's time for all God-fearing Americans to be out of bed and hard at work."

"Twelve o'clock!" Meryl exclaimed. "You've got to be kidding. I've never slept that late in my entire life. I guess I was more exhausted than I realized."

"Did you by any chance have a hot date last night?" Morgana asked in a hopeful voice.

Meryl gritted her teeth. "You know better than that," she snapped. "I just got in yesterday at noon and then I taught a late class at the new studio." Instantly she regretted her terse words. It wasn't Morgana's fault she hadn't slept and that her head was splitting, she reminded herself quickly. But still . . .

"Now, don't go and get your dander up any more than it already is. I just keep hoping that you'll give in and date someone besides staid ole Tucker Hammond, that's all," she said peevishly.

Meryl let that last statement slide by without comment. She was in no mood to humor her sister this morning. They had been over this same territory until she was sick of hearing about it.

"Why are you so charming and chirpy this morning?" Meryl inquired instead.

"I thought you'd never ask," Morgana replied with a sarcastic edge to her voice, though Meryl could hear the thread of laughter that promised to break through.

A tired sigh escaped through Meryl's lips. "Well, let's hear it." She was prepared to hear about another of her sister's latest shenanigans.

"On second thought, maybe I'll save it for later, seeing as how you're in such a grumpy mood."

"Morgana!"

"Oh, all right. I'm not going to let you or anyone else dampen my spirits. Are you free to come to dinner at my apartment tonight?"

Meryl counted to ten. "Is that all you called for?" What little patience she possessed was rapidly ebbing away. Her head felt like it was being used as a tennis ball with each passing moment, and the taste in her mouth was wretched.

Morgana laughed. "But this is a very special dinner party, my love."

"Oh, how's that?" Meryl responded, still unconvinced.

"Are you sitting down, for starters?" Morgana asked. "If you're not, then you'd better anchor yourself." There was a short pause. "I'm going to introduce you to the man I'm planning to marry," she added calmly.

Meryl was anything but calm. "What!" Suddenly realizing she was shouting, she lowered her voice. "I don't believe . . . When? How?" she spluttered, only to stop in midstream when she again heard Morgana's shrill laughter cut through the wires with roaring intensity. She held the phone slightly away from her ear until all had quieted on the other end.

"Oh, Meryl, he's a hunk. A real hunk. And so sweet, so generous. He's everything that Stan wasn't, and much more besides."

A warm glow of pleasure filtered its way through Meryl's body. "Oh, Morgana, that's wonderful. But I'm mystified. When on earth did all this come about? It's . . . it's all rather sudden, isn't it? When I left three weeks ago, you weren't even dating anyone, were you?"

"That's true," Morgana admitted, "but who said anything about love being on a timetable?" Her voice was overflowing with excitement. "Anyway, I've been with him as often as our schedules would permit, but that has been enough to know I've met the man of my dreams and that I'm in love."

Meryl laughed. "Well, who am I to argue with that? Am I safe in assuming that I'm to meet this miracle man at dinner this evening?"

"Right," Morgana quipped. "And do be early, as we have scads to talk about. You know I'm dying to hear all about your tour."

Meryl laughed again. "You can count on it. In fact, wild

horses couldn't keep me away. I haven't heard you sound this happy in years."

"I don't recall ever being this happy even when Stan and I first married."

Meryl hesitated. "I hate to mention this, but what about Jay? How's he taking this latest development?"

Morgana's tone was flippant. "Jay? Who cares what he thinks? He's only my agent, Meryl, not my keeper."

"Oh, come now, Morgana, you know he's crazy about you, and there was a time when you encouraged—"

"But that was ages ago," Morgana interrupted loftily. "And besides, all Jay thinks about is the money angle. He's been pushing me to accept any and all modeling jobs that are offered."

"Well, that proves you're still in demand, doesn't it?"

"Not really. I can get all the small uninteresting jobs I want, but lately the big ones have gone to others—the younger ones."

Meryl would have been deaf not to have heard the bitterness underlying each word Morgana spoke, and immediately she was sorry she had broached the subject, which never failed to upset her sister.

"You sell yourself far too short. And anyway, I think you're wonderful, and I love you," Meryl said by way of apology. She couldn't stand to see Morgana suffer. She guessed it stemmed partly from being twins; whatever affected Morgana affected her as well. And partly because she had always felt responsible for her sometimes scatterbrained, sometimes self-centered twin. More times than not, this was more of a curse than a help, Meryl thought.

"I love you too, and I'll see you about six. Okay?"

"I'll be there."

After hanging up the phone, Meryl eyed the bed and contemplated crawling back in it, snuggling under the covers, and nursing her headache. But having already slept too late as it was and then talking to Morgana much longer than she'd intended, she couldn't allow herself that luxury. Nor could she let herself dwell on Morgana's bombshell. She would have to tuck that away for later scrutiny. Instead she quickly swallowed two aspirin, hoping to ease her throbbing head.

She had a luncheon date with Tucker at two o'clock. Tucker. She sighed. Tucker was becoming a problem that she didn't know quite how to handle. Why was she afraid of him? she chided herself as she rubbed her throbbing head. He was just another man, wasn't he? She could repulse him anytime she pleased. She'd made a vow no man would ever have her love again. That lay dead and buried in the dark corner of her heart with Reese Corbett's name on it.

But Tucker did not know this. She knew he was in love with her and wanted to marry her. It was only a matter of time before he popped the question. What then? She could do worse than Tucker Hammond, she reminded herself. He would never demand more than she was willing to give.

Yet she had already been through one less-than-perfect marriage, and unless she could have the magic she'd found with Reese, she'd be better off to remain alone. After Reese, she had given up her dream of ever lying within the protective custody of a man's arms. Besides, having a home and family was no longer important to her. She had found her niche in life without a man. Her career and her independence were the two things she valued most in life now.

But at times the craving for a warm body to curl up to after a long, hard day's work, a home with the patter of a child's footsteps, was an almost tangible dream. When that happened she would feel an ache in every pore for what might have been.

For the most part, however, she was content with her life. She had a lovely town house, beautiful clothes, her health, friends, and a sister whom she loved to distraction. Even more important, she had her career, which she enjoyed and poured herself into more and more with each passing day. That was enough.

Or was it? she asked herself fretfully. At this moment, she thought not, with the pain still pounding away at her temple.

She was tired to the point of exhaustion. Not even the prospect of having her own syndicated television show perked her up.

"You're just a glutton for punishment, Meryl Stevens," she mumbled aloud as she crossed the room to stand in front of her closet and survey its contents.

She yanked a white Dior two-piece suit off the hanger and a paisley print silk blouse to match. She laid it on the bed and eyed it carefully, making sure it was just right. Trying to psych herself into mustering up a show of enthusiasm, she scooted into the bathroom for a refreshing shower.

She breezed into the posh Memorial Drive Country Club exactly on time, looking like a million dollars. Her suit clung to her willowy silhouette, giving a hint of hidden allure. And her cap of shiny dark curls called attention to her golden beige skin and soft, expressive eyes. She seemed to radiate an inner blush of confidence and a vibrant but subtle sensuality. She turned more than one male's head as she glided across the room.

Tucker Hammond peered over the rim of his glass, his eyebrows massing together to create a deep frown. He despised the way other men looked at Meryl. Jealousy formed a hard knot in the pit of his stomach. She was his, dammit, or soon would be, he hoped. Then he would personally see that no man looked at her like that ever again.

Showing none of his inner tension, he stood up as she was shown to his table, and smiled. "Hello, my dear, you're looking beautiful as usual." He leaned over and pecked her on the cheek before pulling out a chair and seating her as if she were a piece of rare and expensive porcelain.

Meryl smiled. "Hello, Tucker, it's good to see you." And it was. To her surprise, she had missed this seemingly mild-mannered man, who underneath that urbane charm was a shrewd and relentless businessman. He was impeccably dressed as usual in a dark three-piece suit that placed emphasis on his mop of silver hair and deep green eyes. All were compatible with his stocky but well-preserved frame. At fifty, he could hold his own anywhere.

"Well, tell me, how was your trip?"

"It went smooth as silk as far as the work was concerned, but being away from home for three weeks is just too long. Actually, I'm exhausted."

Tucker frowned and leaned forward, his sharp eyes missing nothing. "I can tell," he said bluntly. "Even your makeup can't cover up those dark circles beneath your eyes." He pursed his lips. "It's obvious you've been keeping late hours."

"Yes," she said patiently, "I've been keeping late hours, but not for the reasons you're hinting at." She failed miserably at keeping the censure out of her tone.

He flushed but offered no apology for his implied interrogation. Instead he turned and motioned for the waiter standing quietly in the far corner. "Are you drinking anything today?" he asked Meryl while the waiter hovered over his right shoulder.

She smiled. "No, I think I'll have a glass of club soda with a twist of lime."

"Make that two," Tucker tossed over his shoulder, sending the waiter scurrying for their drinks. Then he faced Meryl with a smile relaxing his features. "Are you hungry?"

"Not really, but I need to eat something anyway. My head feels twice its normal size." She sighed. "Most likely the result of no food or sleep."

Again Tucker voiced his concern. "We can postpone this conference until later if you'd rather." He spread his hands. "I just wanted to keep you posted on the latest word."

"And I want to hear it too," she readily assured him. "As soon as I get something in my stomach, I'll be fine."

There was a moment of silence while the solemn-faced waiter placed their drinks in front of them.

"Why don't we go ahead and order now," Tucker said, his brow raised in question.

"I'll have a large spinach salad with the special dressing," Meryl told the waiter.

Tucker handed him the menus. "And I'll have the cold boiled shrimp and a spinach salad."

Once the waiter had departed, Tucker lifted his glass, waited for Meryl to follow suit, and then toasted her with an infectious grin.

"To Meryl and a successful TV debut."

She smiled sweetly. "Thank you."

They drank, and Meryl savored the refreshing liquid as she eyed Tucker carefully.

"What do you really think our chances are of getting the group of men to put up the money to produce the show and then to interest a syndicator in selling it to television stations?" she ventured to ask after enjoying several sips of her drink. "I'll have to admit that I'm scared," she added with a sigh.

"You're worrying needlessly," Tucker replied quickly. "The chances are good, extremely good. In fact, I think I've about convinced the corporation that you're a hot commodity. And that they could stand to double their investment by backing you even in this somewhat risky enterprise."

Meryl clasped her hands tightly together, suddenly feeling the long-overdue excitement begin to bubble within her. "Oh, Tucker, you have no idea how much this means to me." Her eyes were glazed with awe. "For two years I busted my buns, literally"—she smiled—"just for this chance, never thinking in a million years I'd get it."

Tucker answered her smile and covered her clasped hands with his large one, patting them gently. "Well, it's not in the bag yet, my dear, but it's so damn close I think we're safe in celebrating. But on the other hand, let me caution you that there's still a chance, though a minute one, that it could fall through."

There were shadows in his stone-cut face and the lines around his mouth hardened visibly. "These men are so damned cautious and conservative."

Meryl withdrew her hands and made room for their salads. Seeing that they needed no refills on their drinks, the waiter took his leave.

"Don't worry," she said after a moment, "I know we're not home free as yet, but at least it's something more than just a dream. When do you think we'll get the final answer?" she asked while pouring the hot dressing over her salad. Then she smiled ruefully. "I'll be a mental case if they don't reach a decision soon."

His countenance softened. "You just leave everything to me." He paused significantly. "Have I ever let you down?"

She shook her head. "No. As a matter of fact, you haven't. And you know something else? I suddenly feel wonderful." She grinned. "Even my headache seems to have vanished into thin air."

Tucker's eyes gleamed. "I'm glad. You know that all I care about is making you happy, don't you?" His voice had lowered, his words for her ears alone.

Meryl tried to remain calm and unflustered. Although she had known this was inevitable, she still wasn't ready. "I . . . I know," she replied softly. "And . . . I thank you for it."

He covered her hand with his once again. "I want more than your thanks."

With a delicate motion she drew away. "Not yet, Tucker," she said, her eyes gazing out the glass-covered wall to the golf greens beyond. Everything appeared peaceful and quiet, she thought, wishing desperately some of that tranquillity would rub off on her. "But maybe soon," she added, returning her eyes to his.

"I can wait," he told her. "Forever if need be. I have infinite patience when it concerns you. Haven't I already proved that?"

"In more ways than one," she said barely above a whisper, while fighting off the helpless feeling that was threatening to overwhelm her. "But don't you see, you may be wasting your time—"

"I'll never accept that," he declared tightly.

Suddenly an oppressive silence fell between them, each battling his own inward problems.

Then Tucker ventured to speak. "You've got to forget him, Meryl, whoever he is, wherever he is. You've simply got to quit punishing yourself for the past. Don't you think you've played the martyr long enough?"

Meryl was appalled. "Is that what you think I'm doing?"

He suddenly looked uncomfortable. "No. Forgive me," he clipped. "I didn't mean that, but dammit, Meryl . . ."

Meryl felt a burning sting behind her eyes. "Apparently that's what everyone thinks," she said bitterly. "But nothing could be further from the truth. Just because I . . ." She jabbed at her food. "Oh, forget it." She had no intention of discussing her past problems with Tucker. After all this time, the pain associated with her affair with Reese was still tender to the touch. It was like a wound that hadn't quite healed.

Every once in a while Nelda mentioned it to her, but those times were few and far between. Morgana had finally given up and rested her case long ago when Meryl made it quite plain to both her and Nelda that she had no intention of telling them the name of the man she had been involved with and who had hurt her so deeply.

"All right," Tucker said with a sigh. "I won't push the point *now,* but just remember, I'll be around when you come to a decision about your future."

"I don't want to use you, Tucker," Meryl said faintly. "As I said before, you have too much to offer."

"You still don't understand, do you? I want to be used." His voice was vibrant and warm. "In any way you want to use me. Just remember that."

Meryl shook her head as if to clear it. "What do you say we change the subject." She attempted to smile. "This is supposed to be a celebration, or have you forgotten?"

Tucker smiled. "When I'm with you, I have a tendency to forget everything. All the big deals that keep my brain in constant motion seem unimportant compared with my fervent desire to make you happy, to remove that haunted look from your beautiful eyes."

With a rush of affection, she reached out and laid her hand over his. "Oh, Tucker, you do know how to make a lady feel special. And I do care . . ."

Tucker lifted her slender wrist to his lips before he spoke. "I know you do. Why do you think I keep badgering you to give us a chance? I know I could make you happy, happier than you've ever been in your life."

She shrugged. "I guess I'm either hardheaded or just slow to trust." Suddenly she hated herself for not being able to turn loose of the past and let this capable man become a permanent part of her life. He could make her happy. She was sure of it. Then *why* was she holding back?

"Are you about ready to go?" he asked following a moment of silence.

His tactful question alerted her to the time. She looked at her watch and was appalled when she saw how late it was. Morgana was going to kill her. She would have just enough time to go home and change clothes and get to her sister's house before the evening's honored guest was due to arrive. So much for her and Morgana's gossip session, she thought.

"Is something wrong?" Tucker inquired, his bushy brows drawn together in a frown. "Suddenly you looked panic-stricken."

She laughed and shook her head to the contrary. "No, nothing's wrong, not really. It's just that I'm supposed to be at Morgana's in about an hour for dinner, and I still have to get home, change clothes and then drive all the way across town to her new condo out by Hermann Park."

"You should have told me," Tucker chastised sharply. "I certainly wouldn't have kept you so long had I known you had other commitments."

Meryl smiled as she reached for her purse beside the chair. "It's not your fault. It's mine. Besides, our getting together this afternoon was much more important than gossiping with my sister." She paused, a grin spreading across her lips. "Although Morgana did have some startling news this morning when she called me."

"Oh?"

Meryl watched as Tucker signed the ticket before she spoke again. "Morgana's in love."

"Again."

She laughed deeply. "That was my reaction exactly—at first," she clarified. "But now I'm not so sure that it isn't the real thing."

"You really think she's serious this time, huh?" Tucker asked as he held Meryl's chair for her and they walked toward the front of the club.

Meryl's brows knitted. "For some strange reason, I do. But then again, maybe it's because I want it so badly for her. Even though getting rid of Stan was a blessing, Morgana hasn't been happy since." She paused, her eyes glistening. "I wish you could have heard the change in her. The lilt was back in her voice, and she sounded so excited, so . . ." Meryl broke off as if groping for the right word. "I don't know, maybe 'animated' is the word I'm looking for."

They were now standing beside Meryl's car, soaking up the beauty of the April afternoon. Looking up, Meryl noticed there wasn't a cloud in the sky. It was as clear as a bell. She squinted against the harsh bright light before digging into her purse for her sunglasses.

"You and Morgana are as close as ever, aren't you?"

It was more of a statement than a question, Meryl thought as Tucker opened the door of her recently purchased red sports car and waited for her to get in it. Did she detect a thread of jealousy in his tone, or was it just a figment of her imagination?

"Of course," she quipped rather emphatically. "Whatever affects Morgana affects me." She shrugged and looked up at him as he leaned his arm against the top of the car. "With twins, I guess that's a way of life. Or at least it's that way with us, having only each other to depend on for most of our lives."

Whether he agreed or disagreed, Meryl couldn't tell. His features showed no emotion.

"Well, give her my best," he said with a polite smile. "Be careful, and I'll be in touch in a day or so."

Meryl disliked having to hurry. She also disliked being late for an appointment even if it was just to her sister's for dinner. And to make matters worse, she was battling the freeway at the worst possible time of the day. The late-afternoon traffic was horrendous. It was all she could do not to honk her horn in frustration and thrust her foot down on the accelerator in hopes of getting the traffic moving.

But then she realized she wouldn't be in this predicament if she hadn't dallied so long over lunch with Tucker. As it was, she'd had barely enough time to put on fresh makeup, slip into the pair of silk jeans that matched her blouse and blazer, and make a quick phone call to Nelda to make sure there were no tragedies at any of the studios before she was on the run again.

Now, as she fought to calm her frayed nerves, her thoughts turned to Morgana. She couldn't be more pleased or less surprised. She had always known that when her twin fell in love, really in love, it would be impetuous—hook, line and sinker all the way. And it seemed that she had at last found a man who could offer her the happiness she deserved and give her the stability she needed. With her modeling career beginning to flounder, Morgana had been through some tough times lately.

It seemed ironic to Meryl that when her career was at its best Morgana's was on a treadmill downward. Because of this, Morgana was oftentimes bitter and leaned toward self-destruction, which placed a heavy burden on Meryl. She could not stand to see her sister unhappy. And it worked both ways. When she had come back from Galveston two years ago, Morgana was there waiting to pick up the pieces, and virtually alone she helped Meryl glue the tiny pieces of her life back together. In many ways Morgana was an extension of herself.

But lately, as much as she hated to admit it or even think it, she sensed an underlying thread of jealousy on Morgana's part. She could understand why Morgana was bitter concerning her own career. When a model began to fade, she was no longer tolerated by the fashion houses or the magazines. And to hear Morgana tell it, she was fast approaching that point in her career. But Meryl wasn't sure that was true. Morgana stayed much too busy and made too much money for Meryl to believe that most of Morgana's paranoia was not exaggerated.

Yet it hurt Meryl deeply to think that her own sister could actually be jealous of her success, especially when Morgana had always been the successful one, beautiful and talented, with the world at her feet.

Still, it made no difference in how Meryl felt about her sister; she loved her more now than perhaps she ever had. For some reason, she had always felt responsible for Morgana, and that sense of responsibility had never lessened over the years.

Now it seemed as though Morgana had found a replacement for her faltering career—a man who would love and cherish her above everything else. A sigh rippled through Meryl. But then again, Morgana wasn't known for her ability to choose men. Since her divorce she had been through several affairs and several broken hearts, but marriage was never mentioned.

So all Meryl could do now was keep her fingers crossed and pray that this newfound happiness for her twin would work out for the best. As far as she was concerned, she intended to do everything in her power to see that it did work. She wanted desperately to see Morgana settled and happy.

* * *

Morgana met her at the door. She grabbed Meryl, held her close for a split second, then tore into her. "It's about time you got here, Meryl Stevens," she all but shouted. "Where on earth have you been? I've been ringing your phone off the wall for the last two hours."

Meryl chuckled as she returned her sister's brief hug and took in her lovely flushed face. It had always been a mystery to Meryl how twins could be so different in looks and temperament. Whereas she was dark and of average height, Morgana was just the opposite. She was tall, around five-feet-nine. The natural wheat-colored hair that swung loosely about her shoulders was the perfect foil for her peaches-and-cream complexion, further enhanced by high cheekbones and bright blue eyes.

If her lovely lips were often petulant and tiny wrinkles were beginning to appear around her eyes and mouth, brought on by constant dieting and worry over her career, they went unnoticed by Meryl. She thought Morgana had never looked lovelier.

"Sorry," Meryl said at last. "I had great intentions, but unfortunately they took a flying leap out the window the moment I met Tucker for lunch."

"What did 'dear old Tucker' have to say that was so important you couldn't tear yourself away?"

Meryl was evasive. "Oh, we just had to discuss a little business." She shrugged. "With me being gone for three weeks, he just wanted to touch base." And she wasn't lying, not really, she reassured herself. But she wasn't ready to tell Morgana about the television contract. Not yet. Not until it was a sure thing. Anyway, this was Morgana's day in court, not hers. She didn't want to do or say anything that would overshadow Morgana's news.

"Well, it doesn't matter, you're here now and that's all that counts." Her eyes sparkled as she held out her hand for Meryl's blazer and purse.

"Okay, let's have it," Meryl demanded as she followed

Morgana into the lovely ultramodern master bedroom, where she dropped the purse and jacket on the bed. "I want you to tell me every itsy-bitsy detail," she added, following Morgana into the kitchen. It too was ultramodern in decor, as was the rest of the condominium.

Morgana's eyes flashed boldly with excitement. "Mix yourself a drink while I put the finishing touches on dinner." She paused and looked down at her watch. "The guest of honor is due in exactly thirty minutes, which doesn't leave much time to fill you in on all the details."

Meryl hid a smile as she viewed Morgana's obvious nervousness. She had never seen her sister in such a state; she was behaving like a young girl about to make her prom debut. She was dressed in a pair of pink silk pants and a matching top. She looked stunning, especially if one counted the inner glow that surrounded her like a halo.

"Why don't you let me slice that roast beef," Meryl remarked dryly, "before you end up adding a finger to the delicacy."

Morgana made a face at her. "You just sit tight, sister dear. I have everything under control." She paused to throw a mischievous grin at Meryl before she resumed her task. "All you have to do is listen."

"All right," Meryl said, offering her hands up in mock defeat. "Go ahead, you have my undivided attention." She then positioned her elbows on the small wrought-iron ice-cream table adjacent to the counter and cupped her chin in her hands.

Morgana took a deep breath. "Well, first of all, I guess I'd better tell you his name."

"I was beginning to think this superman didn't have one," Meryl interrupted with a grin.

Morgana turned and glared playfully at her. "Well, he does, and it's—"

Suddenly the musical chimes of the doorbell aborted her sentence. Sheer panic overtook Morgana as she whirled around. "Oh, Meryl, that's him, I just know it is, and he's early. Would you please go let him in while I give my makeup a glance and discard this god-awful cooking smock?"

"For heaven's sake, calm down! Of course I'll let him in." Meryl laughed. "I can't wait to meet this superman."

Following on Morgan's heels as she fled to the privacy of her bedroom, Meryl maneuvered through the den to the front door.

A welcoming smile plastered on her lips, Meryl jerked open the door. "Hello," she said, "I'm . . ."

Meryl hung on to the doorknob as she reeled against the sudden and staggering blow to her heart, the blood slowly draining from her face.

"*You!*" she mouthed, before closing her eyes against the dizziness that drifted over her like a mist.

Chapter 5

IF MERYL WAS STUNNED, REESE CORBETT WAS DOUBLY SO. FOR an endless span of time neither moved, or spoke, or even breathed.

Meryl, paralyzed by shock, continued to clutch the door-knob for dear life while Reese paled visibly and blinked his eyes several times, positive that his mind was playing a malicious trick on him. But then, when she continued to stand motionless before him, he came to the conclusion that she was indeed real, *achingly* real.

She was as lovely as he had remembered. If not lovelier, he thought as his head ceased to reel and he began to focus on her features. Even though he hadn't so much as laid eyes on her for two years, he carried memories of their magic time together in the center of his heart. A day never passed that he didn't think about her.

And his yearning for her had increased twofold over the past few months. He had wanted desperately to seek her out, to tell her it was all over and that he was at last free to love her, to marry her. But something had held him back. Had it been pride? After all, he had gone back to the cabin with his heart on a silver platter, only to find her gone, with no forwarding address, no nothing. And perhaps a gut instinct had warned him that he would not be welcome in her life even though the circumstances had changed. Maybe, too, it had been the look on her face and in her eyes that day in the cabin when she had turned on him with such scorn in rallying around and clinging to her high ideals like a drowning man to a life raft.

So he had once again backed off, and in spite of his continued obsession for this woman, he had somehow managed to regroup and get his life back on track as best he could.

But the gods had suddenly smiled on him. She was here. Now. In the flesh. And he longed to reach out and fold her close within his arms and never let her go.

Another impossibility. He saw it. He knew it. He saw it in the coldness that radiated from her rounded eyes. And he knew it in his heart. Or where his heart should have been, he clarified bitterly. He was positive that nothing in his entire body was still intact, especially his heart. It was as though she had reached down his throat and grabbed that vital part of his body and stomped on it until it was no more.

Yet he was completely at her mercy; powerless to do anything other than just stand there and stare and drink in her beauty, still clinging to the hope that she truly wasn't an illusion, a dream. She seemed taller and much thinner, her eyes larger, but her face was as perfect as ever. God help him, he still wanted her and, yes, loved her. And now that he had seen her, he would never let her leave him.

Not again. Not this time.

He was the first to recover, though he spoke softly and moved as if still in a trance. He behaved as though he were a blind sculptor memorizing the face he aimed to recreate as he raised his hand and moved his thumb along the ridge of her brow, down the line of her cheek, across her lips. He touched the vibrant sheen of her dark hair. And remembered.

"Meryl, it is you, isn't it?" His voice was trembling with heartrending emotion.

Meryl stood like a statue split in two. One part of her entombed body was screeching: *How dare you do this to me?* longing to recoil from that tender, yet knowing touch, while the other part of her craved more of the same. *It had been so long.*

Suddenly Meryl was forced to react physically, but only because she had no choice. She heard the soft thudding tread of Morgana's footsteps as she made her way into the entry hall.

Meryl felt as though she was suspended by strings, that she had no control as she listened to a protective inner voice that kept repeating the same message. *Hang in there, Meryl. Just a while longer, that's all. Then you can disappear into your own little world and quietly have a nervous breakdown. But for now, you must be strong. You must protect yourself and Morgana at all costs!*

Instantly she became a cunning actress, a role she had never envisioned for herself. She was not only fighting for her own sanity, but again she was determined to protect Morgana, who, even more than herself, was the innocent victim.

"Hey, you two"—Morgana's musical voice effectively unhinged the smothering silence—"why are you still standing there?" She turned toward Meryl, a slight frown on her face, and added, her tone mildly chastising, "I thought at least by now you'd have a drink in his hand and be chatting like old friends."

If it hadn't been reminiscent of a scene out of an old horror movie, Meryl would have burst into laughter at the irony of the situation. But there was nothing funny, unless being caught with a lighted stick of dynamite in one's hand could be called funny, she thought bleakly.

She tossed her head back and met her sister's eyes with a plastic smile frozen on her lips and injected a false brightness into her voice. "That's exactly what we've been doing, introducing ourselves and getting acquainted," she lied. Under no circumstances could she let Morgana know of her past with this man. One broken heart in a family was enough. Furthermore, she had to be careful that Morgana didn't see through her charade.

Meryl held her breath, waiting to see if Reese would refute her lie, but he didn't. Like the perfect urbane gentleman, he smiled at Morgana and agreed, "That's right, but we were just heading for the den," he said calmly. Meryl couldn't help but notice that a muscle ticked in his jaw, showing he was not as cool as he appeared.

If Morgana noticed anything amiss, she didn't show it. Instead she threw her arms around Reese's neck and gave him a deep, searing kiss. "Hello, darling," she purred. "I'm so glad you were able to get away from the clinic early. I've been dying for you to meet my twin, Meryl."

Meryl turned away as a blinding, stabbing pain pierced her heart. Had Reese responded with equal fervor? She couldn't bear to know. Jealousy of her own sister was already beginning to work on her. How on earth, she wondered, could something so bizarre be happening? There were so many unanswered questions swirling around inside her head. Had Reese known all along that she was Morgana's sister? If things had progressed as far as Morgana had insinuated, then how could her name have failed to come up in their conversations?

But then she quickly reminded herself that she hadn't known his name either. Yet, she hadn't seen Morgana for three weeks, so it was understandable on her part. It just didn't make sense. But what did make sense was that she had this evening to get through without falling apart.

They were seated now in the den, with the exception of Reese, who was standing with his foot propped up on the hearth. Surrounding them were modernistic paintings that loomed over the plush ultramodern furniture and the glass end tables. They were in turn tastefully ornamented with more glass—figures from the various countries where Morgana had traveled as a successful model.

"I don't remember if I mentioned to you that Reese is a doctor," Morgana was saying from the bar, where she was busy mixing drinks. "And a very successful one at that. A plastic surgeon," she added almost as an afterthought, and then seemed to shift her eyes rather quickly away from Meryl.

Meryl was sitting rigidly on the couch adjacent to Reese.

She made sure her eyes never once veered in his direction as she made an effort to digest what Morgana had just told her. *A plastic surgeon.* How could it be, she asked herself, swallowing the hysteria that bubbled within her, that she had known every square inch of his hard body intimately but hadn't even known what kind of doctor he was? The hysteria was close to rising to the dangerous level.

She stood up abruptly and met Morgana halfway, intercepting her amaretto sour from the tray, desperate for something to occupy her hands. "Thanks," she mumbled, flashing her sister what she hoped was a sincere smile before lowering her shaky limbs back onto the couch.

Morgana then turned to Reese, who was still quietly standing to himself. "You're awfully subdued, darling," she said. "Did you have a hard day?"

Reese had to force himself back into the conversation with what he hoped was a pleasant smile, though his insides were clamoring with despair and weakness. God, what must Meryl be making of all of this? Morgana had talked about her sister endlessly, but she had never once called her by name. He was sure of it. In fact, he'd stake his life on it. Because if she had, he would have made the connection immediately. Even now, he couldn't believe it. Twin! No. It seemed impossible. They didn't look like sisters, much less twins.

And to compound his dilemma was the fact that he had no way in hell of knowing what Morgana had told Meryl concerning their relationship, but whatever it was, it wouldn't be the whole truth.

Only he knew the truth, but unfortunately it wasn't the kind of truth that would set him free, he thought with disdain. It was all he could do to keep from vaulting across the room and snatching Meryl up in his arms and devouring her lips with his and begging her to forgive him. Forgive him for not taking a chance and coming to her immediately after his divorce had become final. Now fate was dealing him another cruel blow—a twin sister in the middle.

He swallowed the lump in his throat and tried to squelch the raging desire that burned through his veins as he took in Meryl's slender gracefulness. She was holding herself like a queen, showing to perfection the burgeoning fullness of her breast, those same breasts that he had wooed time after time into a pulsating hardness with his mouth and tongue.

How had he stayed away from her for two long years? he asked himself as the desire for her continued to surge through his body like adrenaline.

Realizing that Morgana was waiting for his reply with a frown dotting her forehead, he finally said, "No, not too bad." He shrugged. "Just seemed to have more paperwork to do than usual, that's all," he finished lamely. *Watch it, Corbett! You'll have to do better than this. If you're not careful, you'll raise Morgana's suspicions with your less-than-enthusiastic attitude. It's obvious Meryl doesn't want her to know of your prior acquaintance. So watch your step!*

"Well, just wait until you've sampled what I've prepared for your palate." Morgana laughed. "I guarantee it'll perk you up. And speaking of food, why don't you and Meryl keep each other company a moment longer while I put the finishing touches on dinner."

Meryl quickly spoke up to the contrary. "I've got a better idea," she said breathlessly. "Why don't I go to the kitchen and let you stay here and talk to . . . to Reese."

"Huh! Not on your life, sister dear," Morgana retorted airily, though a smile encased her lips. "This is my chance to shine in the kitchen, and I will not have it usurped by a delicious cook. I'll call you when dinner is served," she flung over her shoulder as she flounced out of the room.

The moment they were alone, the tension in the air spread like cancer.

Meryl sat numb, clasping her hands so tightly together that she didn't even feel the pain when her nails dug into the tender palms of her hand. But she couldn't control her eyes; her vision now clear, they migrated toward Reese.

He had changed. For one thing, he was older. Time had taken its toll, etching deeper grooves into the planes of his face. And the creases on either side of his mouth lent credence to the fact that laughter would have a difficult time passing through those lips. And his eyes. They were still strangely beautiful, but again, they were imbued with signs of deep suffering. Worse than when she had first met him, she thought sadly.

Otherwise he looked great. Still the same hard-toned physique, actively fit. Age and time had done nothing to change that. He looked rakish in a gray pullover shirt, the exact color of his eyes, and a pair of tapered gray slacks that covered the muscled strength of his thighs, only to draw attention to his disturbing maleness. . . .

And to think he was going to marry her sister! She snapped her head up, praying he hadn't noticed the direction her eyes had taken.

But he had. Where she was concerned, his eyes missed nothing. His senses refused to respond to the tight rein he was putting on them. Unwillingly he felt the ache of his own arousal, the close-fitting knit pants he was wearing suddenly feeling too tight.

Out of sheer desperation, he broke the silence. "Alone at last," he said before gulping down the last of his drink and setting it with a clinking sound on the mantel. "You know we have to talk," he added urgently, tersely.

"No . . ." She wet her parched lips. "We . . . we have nothing to . . . talk about." How could fate tempt her like this? she cried inwardly. Especially now, when she had finally gotten her act together and was content, if not happy.

Reese's eyes darted past Meryl toward the kitchen before fervently settling back on her. "You can't mean that." He spoke with heat. "Of course we have to talk!"

She listened in shocked disbelief to his self-assured demand, her blood pressure steadily rising until she could hear her ears pounding.

"How dare you say that to me when you're as good as married to my sister," she spat. "Or is your ex still standing in the way of that union, too?"

"What the hell is that supposed to mean?" Reese countered sharply, only to have to abort the remainder of his inquiry as Morgana began making her way back into the den.

Morgana smiled delightedly. "Well, I'm glad to see you two are finally making friends." She waltzed over to Reese and looped an arm through his and began running a finger up and down his tanned skin, looking up at him adoringly. "Tell me, darling, what do you think about my ravishing twin? Isn't she everything I told you and more? Has she been telling you all about her zooming career in the world of physical fitness?"

"Your sister's beautiful indeed, Morgana, but no, she hasn't said a word about her illustrious career," he replied smoothly.

Meryl shivered inwardly, detecting the note of unleashed violence that punctuated each syllable.

Throughout dinner Meryl reacted as though she were underwater. Her every movement seemed to be weighted, heavy, slow. Morgana's carefully prepared meal of succulent prime rib, tiny new potatoes and carrots, fresh green beans, and ambrosia salad tasted like paste in her mouth.

Again, if Morgana noticed her less-than-amiable attitude, she failed to say anything, much to Meryl's relief. Her heightened nervous system could not have handled her sister's scrutiny or her sometimes caustic tongue.

For the most part, Meryl listened to Morgana's chatter, interrupted on occasion by a comment from Reese. Then suddenly Morgana made a statement that penetrated the fog around her brain like a gunshot.

"What did you say?" Meryl asked bluntly, not believing what she had just heard.

Morgana paled and shifted her eyes toward Reese as if asking for support. "What I said was that I'm going to let

Reese do a face-lift on me." Her chin lifted a fraction of an inch in a show of defiance. A look Meryl was very familiar with.

"Now, Morgana, I told you," Reese interjected patiently, "I—"

Morgana waved a hand in the air, cutting him off before he could utter a protest. "I know, I know. It all depends on whether or not you can fit it into your busy schedule," she finished petulantly.

Meryl's eyes bounced back and forth between the two of them, concern turning her eyes coal black. "Morgana, have you lost your mind?"

Morgana's lips formed a taut line. "It's made up, Meryl. Don't try to change it."

"But . . . but that's absurd! How can you improve on perfection?" Then, before Meryl could get an answer, her eyes swung around to Reese. "Surely you haven't encouraged her in this madness?" she accused harshly.

An expletive savagely sprang from Reese's lips as he shoved a hand through his thick hair. "Of course I haven't," he retorted, "but as you well know, your sister has a stubborn streak up her back a mile long."

"Both of you quit talking about me as if I weren't here," Morgana cut in, a whiny edge to her voice.

Still looking at Meryl, Reese continued. "I'm afraid her mind is made up, and if I don't do it, someone else will." He sighed. "At least if I do it, I know it will be done right."

Meryl's eyes darted back to her sister. "What made you come up with such a cockamamie idea in the first place?" She paused, gnawing at her lower lip. "It reeks strongly of Jay Johnson's handiwork," she added sarcastically.

Morgana fidgeted uncomfortably. "Well, as a matter of fact, we did discuss it, but," she went on hastily, "he didn't encourage me one way or the other. He left it up to me, and I'm the one who contacted Reese."

So that's how she met him, Meryl thought before listening to what Reese was saying to Morgana.

"I want you to be absolutely sure that's what you want to do." His eyes softened suddenly. "But I have a tendency to agree with your sister: it's hard to improve on perfection."

Blind jealousy purged Meryl's body like poison, and no matter how hard she tried to keep it at bay, she could not. *Don't panic. Remember, it's purely physical. You're just remembering how it felt to have his hands caress your body. You don't love him anymore. You can handle it.*

"Oh, Reese, you certainly know how to make a woman feel good," Morgana cooed before smoothly changing the subject. "But what do you say we discontinue this boring conversation and adjourn to the den for coffee."

Once they had exited the dining room, Meryl knew she had reached her limit of endurance. Her head was throbbing again and she attributed it to nothing more than high-voltage tension. She longed to put as much distance between her and Reese as she possibly could. God, it seemed as though they'd never been apart. *She needed time to think!*

Fifteen minutes later, Meryl stood up and leaned over and pecked her sister on the cheek. "It was wonderful, love, but it's time I took this tired body of mine home and put it to bed."

Morgana frowned. "But it's early yet . . ."

"You know me," Meryl said, adopting a casual tone. "I have to have my beauty rest."

Reese stood up and deliberately held out his hand. "Nice meeting you, Meryl Stevens," he drawled. "I hope to see you again—soon."

The blood surged to her head. He was deliberately challenging her and enjoying it to the hilt. She wanted to slap his arrogant face. It took every ounce of fortitude she possessed to reach out and touch his fingers.

"Dr. Corbett." Her voice sounded foreign and cold even to her own ears. But hopefully he got the message, she thought. There would certainly be no "again soon" for them.

The slight but gripping pressure she received made it abundantly clear that he hadn't been rebuffed in the least.

Then Morgana was speaking eagerly. "Oh, for goodness' sake, Meryl, call him Reese."

Would this nightmare ever end? she wondered as she smiled through stiff, contrived lips, fighting to control the tingling in her hand from his touch and the dizziness that washed over her. She just prayed she would get out the door before she disgraced herself by losing the contents of her stomach.

The task of driving home was no easy one. Her mind was a seething caldron of contradictions. She still couldn't believe that the man her sister proclaimed to love was none other than Reese. *Her* Reese. No, she quickly admonished, he was no longer hers. Had never been hers. And furthermore, she didn't want him. Didn't care if she ever saw him again. *What a liar you are*, she thought, clutching the steering wheel so hard she was afraid her knuckles would crack.

"Oh, damn you, Reese Corbett. Double-damn and triple-damn you!" she vented aloud as she sailed down the freeway, ignorant of the fact that she was speeding. Just when she was beginning to make an inroad into a new life for herself, one that she could be proud of, *he* had to come back into her life, opening the floodgate of memories she'd tried to dam up, his mere presence cruelly emphasizing the loneliness she'd tried to ignore. . . .

After she had arrived home from the cabin, the first few weeks had been a living hell. She had been afraid she could not survive without him; she missed him so much. It was like a sickness gnawing at her insides twenty-four hours a day.

She had been helpless against the unbearable emptiness that kept dragging at her like a menacing undercurrent, threatening to suck her under. For the longest time, she would reach out for the warmth of his body during the night, only to find coldness. Then, in the wake of the morning sunlight, the images of his face in the throes of lovemaking, their shared laughter over some silly incident continued to hammer away at her, carving a deeper hole into the emptiness of her life and filling her with bittersweet pangs of longing.

How could she go on without him? In just three short weeks he had become her life. The culmination of all her dreams, her fantasies. But reality had come hard; she learned that one's dreams have a way of being swept into thin air like leaves on a blustery fall day, leaving devastation in their wake.

Yet, throughout those days overflowing with pain, she had clung to the hope that in spite of what it had cost her, she had indeed done the right thing. She still believed that right was right and wrong was wrong. And to have continued to be a part of Reese's life would have been wrong.

By clinging to this sacred principle she had been able to stop wallowing in self-pity and "what might have been" and make her life count for something.

The idea for the exercise studios had turned into a reality in just the nick of time or she might not have made it through the trauma.

As for that aspect of her life, Meryl couldn't have been more satisfied. She had proved to herself and to others that she could be a success and obtain an individuality she never had as a married woman. This was the part of herself she displayed to the outside world. Others thought she had it made.

And most of the time she thought so too. Except when her nights were filled with erotic memories that just wouldn't rest. But she had fought like a crazed person, determined to forget him. And laying her memories to rest was the last major hurdle she had to jump. She had likened losing Reese to losing a limb. It had crippled her, but she had survived and would continue to do so. Or so she had thought. But now . . . Oh, God, what now?

The jolting sound of a horn honking brought her out of her kaleidoscope of memories back to the present, the awful stark present. But if she didn't stay in her lane on the freeway, she wouldn't have to worry about the present or the future, she reminded herself severely. She would be a statistic in the city morgue.

Although she forced herself to pay closer attention to her driving methods, she still was powerless to stop her emotions from churning.

Suddenly her thoughts shifted to Morgana. *Morgana and Reese!* Together. A couple. Oh, God, she prayed as she fought to control· the sickening humiliation that drew her stomach up into a tiny knot. Did Reese return Morgana's feelings? Somehow she didn't think so. Oh, who was she kidding? Of course he cared for Morgana. She couldn't see it because she didn't want to. She was blinded by her own feelings. But they didn't count. She was past, Morgana was the present. And Morgana must come first.

Suddenly unbidden memories of a time long ago came to her mind. It was the only time she and Morgana had had a serious disagreement. She recalled it as if it had been yesterday. . . .

It was immediately after the senior prom and they were in Morgana's room and Morgana was furious.

She had turned on Meryl, fire shooting from her eyes. "Why did you do it?" she had demanded.

Meryl had been flabbergasted by her action. "I . . . I don't know what you're talking about," she said.

"Oh, yes you do! Alton was my date. How dare you encourage him to pant after you?"

"That's not true, and you know it," Meryl shouted back.

"Oh, isn't it? How do you explain the minute my back was turned he sniffed you out like a dog in heat? He wouldn't have done that if you hadn't encouraged him. I just know he wouldn't." She then fell on the bed and began sobbing like her heart was broken.

Meryl was horrified. She stood like a zombie and stared at her twin, her mouth gapping open. "Surely you don't think I'm interested in Alton, just . . . just because he was being nice and talking to me?"

"That's the problem, they're always just coming up to you

and being nice." Every word she enunciated dripped with sarcasm.

"Morgana, don't! You're wrong. Why won't you listen to reason?"

Morgana jerked herself upright on the bed and glared at Meryl. "Don't lie to me." She gulped back the tears. "Everyone thinks you're beautiful and intelligent and that I'm just a dumb blonde with no sense."

"That's pure rubbish if I ever heard it!" Meryl spat back, now furious herself.

"I know it's true, every word," Morgana countered dully. "You're better at everything. You make the best grades, have the most friends. There's not anything I can do better than you," she finished dully.

Meryl felt as though her heart had caved in. She'd had no idea Morgana was harboring such resentments against her. But what frightened her even more was that she didn't know how to deal with them.

Morgana began crying again, and Meryl couldn't stand it. She knelt down beside her. "Please, don't cry," she begged. "I'm so sorry if I've hurt you. But what you've said is only partly true. If I do make better grades, it's because I try harder, and the same thing applies to friends—boys as well as girls. I've always felt I had to, because I was always envious of your lighthearted attitude and your blond beauty. Don't you see?" Meryl's eyes were pleading.

Morgana had finally stopped crying, but she didn't look convinced. "You're . . . you're just saying . . . saying that," she stammered.

Meryl was crying. "If only you knew how insecure I am, you wouldn't be envying me at all. But I'm so sorry if I've hurt you. I'd rather die than do that." And she was. Morgana was all she had, and she couldn't stand the thought of anything separating them.

"Well, maybe when we . . . we go to different schools, we won't be in competition with each other," Morgana said.

Meryl shook her head. "No!" she refuted. "I don't want us

to go our separate ways. We've always been together. Please, Morgana, don't let Alton come between us."

Morgana sighed. "It's not just this thing with Alton, don't you see? It's . . . everything."

It was at that precise moment that Meryl began to live her life apart from her twin. But she had felt down deep that Morgana had turned on her because of the fickle attention of a mere boy. But through the years she had never forgotten it. It was a lesson she had learned well.

Exhausted now both in mind and in spirit, she wheeled the car into the covered parking area and made her way slowly to the rear door of her town house and locked the door behind her.

Forcing her weary limbs to function, she headed straight toward her bedroom with only a short detour by the bathroom, where she hastily brushed her teeth. She then shed her clothes and dived naked between the sheets, curling the crisp clean sheet under her chin.

She was so tired! If only she could get one decent night's sleep. But the moment her head touched the pillow and she closed her eyes, Reese's face danced across her vision, as did the memory of his fingers gently caressing her face.

She ached for him. Oh, God, how she ached to feel his arms around her, his mouth searing her skin. . . . Suddenly a tight band formed itself around her ribs, making it impossible for her to move.

She knew. With the force of a sledgehammer pounding her brain, the truth hit her. The electrifying truth. *She and her sister were in love with the same man!*

Chapter 6

No! Oh, God, no. Don't let it be true, she begged as she lay stiff as a rod and stared at the ceiling. She couldn't still be in love with Reese. Impossible. It was just lust, she told herself. It had to be. She was simply confusing lust with love. That's all. She felt warm tears seep from the corners of her eyelids and bathe her cheeks. *Don't freak out!* she pleaded with herself. Don't think.

But there was no way she could keep from thinking. Her brain simply refused to take orders from her tired body. From the moment she had opened the door and seen Reese standing on the threshold, her life had once again become a chaotic nightmare. Suddenly and without warning her past had caught up with her and crashed violently into her complacent life.

She dragged the back of her hand across her cheek to remove the moisture that was now dripping into her mouth, the salty taste of the tears stinging her tongue.

"Damn you, Reese Corbett," she hissed aloud, using the pillow as a punching bag. "How could you do this to me? To Morgana?"

Then another chilling thought struck her. She wondered if Morgana was aware that the "love of her life" was more than likely still a married man? She, Meryl, believed that Reese had never obtained his freedom, because she had always harbored the hope that he would have tried to contact her if his divorce *had* gone through as planned.

A laugh filtered through her lips as she rolled over and

again punched her pillow, but it held no mirth. But then, it wouldn't be the first married man her sister had been involved with since her divorce, she reminded herself dispiritedly. For the thousandth time, Meryl asked herself how she and Morgana could think identically in so many ways, yet be so different in others. Once she had faced the truth that Reese was a married man, she could not have lived with herself if she had continued to see him.

And nothing had changed, she thought with another wave of despair. He was still forbidden fruit, and she must avoid him at all cost. He had shaken the foundations of her secure life, but she would *not* allow him the luxury of completely destroying what she had worked so long and hard to build.

Nor would she ever again compete with her sister for the affections of a man. Or play havoc with her sister's happiness, no matter how much the thought of them together slashed her heart to ribbons.

How long she lay there before the sound of the doorbell made it through her muddled senses, she didn't know. But whoever was on the other end of it—and she'd bet anything it was Morgana—was persistent.

"Damn!" she mumbled, flinging the top sheet back and blindly reaching for the robe that draped across the end of the bed. Positive that it couldn't be anyone other than her sister at this ungodly hour, she didn't bother to arrange her hair in any kind of order or to mask the traces of tears that still clung to her cheeks.

"Cool it, Morgana!" she called as she raced for the door, her fingers fumbling with the tie on her robe. "I'm coming, just give me time."

Automatically flipping on the front porch light and making sure the chain was unlatched, she jerked open the door. For the second time in one day, Meryl was thrown into stunned immobility. In one quick blink her vision encompassed a haggard-looking Reese staring at her through piercing velvet eyes.

A whimper broke through her lips as she clutched the robe

tighter around her neck with one hand while she strove to slam the door in his face with the other.

But he was too quick for her. "Oh, no you don't," he vented harshly, before positioning a foot in the crack of the door and pressing his arm roughly against it. "I've got to talk to you!"

Meryl was powerless against his strength. For a moment they waged a battle of wills. Ultimately she lost. She was no match for his determined brute force. She finally dropped her hand from the door and turned her back on him.

"Go away, Reese," she said tonelessly as she wrapped her arms around herself defensively. "We . . . we don't have anything to say to one another." Her heart was beating out of control.

"Oh, but I think we do," he replied tersely. "We have two long years to talk about."

She heard the quiet click of the door behind her and knew with a sinking feeling that he was now in the room with her. Still she did not turn around. She was afraid if she so much as moved an inch, her legs would buckle beneath her.

"No . . . no . . . just go away. I . . ." Her voice broke treacherously as she tried to stem the flow of tears. The bitterness was there, burning with its destructive flame. Oh, God, she cried silently, make him go away and leave *me* alone.

But her plea was not to be granted. She knew it when he came to stand behind her; she smelled the very scent of him—that musk scent that was his alone. She fought against succumbing to the blackness that threatened to engulf her by concentrating on the ordinary things around her.

Her eyes followed the shadows that danced around the walls, compliments of the full moon that sprayed its beam through the open draperies. She listened to the eerie sound of an ambulance as it raced through the inky blackness; and somewhere in the distance she was aware of a car door slamming, followed by the sound of voices.

But nothing could obliterate his presence.

Yet he did not touch her, merely moved a step closer. "Don't . . . don't send me away," he pleaded softly, his warm breath feathering her neck.

Beware, Meryl. He's seducing you with honeyed words. It's happening all over again. Put a stop to it now. She forced her legs to move, stretching the distance between them.

"I mean it, Reese, I don't want you here," Meryl responded, at the same time reaching for the lamp on the table nearest her. After switching it on, she spun around to face him, a mutinous look on her face.

"Please, just go," she stressed again, trying to ignore the slight waver in her voice. Oh, God, she didn't want him to go, and she did want to talk to him. But she was still hurt, angry and confused. And what good could possibly come of it? She knew he had never really loved her; their relationship had been based on lies from the beginning. But if, *just if,* he did still care, it would mean only more pain. There was the past . . . and Morgana. Visions of her sister's laughter and radiating happiness as she gave Reese that searing kiss were stamped vividly on her mind.

"Well, now that I'm here, wild horses couldn't chase me away, not until I've had my say, that is," Reese said, a grim smile creeping forbiddingly into his features, drawing his lips into a thin line. The well-mannered mask had completely disappeared, leaving his eyes narrowed slits of determination.

To her dismay, he then stalked across the room and stood by the window, his hard, muscular frame becoming an unmovable object.

She forced her face to show no emotion. She would not let him see how his being here so completely unnerved her. "What exactly do you want from me?" she whispered dully. And then, before he could answer, she rephrased the question. "Surely you don't think we can just . . . just take up where we left off two years ago?" Now, she thought—now he'll mention Morgana. She had opened the door. . . .

As Reese's eyes searched her face for a ray of hope in her set features, he thought he had never seen her look more enchanting. Her hair was beautifully tangled atop her head, her slender form delightfully curved and soft. And her nakedness was an alluring silhouette beneath her flimsy robe. He closed his eyes briefly, fighting off a spasm of shivers, as his flesh was remembering her touch, his loins constricting as his mouth went dry and his skin burned. He thought he would surely die from wanting her.

"Everything," he announced quietly. "I want everything." His voice had softened now to a mere whisper, but there was a finality to it that left no doubt that he meant what he said. "Oh, God, Meryl, what I'm trying to say is that I still love you and want to marry you. I want to wake up every morning with you beside me. I want to watch you grow round carrying my baby." He paused and drew a shuddering breath. "I want—"

"Don't!" she cried again as she marched into the kitchen and yanked open a cabinet door. She then unconsciously began scooping coffee grounds into a filter. She had to do something to counteract her nerves or she would soon dissolve into helpless tears.

He followed her, his eyes soft and pleading. "Meryl, please hear me out. You don't know how many times during the last few months I've picked up the telephone to call you, but I was scared, dammit. Go ahead and laugh. I know it sounds ridiculous, but as God is my witness, it's the truth. I . . ."

Rage. Boiling hot rage swept through her body, replacing the blood in her veins with fire. She pivoted on her bare feet, at the same time clenching her hands beside her body to keep from striking him. *Did he think she was nothing but an imbecile who would swallow anything that flowed from his tongue?*

"Why, why, you . . . you . . . hypocrite! You . . . you bastard," she spat. "How can you come here and say that to me after . . . after . . ." She couldn't go on. The words were jammed in her swollen throat.

Reese literally bolted across the room, coming to stand only inches from her. His jaw was set as though in concrete. "You're not the only one with an ax to grind. Neither are you without fault in all of this," he spat sarcastically. "Why did you run out on me? You knew I was coming back."

"Oh, I did, did I?" she screeched, her eyes blazing. "You were married! With obligations! In light of those minor details, how was I supposed to know you were coming back?"

"Because I loved you, that's why!" he roared.

"Well, that just wasn't enough," she countered hotly. "I didn't play around with married men then, and I don't now."

"What's that supposed to mean?"

"You know very well what that means, Doctor!"

"Like hell I do."

"Like hell you don't!"

"Just hold on a minute!" Reese grated, once again closing the gap between them and bringing the ragged contours of his face to hers, nose to nose. "So I wasn't entirely honest with you, I'll admit that, but believe me, I've lived to regret every second of that day." His face was ashen. "But I'm not married now. And there's something else you don't know . . ."

"I don't want to hear it," she said tersely.

It was all Reese could do to keep from attempting to strangle her. "Dammit, Meryl, why do you insist on pushing me over the brink!"

Meryl quailed before his anger. Then suddenly the punch went out of her. She felt like an overinflated balloon that had just burst. She came crashing back to reality with a thud.

Her shoulders sagged in defeat. "All this is irrelevant, you know," she said tonelessly, keeping her back turned. "It just doesn't matter any longer, Reese. You've got to understand that I'm not the same gullible person I was two years ago. I've changed." She paused while she poured the water into the automatic coffee maker. Then she turned around and faced him, leaning her back against the countertop for support. "Marriage is no longer important to me. It's at the bottom of my list of priorities. And as far as children are concerned, I'm too old to have them," she stated flatly, without emotion, all the while her stomach was churning like she was on a roller coaster.

But it was imperative that she talk tough, that she hide behind this wall of indifference. Every time a child was mentioned in connection with herself, it threw her into a mild panic and brought to mind in full living color the agonies she had suffered because of this flaw within her. She could not bear to see the condemnation on Reese's face that she had seen so often on her husband's.

Although she noticed Reese had paled visibly, his voice was calm. "Okay, so you don't want children. I can accept that."

Don't do this to me, Reese, she wailed silently. *Oh, don't, please don't. Can't you see, it's too late.* "No!" she cried again, rigorously shaking her head. "You've got your nerve coming here, saying those things to me. It's absurd! It's ludicrous!" she shouted. Visions of the months of heartache and pain she had endured at his expense, to say nothing of the guilt that had nearly driven her crazy, suddenly blinded her to all else. And not one word had he uttered about Morgana. *Damn you, what about Morgana?* she demanded silently.

"You're right," he expressed harshly, "I have no rights where you're concerned. But it would have been only a matter of time before I would have sought you out and told you the truth." His shoulders sagged in dejection. "Will you please stop banging around in this kitchen for a goddamned minute and sit down and listen to what I have to say? At least grant that one favor."

He was doing it to her again—standing behind her, within touching distance, seducing her with his electrifying closeness. She tried to move sideways, but he stopped her cold, reaching out and cupping her chin with his fingers and turning her gently around to face him.

"Please," he whispered.

He bent closer still, and Meryl stood as if embedded in cement and felt his breath fan warmly across her cheek. She knew she should turn away, yet she was incapable of moving. In that instant another terrible truth struck her: she could hate him, abuse him, run from him, but she could not rid herself of wanting him. After two long years, he still had the power to turn her insides topsy-turvy.

She nodded her assent, as she was incapable of uttering a word. To her relief, he stepped back and let her pass. She quickly poured two cups of the steaming black liquid and followed him into the den. Trembling, she sat down on the couch and waited for him to do the same.

It was a moment before he spoke. "I'll come straight to the point," he said brutally. "When I came back from Galveston, all hell had broken loose. Jason was in intensive care, and Kathy . . . his mother, was out of town. With one of her lovers, I might add, just for the record."

Meryl sensed there was no pain in those tersely spoken words, only bitterness.

He went on. "I spent every moment with him I could. The only time I was away for any length of time was when I flew back to Galveston to explain things to you." If he noticed Meryl gasp, he ignored it. "So you can imagine what my life was like for the next few months. I lived in a vacuum. I shuttled back and forth between the clinic and the hospital for God only knows how long." He paused and fumbled in his pocket for a pack of cigarettes, yanking one out and lighting it. Meryl couldn't help but notice how his beautiful hands shook. Suddenly he bounded off the couch and began pacing back and forth in front of her like a caged lion, only to abruptly discard the cigarette in the nearest ashtray with a grimace.

"Kathy fought me every step of the way. She still refused to give me a divorce, even though it was obvious she didn't want me. But she didn't want anyone else to have me either—not even her own son. She used him to keep me in line," he expressed bitterly. "And as you well know, it worked . . . until . . ." His voice broke and he stopped his pacing and stared at Meryl.

Pain mingled with tears poured from his eyes. A cold chill raked Meryl's body as she grappled to understand what he was trying to tell her. Without thinking of what she was doing, Meryl sprang to her feet and went to him and folded her arms around his tense body. The tears threatened his composure as she held him close within the circle of her arms.

"Jason died, Meryl." His voice was barely audible. "My three-year-old son died six months ago of heart failure, and there wasn't a damned thing I could do to stop it."

She could only hold him, rock him in her arms, hoping to absorb some of the pain that continued to torment his battered soul. She closed her eyes as the tears trickled down her cheeks as the horror of what he had told her registered. Her face was a tortured mask as the horrifying picture of Reese cradling his son's lifeless body in his arms flashed before her eyes. And to think she had known that his son had been ill, and she hadn't even asked about him. But, dear God, she'd had no way of knowing he'd been *that* sick.

"Oh, God, Meryl, I wanted to die too," he said in a hoarse and tormented voice, his body weighing heavily against hers as he buried his face in her riot of curls, his arms a velvet prison encircling her.

Meryl's heart soared with an overriding sense of relief. She was where she longed to be—gathered close in his gentle embrace once again. It was the most devastating, yet wonderful feeling she had ever hoped to experience. Something she thought had withered up and died within her flowed back to life. She buried her face into his shoulder and ceased to fight the overwhelming realization that she needed him as never before. The reason was simple: he needed her. They came together, one's weakness absorbing the other's strength.

Reese felt the misery, the abiding hurt, the doubts evaporate like mist on a sunny day as he held fast to her lissome frame, cleansing himself of the hollow feeling that had been a part of him for so long.

This physical closeness was a time for healing, blotting out all other conscious thought. And for a moment the hot driving passion that always simmered between them was overshadowed by the simple need to hold.

Serenity drifted around them as their bodies molded together in an embrace that soothed their pain and provided comfort from the loneliness that haunted them both.

Meryl was the first to stir. It was at that precise moment the soothing comfort turned into a raw, aching need.

Reese's body jerked violently, and with a stifled moan, he locked his arms tighter around her, making it hard for her to breathe. She was acutely aware of his arousal as it pressed against her stomach. In that instant, they both went rigid.

Then Reese moved as if to pull away.

Meryl yearned to let him go before she drowned in the sensations that were threatening to sweep her away without conscious thought or reason, but she could not. She had to give in to her own desires, if only for the moment.

No! she groaned inwardly, and clung to him, running her hands through his hair, drawing him closer.

"Meryl," he rasped, looking down at her, a question burning in his eyes.

She pressed a finger against his lips, giving him her answer. *Just this once,* she promised herself. *After all, he was mine first.*

Needing no further encouragement, Reese slowly touched her plump lower lip with his tongue, stroking it gently, savoring the exquisite sweetness of her lips. As he held her, he realized anew that he only felt alive in her embrace. The rest of his life would be like a desert of despair without her. And if he allowed himself to dwell on the possibility of that happening again, he would shatter into a million pieces from the impact.

Then his mouth closed over hers, reverently, tenderly, like the touch of a butterfly on a flower petal. But his insides were begging for more, much more. It had been two long years since he had kissed her.

Meryl craved more, sensed he was holding back. "Reese," she whispered into his mouth as she dug her fingers into the back of his neck and slipped her tongue deep into the delicious crevice.

That proved to be Reese's undoing. He groaned and then ground his lips into hers, kissing her hotly, deeply, until they were both moist and panting.

Just as suddenly as it began, it ended.

Meryl felt him take a long shaky breath; then he released his viselike grip on her and firmly eased her away from him.

Wordlessly she stared up at him, becoming more confused than ever when she saw the misery in his velvet eyes.

"I . . . I can't. We . . . we can't," he stammered harshly. "Don't you see . . . I don't want you to come to me out of pity." His eyes implored her as she stood like a statue, empty and stunned. "There . . . there are painful barriers we still have to erase."

That last statement brought the whole episode into perspective—like a blow to the head. It was almost as though she were living an instant replay of another time, another place, as shame and humiliation washed over her, replacing the passion and the need.

How could she have so blatantly offered herself to him after all that she had said to him to the contrary? He was right: nothing had been settled. There were still too many ghosts separating them. She had sacrificed it all—her pride, her self-respect, and Morgana—for a moment of passion. *God forbid!* She felt sick.

But her indulgence in self-pity was short-lived. Reese was seemingly in total control of his emotions once again and talked to her as if he had her undivided attention. In spite of her efforts not to do so, she found herself hanging on to his every word.

He was massaging the back of his neck as he stood by the open window, staring out into the inky blackness. "There was nothing anyone could do," he was saying softly. "It was a birth defect that couldn't be corrected."

Meryl kept her gaze on his neck, helpless as she heard the pain return to his voice.

"It was shortly after the funeral that Kathy agreed to give me a divorce. But by then both my work and my life were in shambles. I wasn't fit to be around another human being." He paused and turned to look at her with his heart in his eyes. "You'll never know how much I needed you—your comfort, your laughter . . . But I had nothing to offer you then except a broken shell of a man. When I was finally able to put my life back together, I got cold feet, as I've already told you."

"Please, Reese, don't . . ." *You're not being fair. You're doing it to me again. Damn you! You know I can't stand to see you like this.*

"Let me finish . . . please." He was pleading again, and Meryl was powerless to deny him.

"Another reason I didn't try to contact you was my work."

She looked puzzled. "Your work. I . . . I don't understand. I thought you just catered to vain, beautiful women." She tried to keep the sarcasm out of her voice, but she failed miserably.

He winced, but his tone remained even. "Cosmetic surgery —which I devote very little time to, by the way—is merely a means of providing me with a steady cash flow to work on a project that is near and dear to my heart."

Meryl looked skeptical. "Oh?"

Reese went on as though she hadn't spoken, although the backward curl of his lips was not lost on Meryl. "Behind the scenes I do research and perform surgery on children and occasionally adults, but mostly on children whose faces are grossly deformed from severe birth defects." He paused and flexed his shoulder muscles wearily. "I do what I can to help them lead as normal a life as possible, but even at that, there are some who are beyond help."

Meryl felt like a fool. Here she was thinking that Reese spent all his time and efforts on cosmetic surgery, which she thought was a waste of valuable time and talent, only to find that he was involved in doing a service for the helpless and the needy. For reasons she didn't wish to pursue, a warm glow curled around her heart.

"But . . . but I still don't understand." A perplexed frown marred her features. "Why all the cloak-and-dagger stuff? What I mean is, why do you feel the need to keep this talent hidden when it's something to be proud of?" Her eyes dimmed suddenly. "Although I've never actually seen a person with that type of deformity, I've seen pictures. I . . . I think it's wonderful that someone cares enough to help them."

Reese sighed. "Well, as much as I appreciate your pat on the back, every one of us in this field has a long way to go before we can label ourselves successful."

"Maybe so," Meryl concluded softly, "but at least you're in there trying. But that still doesn't explain the secrecy."

He shrugged. "The secrecy, as you call it, is not what I do per se as much as it is the image I must project while I'm doing it."

"You're still not making sense to me." She moved her head in frustration.

"It's simple, really," he explained patiently. "The bulk of the funds needed to carry on this work come from huge grants and donations. Without them, I would be helplessly crippled in my endeavor, as would my colleagues. So I'm forever in the limelight, attending charity functions, or prodding others to hold these functions. It takes years and millions of dollars to do the plastic surgery and bone reconstruction on these individuals, and as a result, no one person could afford to have it done. Hence our depending on the general public." He expelled a harsh sigh. "And that compounds the need for me to keep a low profile and not air any dirty laundry, if you get the drift of what I'm trying to say."

The third time around, it finally soaked through her thick skull. "In other words," she said softly, "there can't be any scandal attached to your name or it will place your work in jeopardy. Those firms and the little old ladies who fork over their money want you to be as fresh and pure as driven snow. Right?"

"You've got it," he replied swiftly, and then his eyes pinned hers. "But neither could I come to your doorstep pleading my case until I had something to offer you." He paused, reached out and carefully traced a line down one side of her cheek with a finger. "Though I never once stopped loving you," he added softly.

Her eyes fluttered shut as she prayed for the pain that suddenly stabbed at her heart to go away. But it did not; it continued to flay her relentlessly.

His alliance with Morgana loomed like a destructive time bomb waiting for the right moment to explode in their faces. Furthermore, she couldn't let him breeze back into her life and take over her person. She would fight him every step of the way if she had to.

"You're too late," she cried, feeling the nerve ends snap, the last vestiges of control slipping. "You inform me one day you're married. Then two years later you waltz back into my life and announce you want me back, thinking we can just pick up where we left off and everything will be rosy."

"I didn't say that," he began vehemently, then stopped himself, forcing the emotion down, lowering his voice. "What I said was that I love you and that I want to marry you. This time it's totally different. Before, I couldn't offer you anything—now I can offer you everything."

Her shoulders sagged in defeat. "All this is irrelevant, you know," she said dully. "There's still . . . Morgana."

Another terse expletive ripped past his lips as he stepped back and walked away, tightening his fist into a ball. *Easy, Corbett, easy, he warned. Remember, Rome wasn't built in a day. Back off, give her breathing room before you screw up your chances of ever getting her back.*

He swallowed his impatience. "Forgive me if I appear dense, but what does Morgana have to do with us, pray tell?"

Meryl couldn't believe her ears. She knew her face must have registered her shock, because she saw his face darken along with the confusion in his eyes. He was either a damned good actor, she thought, or he was truly baffled by her statement.

Then sound reason came to her rescue. Of course he knew what she was referring to. He was up to his old tricks again; he was trying to deceive her.

"I can't believe your nerve!" she snapped acidly. "How can you stand there and play dumb when you *know* that you've encouraged Morgana. Otherwise . . . otherwise she wouldn't have fallen head over heels in love with you." Meryl hated herself for the catch in her voice when she longed to appear strong and uncaring. *Oh, what a tangled web we weave, only to be deceived.* How true, she thought bleakly. Oh, how true.

"That's a lie!" he thundered, taking Meryl completely by surprise.

"What did you say!" she asked sharply.

"You heard me, and I meant exactly that. I'll admit I've taken your sister out to dinner several times and visited with her at length in the office, but I swear that I've never given her any reason to think that I'm in love with her, or vice versa." It was obvious he was barely hanging on to his temper, the way his face settled into harshly defined lines. "If she feels anything for me other than friendship, it has got to be infatuation." He shoved his hand through his hair in frustration; at the same time, his eyes pleaded with her for understanding. "For God's sake, Meryl, I've never even slept with her!"

She listened, wanting to believe what he had just said with undeniable conviction. She'd be a fool not to admit her heart had sprouted wings on learning he hadn't taken her sister to bed. Somehow she knew she couldn't have borne that. But then her heart immediately took a plummeting dive back to earth as the pain reinforced itself. The scars of the past were still there and remained extremely tender to the touch.

Her wounded eyes flickered over him as a hushed silence fell over the room. "I . . . I can't tell you . . . what you want to hear," she whispered, shaking her head. "Not now . . . not ever."

Reese stepped back, the muscles in his jaw working grimly.

"I refuse to accept that," he said heavily, and walked

slowly toward the door, then stopped and half-turned to face her. "I'm going now. But remember this. I can be just as determined as you. I love you, and I don't intend to give up."

Meryl stood unflinching as she watched him go; while on the inside anger, hurt, and confusion tangled into a burning knot of anxiety. She was treading on the thin edge of complete emotional collapse, and she feared it would take very little to push her over the side.

"You've really done it to yourself this time,' she moaned aloud before sinking onto the couch and burying her head in her hands.

Chapter 7

BRIGHT AND EARLY THE NEXT MORNING, MORGANA CALLED.

For twenty minutes thereafter, Meryl listened to her twin sing Reese's praises, until she thought she would scream. Morgana asked her over and over didn't she think he was indeed wonderful and didn't she think he'd make an exciting husband. Somehow Meryl must have inflected the correct amount of enthusiasm into her voice, because Morgana seemed satisfied with her answers.

After promising to call Meryl to have lunch with her after she returned from a short modeling assignment out of town, Morgana finally said good-bye, but not before adding a bubbly rejoinder: "Gotta run now, sis. I'm meeting Reese at his office in thirty minutes." *Nothing like tightening the screw!*

It had been a week now since that conversation had taken place. And a week since Reese's frantic attempt at reconciliation. So far, she had heard nothing from him. But she knew he hadn't given up, that he was keeping a low profile, hoping she would eventually see things his way. Of course she would not. Could not.

Nor could she blame it all on Morgana, either. There had been too many changes. Once, she had been eager to please him; she would have married him in a minute if he had been free to ask her. She had been willing to give up everything for him, deny him nothing. Then he had left her. She had been forced to survive without him. And now that she had an inkling of who she was and of what she was capable, she did not want to give it up.

Once a dream was shattered, trust came hard the second time around. Time and distance were the only answers. Yet, given all the time in the world and all the excuses she could manufacture, she wasn't sure it would change the situation or her feelings.

Chewing on her lower lip, she stood at her office window and stared out into the deepening shadows of the late evening. No matter how hard she tried, she could not quiet this jumble of conflicting emotions.

If she were honest with herself, she would admit she was desperate to recapture what they once had had and then lost. All the while, that other self was mocking her, calling her an utter fool. *It would never work; one could never go back.*

Her head lobbed against the glass as the numbness she prayed would last suddenly disappeared, leaving a dull throbbing ache in its place. Maybe if she hadn't had such a terrible day, things would not look so bleak to her. But her problems kept revolving in her brain like an automatic tape she was powerless to shut off.

"How much longer do you intend to stay here fretting, my friend?"

Meryl whirled around with a start, her hand flying up to her throat defensively. "Oh, Nelda, you scared me half out of my wits." She sank down on rubbery legs into her padded desk chair. "I thought you left thirty minutes ago."

Nelda arched a brow. "Well, to be truthful, I had just opened my car door when I decided to come back and shoo you out the door right along with myself. I don't need to remind you what an awful day this has been for you." She paused. "Do I?"

Meryl massaged a throbbing left temple. "No, as a matter of fact you don't." A wobbly smile showed her perfectly even teeth. "Do you think I was a fool to settle the claim out of court? Tucker does."

"Oh, Meryl honey, of course I don't," Nelda responded with feeling. "And as far as what Tucker thinks . . ." She stopped and rolled her eyes upward. "You know how tight fisted and conservative he is. What else could you expect of him?"

Meryl sighed. "I know, but I've always taken his advice in the past, so I can't help but feel a trifle upset at going against his wishes." She smiled wryly. "But not enough to have changed my mind."

Meryl, along with her health studios, Body Perfect, had been named in a lawsuit for negligence by one of their clients, who claimed bodily injury as a result of an exercise class held by a newly hired employee, a young girl who Meryl guessed had not adhered to the rules and regulations. The woman had said that she had suffered permanent back injury and could no longer hold down a job. Participants in the exercise classes were handed a sheet of paper supposedly exempting Body Perfect from libel in the event of accident.

But in this particular case, it couldn't be proved that Anne, the student instructor, was not at fault. So the woman had hired an ambitious lawyer who saw a chance to make a name for himself and pick up some easy money by dragging Meryl's name through the mud.

"Just think what a jury trial would have done to Body Perfect's good name, and yours as well," Nelda was saying. "Especially now that you have a book that's on its way to becoming a best-seller, not even counting your pending television deal." She shook her head. "I definitely think you did the right thing by settling out of court. However, I hope you'll let this nasty episode be a lesson to you."

Meryl smiled ruefully. "You don't have to worry about that. Tucker will never let me forget it for one moment. He thinks I'm much too softhearted for my own good. And maybe he's right. It certainly doesn't speak too highly of me as a business person."

"Pooh! All that's wrong with Tucker is that he doesn't like your having a mind of your own. He wants you to depend on him to make your important decisions."

Meryl grimaced. "Well, if that's the case, I'm afraid he's in for a rude awakening. Hopefully, I'll never again be totally dependent on a man for anything." She began rubbing her other temple. "Anyway, I'm glad this day is over and I'm not facing a court date in the near future."

"Me too," Nelda echoed.

"But while we're on the subject, I want to have a meeting of all our employees." She paused and looked down at her calendar. "Mmmm, let's see," she added, tapping the pencil on the desk, "why don't we make it for Thursday, day after tomorrow. Will that give you enough time to circulate the memorandum?"

Nelda nodded. "I'll get on it first thing in the morning. Just tell me what you want me to say."

Twenty minutes later, Meryl was alone again with her promise to Nelda that she was on her way out still ringing in her ears. With a sigh she gave her desk a cursory glance before getting up and reaching for her purse, only to have the soft ring of the telephone stall her actions. With a muffled curse of frustration, she yanked it off the hook.

"Yes?" she clipped.

"Don't tell me it's another one of those days."

"Oh, hi, Morgana," Meryl said, feeling the tension ease from her body as she once again lowered her tired body into the chair. "When did you get in?"

"About a couple of hours ago," Morgana responded cheerfully.

"From the sound of your voice, you must have had a good show," Meryl commented lightly.

"Oh, it was." There was a short pause as Morgana sighed deeply. "It would have been better, though, if Jay hadn't been along," she added unkindly.

Meryl laughed. "I can't believe you two are at it again. You're worse than two children, always fighting over nothing."

Another sigh. "I know, but lately it has gotten much worse. He has become sullen, loses his temper for no reason at all, and . . . God, talk about possessive! He doesn't want me out of his sight. And I talked about Tucker. Jay's twice as bad as he is. I don't know what I'm going to do about it, either," she wailed.

Meryl finally got a word in edgeways. "You know very well what's causing this latest bout of rebellion, sister dear," she declared soberly.

"Oh, and what might that be?"

"Don't 'oh' me," Meryl replied, more sharply than she intended. "He's eaten up with jealousy, and you know it."

"Well," Morgana returned airily, "he'll just have to get over it, because I've already told him I fully intend to marry Reese Corbett. If I can convince him, that is," she added with a laugh.

Meryl tried to ignore the tremor that shot through her, followed by the sick feeling that settled over her like a wet blanket. Although Morgana had laughed when she mentioned enticing Reese into marrying her, she sounded completely confident of her ability to do just that.

"Meryl, are you still there?" Morgana asked, breaking the lengthening silence that had suddenly fallen between them.

Fighting off the onslaught of depression, Meryl forced her tone to remain cool and even. How she hated having to play this cat-and-mouse game with her sister. "Of course I'm still here. I guess I'm just feeling the strain of this very long and traumatic day." A hearty sigh followed this brief disclosure.

"Oh, did anything happen that I should know about?" Morgana quipped, but the concern was evident in her voice. "Now that I think about it, you don't sound like yourself, and haven't for a while."

Meryl sighed. "Well, for one thing, I spent the day in court, settling out of court, if that makes any sense." She laughed without humor. "It's a long story, so I won't bore you with the details tonight. How about lunch tomorrow, and I'll tell you all about it then?"

There was a slight pause before Morgana answered. "Well, actually, that's what I called to talk to you about, only—"

"Oh, good," Meryl interrupted. "Let's meet at Bennigan's about one o'clock. Okay?"

Morgana laughed. "Hold it! Slow down. You didn't let me finish," Morgana replied, sounding slightly rattled. "I was just going to add that I couldn't meet you for lunch as planned." She paused. "I'm leaving for Paris first thing tomorrow morning," she added in a rush.

"Paris!"

"Yes, Paris. Isn't that great? After all this time, I finally got another top-notch assignment."

"Oh, Morgana, I'm so proud for you," Meryl exclaimed excitedly. "Well, don't keep me in suspense any longer. When did all this come about?"

"Jay confirmed the deal just a little while ago, actually." She hesitated. "However, there's a catch to it. If I don't leave first thing in the morning, there's a chance that I will lose the assignment. But—"

"But what!" Meryl interrupted. "Nothing should stand in your way. Paris is big-time. It's just what you've been waiting for. Don't blow it now!"

"I don't intend to. That's why I need your help."

"You name it." Meryl laughed. "As the old saying goes, 'your wish is my command.' And by the way, don't let me hear you criticize Jay ever again. You ought to be ashamed."

"I know," Morgana muttered sheepishly. "But I don't want to talk about that now, please. It's just a relief to know I can count on you to help me out."

"Haven't I always helped you out?" Meryl reminded her twin without rancor. Then added, "Okay, so let's have it. What do you want me to do? You've got my curiosity aroused, but I hope it's nothing that takes any brain power, because right now yours truly's is mush."

"It's no big deal, really," Morgana replied. "What I want you to do is meet Reese's plane and attend a reception with him in my place." She paused. "Now, does that sound like something you can't handle?"

For breathless seconds Meryl was too stunned to speak. She felt as if she had received a staggering blow to the side of the head as her thoughts splintered in several different directions at once.

She swallowed, hoping to relieve the pressure in her throat, but nothing helped. She still couldn't say a word, not even the simple two-letter word *no!*

"Meryl?"

Her hand flew to her throat. Somehow she had to make herself say something sane and diplomatic without raising any suspicions. "I'm . . . I'm sure that Reese would object to . . . to that," she stammered. She couldn't believe this was happening. Had she heard Morgana correctly? Surely she hadn't asked her to spend an evening with Reese? Impossible! *But she had!*

"Hey, like I said, it's no big deal," Morgana remarked lightly. "It's only a charity dinner with Reese giving a short speech about his work. He'd asked me to go with him right after we first met, only I'd forgotten about it until he called last night and reminded me, along with asking me to pick him up at the airport. From there we're supposed to go straight to the hotel where it's being held."

Meryl's heart was beating frantically. "Why don't you just call him back and explain that you have to go to Paris. Surely he can get a cab from the airport." Her voice was strained.

"I thought of that," Morgana replied, "but I don't know where he's staying. Besides, I can't just leave him in the lurch for tomorrow night. From what I understand, it's an important function, so it wouldn't be fair. Then I just happened to have this brilliant idea about you helping me out." She giggled softly. "If you can't trust your own sister, then who can you trust? What do you say, are you game?"

Still Meryl hesitated, trying desperately to camouflage her feelings while searching for a reasonable excuse not to do as Morgana asked. But as usual, she had opened her mouth and inserted her foot, volunteering her services. An avid refusal now would bring on unanswerable questions.

She stalled. Panic was twisting and turning her insides. One part of her wanted to go, to have Reese's undivided attention for a whole evening. She couldn't deny it would be sheer heaven to sit across the table from him and watch his velvet gray eyes squint with laughter, watch his talented fingers wrap around the stem of a glass, thinking all the while how they felt caressing her body, and more, so much more. Such little things, she thought. Yet so important; the kind of intimacies that take a lifetime of sharing to create. The other part of her cringed from the thought of exposing herself to this kind of torture, knowing that it would be the start of something that could never be finished.

And what of Reese? How would he feel about the exchange of partners? Would he be furious? Happy?

"Meryl, what on earth is wrong with you?" Morgana demanded, breaking into the taut silence. "Has the cat suddenly got your tongue? You're acting rather weird, if you don't mind my saying so." It was obvious even to Meryl's battered senses that Morgana had reached the end of her patience.

Meryl bit down hard on her lower lip and wasn't aware of having done so until she felt the warm taste of blood on her tongue. She had to get a hold of herself! "Morgana," she said at last, "did it ever occur to you—?"

"Don't you dare say no, Meryl Stevens. If you do, I'll never forgive you," Morgana cried childishly. "You know how important pleasing Reese is to me. How can you possibly think of letting me down?"

Meryl knew she was trapped in a tight corner with no way out. She'd be damned if she did and damned if she didn't. She took a deep breath to relieve the pressure within her, then in a voice she could swear wasn't her own, said, "All right, Morgana, calm down. You win. What time does his plane land?"

"Six o'clock," Morgana responded, her tone altering considerably. "Flight 407 from New York City."

So that's where he's been this past week, Meryl thought

erratically as she made a last-ditch effort to pull herself together and reconcile what she had just done.

"I'll be there," she replied flatly.

"Thanks, love, I'll return the favor," Morgana gushed. "You know I will. It's just that I can't stand the thought of Reese asking someone else to go to the dinner in my place." A deep sigh filtered its way through the receiver. "I know you think I'm crazy, Meryl, but I'm nuts about this guy and terribly jealous to boot. And scared," she added on a subdued note. "Scared I'll lose him before I can get him down the aisle."

Meryl couldn't take any more. "Please, Morgana, can we talk about this later?" she pleaded. "I've really got to get home before I fall on my face."

"Okay, okay." Morgana returned once more to her bubbly self, now that she had gotten her way. "Thanks again for getting me out of another jam. You know I love you and I'll call when I get back from gay Paree. I know I'll be leaving Reese in safe hands," she added, stifling her triumphant laughter.

"Good night," was all Meryl managed to choke out before she dropped the phone back on the hook.

She then buried her head in the cradle of her arms and sobbed as though her heart were breaking.

The flight from La Guardia was late. Twenty minutes late. Finding she had to wait only increased her frustration and kindled her nerves to a frightening pitch.

How had she let Morgana talk her into doing this? Had she gone temporarily insane? Or was she doing this because she craved the thought of having him to herself for a few stolen hours? These were questions that kept twisting and turning in her head. She hadn't slept a wink, nor had she accomplished anything worthwhile. All her thoughts and energies had been centered on Reese and this upcoming rendezvous.

She had vowed to herself as she dressed that it didn't

matter what she wore or how she looked. She wasn't out to impress him; just the opposite, in fact. She had then proceeded to make a liar out of herself by indulging in a leisurely bath and dressing with the utmost care. It was a matter of pride, she'd told herself as she chose a black silk gown that left one shoulder bare as it fell in soft folds to her ankles.

It was both simple and elegant, yet bold in concept. As she viewed her reflection in the full-length mirror, she'd had to agree that it was probably her most flattering gown—the black complementing her flawless skin and her dark eyes and hair. Diamond studs in her ears and a thin gold chain centered with a diamond, a gift from Morgana, were her only jewelry.

Now as she stood reed-straight in the rather quiet waiting room and stared out into the dazzling sunlight, she fought to calm her nerves. She was filled with anticipation laced with dread at the thought of seeing Reese again. As far as thinking about spending an entire evening alone with him—well, that didn't bear thinking about.

Suddenly the door to the boarding ramp was opened and secured by a uniformed flight attendant, and Meryl lost control of the natural act of breathing. Reese was the last person out the door. He looked good, endearingly good, she thought with a pang. But there was a stern set to his jaw which she hadn't noticed before, and he appeared older and very tired. He was dressed in an expensive black pin-striped suit, and his thick dark hair was combed ruthlessly into order. The well-cut suit displayed his solid muscular figure perfectly. He was the epitome of a sleek, successful doctor—a far cry from the casually clad jogger she had fallen in love with. Had it been only a week since she'd last seen him?

Meryl knew her face was tissue-paper white as she watched him gaze down and shift his briefcase and newspaper to the other hand. It was then that he looked up and saw her.

Time stood still for Reese. Then an incredulous expression crossed his features, followed by another of pure joy, his eyes lighting up like a torch. "Meryl," he mouthed silently. To her it sounded like a caress.

Meryl found herself helplessly staring at him. Her chemistry sparked alive within her body; she was shaky, as if composed of molten liquid.

Although the room was now a beehive of activity with everyone laughing and talking and hugging loved ones and friends, Meryl and Reese were oblivious of it all. They continued to stand motionless, each one afraid to make the initial move toward normal conversation, afraid of shattering the stolen moment.

To Reese it seemed like forever since he had walked out of Meryl's house, thoroughly frustrated because he hadn't the faintest idea how to solve the problem of Morgana or how to get through to Meryl, to make her understand that no matter what, they belonged together.

Since that night when he'd actually seen Meryl in the flesh, he had been so lonely for her he actually hurt. It was a kind of all-consuming grief, in which he had berated himself for all the things he'd said or done or should not have said or done, but was at a loss as to how to remedy them.

He knew eventually, as he had promised her, he'd have to go to her. Yet he hadn't wanted to harm her or upset her more, hadn't wanted to further alienate her or encumber her. He had given her plenty of breathing room. But, God, he'd hurt with the need to see her, to touch her, to soothe her. He hadn't known what to do.

Leave her alone, his sensible inner voice had commanded. *She doesn't want you anymore, doesn't need you. Just leave her alone. She has made a new life for herself without you. Just butt out once and for all!* But he hadn't been able to let go. It would have buried him to have done so. Still, he hadn't known what to do, hadn't stopped thinking about her, and hadn't stopped wondering.

And now here she was, standing in front of him, a vision of loveliness. Unless he was making a grave error in judgment, she was here because of him. What did it mean? His blood began to pound through his veins, giving him a surge of new life. It didn't really matter what she was doing here, he told himself. He certainly wasn't one to look a gift horse in the mouth.

"Reese . . ." she began haltingly, only to pause and circle her glossed lips with the tip of her tongue. He groaned inwardly at her innocent action. "I . . . that is . . . Morgana had to go to Paris on an assignment, so . . ." Her voice completely faded out. Her eyes were round and shimmering as she looked up into his face, now only a hairbreadth away.

"Oh, Meryl," he whispered for her ears alone, "it doesn't matter why you're here. I'm just glad you are." His warm breath fell like mist across her lips, giving her a further sensation of floating. "I've thought about you every waking hour of every day," he added, his heart reflected in his eyes.

Meryl turned away to keep from completely drowning in their soft depths, trying desperately to cling to her resolve to remain cool and unemotional. Survival was the name of this game, she reminded herself savagely.

"Don't . . . don't, Reese . . . it's not what you think." She swallowed with difficulty. "I only agreed to do this because . . . because Morgana wouldn't take no for an answer." How on earth was she going to make it through the entire evening? she wondered with bleak despair. Especially when she was having to keep a tight rein on her hands in order not to reach out and touch him.

Seeing the unhappiness and fright mirrored in her eyes, Reese choked back an expletive and tried to hold up under the crushing disappointment that threatened to suck him under like quicksand.

Reese drew a deep shuddering breath and forced a smile to his lips. "Lead the way," he said unemotionally, "and I'll follow."

By the time they retrieved his luggage and made their way out of the terminal, the sun had lost some of its sting. But the humidity was high and hovered in the air with smothering intensity, adding to Meryl's discomfort.

The short trek to the car and the mundane task of putting his luggage in the trunk were carried out in silence. Taking for granted that he would drive, Reese opened the door on the passenger side for Meryl and then strode quickly around the hood and settled his long limbs behind the wheel. Once they were on their way into the city and toward the Medical Center complex, the atmosphere was still strained.

Refusing to be left alone with her troublesome thoughts, Meryl broke through the sterile silence. "Where is the dinner going to be held?" she asked conversationally, casting him a furtive glance out of the corner of her eye.

"At the Warwick," he responded, throwing her a rather grim smile before turning his eyes back carefully to the road. "From what I've been told, there's to be a rather elaborate seafood buffet, and then I'm to present my case to a group of elite businessmen and their wives."

"Mmmm, sounds interesting, but what do you think your chances are of selling them on your endeavor?" Meryl asked, a note of warmth creeping into her voice. When they were discussing his work, they were on safe ground. She felt herself relax.

"Extremely good," he commented. "My assistants were told to have everything set up and ready to go. I plan to show photographs and numerous sketches of several of my most severe cases." He paused. "I can't imagine not being able to move the audience with the plight of those patients."

Meryl's eyes softened as they flickered over his profile. "You really feel for your patients, don't you?" Her words were quietly spoken as she continued to watch him and store away in a special corner of her mind each and every one of his mannerisms: the way his hair gently brushed his collar when he twisted his head, the way his muscles rippled in his thighs when he manipulated the brake on the car, the way the dimple in his cheek deepened when he smiled.

He was quiet for a moment, then nodded. "Yes, I do." He sighed. "I see and counsel them and their families so often that, more times than not, they become friends as well as patients. And underneath all that horrid disfigurement, they're warm, generous people groping for a way out of the hopelessness that has a stranglehold on them." He expelled a breath impatiently. "And I'd just about do anything I could, short of selling my soul to the devil, that is, to see that they get help."

"I admire that type of dedication in a person," she remarked sincerely. "There are very few of us who have it, I'm sorry to say. You're one of the lucky ones."

His gaze swept over her briefly. "I'm not so sure about that. Sometimes I think it's a curse." He smiled, easing the lines of tension around his mouth. "Anyway, I didn't mean to get on my soapbox, nor make myself into a saint."

This was a side of Reese that Meryl had never seen, and she was not only impressed, but intrigued as well. And jealous. Yes, jealous. Jealous that he was so thoroughly involved in his work, doing something he really believed in and never lost his enthusiasm for. That was something she couldn't say about herself, she thought disconcertedly. At least not since Reese had come back into her life. Her work, her upcoming television show, her extracurricular activities—everything seemed to have suddenly lost its sparkle.

In essence, Reese had taken her life by storm. Again. She hoped, however, as soon as this ordeal was over, she could once again go on with her life as though Reese Corbett didn't exist. Was she a fool to think she could pull that off? Or was she simply hoping for a miracle?

"I still don't know exactly how Morgana was able to convince you to take her place," Reese was saying now as he turned the car onto the circular driveway of the Warwick Hotel, "but whatever it was, I owe her a debt of gratitude." His fingers were curled tightly around the wheel. Meryl could see his knuckles as they whitened from the pressure he was exerting on them. "This has been one hell of a week. The convention in New York wore me out, plus I haven't been worth a damn since you practically threw me out of your house last week."

His eyes latched on to hers, and he smiled again, though there was little joy in his expression. "But what I was trying to say is, I'm going to make every second we have together count." He meant every word he said as his eyes stared at her with pure male appreciation, delighting in the pearl-white smoothness of her skin, much of it left bare by the seductive cut of her dress, and the graceful way she moved, like a dancer. She was pure dynamite.

"Reese . . . please . . . don't do this." In spite of her effort to hold it steady, her lower lip began to quiver. "I . . . I haven't changed my mind . . ."

"Don't worry," he said, winking at her suddenly, hoping to put a smile back on her face and lighten the mood. "I'll be on my best behavior, I promise." Then, on a more serious note, he added, "Even though I may not be allowed to touch, at least I can look. And that's better than nothing, I can assure you."

Before Meryl could come back with a suitable rejoinder, a valet had opened the door and was waiting for her to get out of the car. She shook her head as if to clear it as she waited for Reese to accompany her inside.

They walked silently across the lobby, down a long hall, before pausing just inside the door of a large room. Unnoticed by anyone, they were free to take in their surroundings.

Reese was correct. The elite of Houston's high society had turned out for this occasion. The massive banquet room in the Warwick was filled with glittering people and beautifully decorated tables graced with vases of rare flowers. Seeing the elaborate display of wealth, Meryl gleaned just how important Dr. Reese Corbett was. It thrilled her to see the response that he had drawn. Excitement, combined with the smell of money, was thick in the air.

Suddenly her tongue circled her lips in trembling anticipation that she was able just this once to be a part of Reese's life and work. Surely that wasn't asking too much. Or was it?

Standing on the outskirts of the milling crowd, Meryl was very much aware of his presence. As though on cue with her thoughts, Reese gently curved his fingers around her arm, urging her forward. At his touch, a tingling sensation danced all the way from her arm down into the recesses of her womanhood, creating a warmth that she couldn't ignore. She felt her face turn the color of the red flowers on the table as she tried to calm her racing heart. God, she was treading on dangerous ground by even letting him so much as lay a finger on her, albeit more out of courtesy at the moment than passion. Even so, she warned herself, she was asking for trouble.

"You're more beautiful than any other woman here," Reese whispered close to her ear as they took a tentative step farther into the room before threading their way toward the front. "I'm proud to have you at my side," he added, a husky tremor deepening his voice.

Meryl forced herself not to react. But each time he spoke in that seductive tone, her temperature shot up a degree higher. She also realized with a sinking heart that it took very little from this man—a mere look, a feathery touch—to upset her entire emotional balance. She shivered.

She cut a sharp glance in his direction. "You . . . you promised," she said through tight, stiff lips, determined to be strong, making it clear she would not tolerate any more of his personal remarks.

A small smile tugged at his harshly etched lip in rebuttal of her sudden waspish attitude and flashing eyes. "I'm sorry," he apologized, though he didn't sound the least bit sorry. "I'll do better," he added, his lips warmly caressing the delicate part of her ear. She sucked air into her suddenly light chest, feeling as though she had just been branded. She could not allow this to continue. Dammit, he had given his word!

"Stop it!" she hissed, biting down on her anger. The fright

that charged through her now was almost a tangible thing, for every intimate word he uttered chipped away at the armor-plated shield she had donned in order to make it through the evening.

Before Reese could respond, however, they were suddenly bombarded by a group of people.

"Reese, you sly old dog, you, how on earth did you, the guest of honor, sneak in without being seen?" a tall sandy-haired man demanded, a wide grin crinkling his features.

"Hello, Thomas," Reese laughed, shaking his hand heartily. "You know I'm good at disappearing into the woodwork when I want to."

Thomas grinned knowingly. "Well, now that you're here, what do you say we get this shindig on the road?" His eyes then turned toward Meryl. "We haven't met, have we?" he asked with a generous smile on his face.

"No, you haven't," Reese cut in swiftly. "Meryl Stevens, meet Thomas Moore, a colleague of mine." Although not touching her, Reese had moved closer. There was nothing separating them but their clothes and the air they breathed.

Meryl extended her hand. "Pleased to meet you, Thomas," she acknowledged with a smile.

From that moment on it was utter chaos. Meryl was introduced to everyone in the group, with none of their names sticking in her mind. None too soon for Meryl, they were finally escorted to their seats at the head table.

Seated on her left was a robust silver-haired man who introduced himself as Emory Cantrell, the chief of staff at the hospital where Reese did his surgery. She liked him on sight.

"Tell me, young lady, what do you think of our boy here? His work, I mean?" he asked, his shaggy brows hooding his sharp piercing blue eyes.

"Oh, I think it's wonderful, although at times I know it must be thoroughly frustrating."

He sighed. "That it is, but he never seems to lose sight of his goal to help these people. That's what makes him such a valuable asset to the medical profession."

A smile gentled her lips. "I know, and I'm proud for him."

"We've been trying to honor him for his pioneer work in this field for months, and finally we were able to get him to agree to it. This is a big night for him. As well as being honored, Reese stands to receive some whopping amounts in donations."

Meryl was appalled. "Do . . . do you mean that this isn't just another fund-raising dinner? That it's a dinner to honor Reese?" She guessed she shouldn't have been shocked, but she was. This was to be a big night for him, a milestone in his life and career. A feeling of guilt stabbed at her conscience. Morgana should have been here sharing all this hype and glitter with him. It was not her place. It was Morgana's. But on the other side of the coin, Morgana had tossed this chance aside, opting for *her* career instead. Meryl felt the sudden need to scream with the injustice of it all.

However, she soon threw off her feeling of gloom and joined in the excitement of the evening. The seafood buffet was delicious, offering numerous delicacies from the ocean. At Reese's teasing insistence, she tried a portion of each. Shortly thereafter, Reese got up to speak, and Meryl concentrated on his every word.

He began by thanking his colleagues and friends for this evening and saying how much it meant to him. Then he talked about his "special people," as he was fond of calling them. He gave a brief history of each patient he presented to the audience, which included pictures of disfigurements more horrible than the mind and eyes could imagine. Both children and adults were included, each one seemingly more pathetic than the last. By the time he finished his presentation, there was not a dry eye in the room, including Meryl's.

She was so proud of Reese and all he stood for, she thought her heart would burst. This feeling of warmth around her heart carried her through the good-byes and remained with her even as Reese settled her comfortably in her car.

When he lowered himself behind the wheel and turned

tired but eager eyes on her, it was all Meryl could do not to grab and kiss him as her heart swelled with hidden pride.

"Well, what did you think?" he asked softly.

A warm, aching tightness twisted in her belly as his deep penetrating stare sent a charge of electricity crackling between them.

Tears glistened on the edge of her lashes. "I think you're wonderful," she eked out between trembling lips.

The smile disappeared from his lips, leaving him looking suddenly vulnerable, uncertain. "Oh, God, Meryl," he rasped, "I want you to mean that more than anything else in the world."

"Reese . . ."

"Shhh," he whispered, and touched a silencing finger to her lips. "Don't say anything—not now. We can talk at my place," he finished, a shudder raking his body while the engine responded to his touch with a muted snarl.

"No, Reese." She shook her head. "I . . . can't. Please take me home."

"Dammit, Meryl, I can't," he ground out, his control suddenly snapping. He then saw, in the dim light, her white face along with the jolt that shook her frame, and his tone softened. "How can you deny us this time together after it was handed to us on a silver platter?" He paused as his eyes wandered over high, pointed breasts that seemed to quiver under his gaze. "You still care; I know you do." His voice dipped to a low timbre. "And you can deny it till the world freezes over, but it won't change a thing."

She wanted to scream her denial as she fought against the sick feeling that clawed its way up from her stomach to her throat. He was right and she knew it. But still that didn't make her decision any easier.

Releasing his breath slowly, silently, Reese turned to face her. "Shall I turn around?"

A heavy silence thundered around them.

Meryl's lashes wavered slightly, but she raised her eyes to meet his again. "No . . . no. Don't turn around."

Chapter 8

His house was as beautiful on the inside as it appeared on the outside. Although dark, the drive circling the front of the sprawling brick structure was so well lit it enabled Meryl to take in the simple elegance.

She halted just inside the dim entrance hall and gazed around. To her immediate right was the den, a large airy room with a high beamed ceiling and walls of glass.

Glass everywhere. She wished suddenly that she was seeing this in the daylight. In her mind's eye, she could picture the sunlight streaming through the glass, stirring the urns and baskets of plants into new life. Next her eyes wandered to the center of the room, dominated by a huge fireplace.

Silently nudging her farther into the lighted interior, Reese said, "Have a seat and make yourself comfortable while I see about drinks." He smiled disarmingly, hoping to put her at ease. She seemed as rigid as a tightly wound guitar string, he thought. God, did she honestly think he had brought her here just so he could attack her?

Meryl smiled feebly in return as she sank down onto the opulent couch next to a table graced with yet another exotic plant. She studied it absently, wondering what kind it was. Then, forgetting about the plants, she let her eyes roam around the room.

It was tastefully decorated with matching crushed-velvet couches and cabinets containing an assortment of memorabilia and exquisite porcelain figurines. Other knickknacks adorned the intricately designed hardwood end tables and shelves. It was fairly safe to assume he was an avid reader, she thought. The shelves were crammed with the latest fiction and nonfiction best-sellers. A massive stereo system took up the wall catercorner to the fireplace.

It was a lovely room and no doubt he enjoyed showing it off. But she still couldn't believe she was sitting here indulging in his hospitality as though it were the most commonplace thing in the world.

During the silent drive from the Warwick Hotel to his River Oaks home, she had longed to tell him she had changed her mind and to demand he take her home. Not once, however, had she been able to utter those words aloud. And she knew why. He still fascinated her.

The human heart was totally unreliable, she reflected. This man had trampled her spirit, plunged her into a hell on earth she had once thought she would never emerge from, and yet she never felt so alive as when she was with him. Her heart said stay, her common sense said flee, and for the moment, it seemed a very unequal contest.

Maybe if just this once she gave in to her body's cravings she would be able to put the ghost of Reese Corbett to rest. She didn't need a man in her life to be fulfilled. Hadn't she already proved that?

Guard that thought, she told herself when Reese came breezing back into the room with their drinks.

"Well, what do you think of my humble abode?" he asked, his lips spread in a pleasing smile.

"It's lovely," she said sincerely, "but surely you don't need me to tell you that?"

"No, I guess I don't, but your approval is important to me." His eyes rested warmly on her face.

"How long have you lived here?" she asked, politely changing the subject, while accepting the glass of wine he held out to her.

He lowered himself onto the couch beside her and instantly began unbuttoning his shirt at the neck. In one quick motion he had removed coat and tie, slinging them haphazardly over the back of the couch.

"Now I can relax," he said with a wink before answering her question. "Not long, actually. Friends of mine owned it and were forced to sell as a part of their divorce settlement."

"Oh, I'm sorry," she replied sincerely, "about your friends' divorce, I mean, but not about your getting the house. It seems their misfortune was your good fortune."

"Well, I guess in a way it was," he drawled. "I used to envy them this three acres and house, so when the crack in their marriage widened into an unbreachable gap, they offered it to me at a bargain price." He paused and watched her take a sip of her wine, noticing how beautiful her hands and nails were as they circled the glass. "But right now I'd rather hear about what you've been up to, then later I'll show you the rest of the house." His eyes dropped to her soft mouth.

A tiny frown marred her smooth brow. "There's not much to tell, really," she remarked absently. If only he wouldn't look at her like that.

"Huh! That's not what I've been told. I hear you have several hot irons in the fire."

Meryl despised talking about herself—especially to him. Once she would have been thrilled to have him drill her with questions. In her eagerness to please, she would have granted him anything. But not now. It was too late. She even resented him asking, yet she was careful not to let her annoyance show.

"If you're referring to my health-and-nutrition studios, I guess I do," she admitted reluctantly.

He scooted closer and looked at her with unflinching eyes. "Tell me, exactly how does your operation work? I've been told that it's first-class all the way."

In spite of herself she was flattered by his sincere interest. She could talk about her work forever and never get tired. Her cool veneer began to melt.

"First of all, the women who participate in our program must have a desire to change their way of life. Once that is established, we—and I mean, by we, myself, along with my staff—set each woman up on a diet and exercise program to fit her own individual needs."

"By attending classes several times a week, we're able to see that she adheres to this schedule. If we find that she is progressing too fast or too slowly, we alter it to meet her needs. We also hold night classes three times a week for their husbands, teaching them the value of nutrition and exercise." She smiled. "I'm proud to say, it's a family-oriented program."

He smiled lopsidedly. "It certainly sounds as though you've got it all together." His voice was gentle but probing. "Do you remember the time we had that discussion about your dream?"

A deep flush stole into her cheeks at his husky reminder. Never once during the entire time she was turning her dream into a reality had she dwelt on that promise given so long ago. And never once had she given him any of the credit for reaching that goal. It had hurt to think about it then, and it hurt to think about it now.

"Well, all I can say is that I've managed to come a long way since those days," she responded. "Because of that, I've made my work my life," she added pointedly.

With forced effort Reese managed to keep his face expressionless and to cover his frustration, refusing to let her rattle him with her rigid and self-protective attitude.

Instead he found himself concentrating on the creamy bare shoulder that was so close to him. It was all he could do to keep a physical restraint on himself when he longed to tease that delectable area of flesh with his warm lips before moving to the swell of her voluptuous breasts. . . .

Damn! He was doing exactly what he had promised himself he wouldn't do.

His burning gaze was not lost on Meryl. In an effort to control her own inner turbulence, she grabbed the glass of potent wine and drained it to the last drop.

Reese stared at her a moment and suddenly vaulted from the couch, desperate for breathing room.

"I'll get you another drink," he offered rather hoarsely, "then we'll take a walk outside. I want to show you the swimming pool."

Eager to cast aside her own disruptive thoughts once she was alone, Meryl hopped up and began to parade around the room, her heels making a tapping sound on the parquet floor. She finally came to a standstill before a portrait hanging above the mantel. Her eyes widened as they focused on it.

It was Reese's son. Although still in the prime of babyhood, he was nevertheless a tiny replica of his father: the same dark hair, full lips and velvet gray eyes.

Meryl felt the tears sting her eyes at the tragic loss of one so young. He was adorable, a grin splattering across his face from ear to ear, reminding her of a dark-haired Dennis the Menace. How had Reese borne the loss? Or dealt with the pain of losing a part of himself? She didn't think she could have endured it.

"He was a chip off the old block, wasn't he?" Reese remarked softly from behind her.

Stepping aside, she turned around to face him. As she knew they would be, his face and eyes were glazed with pain and sorrow. Blindly she accepted the full glass of wine from his unsteady fingers, only to promptly set it on the nearest table.

"When . . . I . . . I stand here and look at this picture, which I do far more than I should, I can't believe that he's dead. It just doesn't seem possible."

"I know," she whispered. "I was thinking the same thing."

"It's the mornings that are the worst," he said helplessly. "When I open my eyes, the first thing I remember is that Jason will never wrap his chubby arms around my neck again or plaster sloppy kisses all over my face. I . . ." He stopped, unable to go on.

He then whirled around and made his way jerkily across the room to stand in front of the wide expanse of glass. His shoulders sagged against it. God, he thought, it was like stabbing a knife in his heart and twisting it every time he talked or thought about his son. And the day that he had buried him . . . well, even to this day he couldn't bear to think about it. The few times he had done so had nearly killed him.

Only since Meryl had come back into his life had he begun to hope, to blot out much of the pain and misery that had plagued him for so long. She had lighted up his life with her beauty, her sweet sympathy and sincerity, but more important, with her presence. He must not lose her again. *So, Corbett,* he warned himself, *no matter how impatient you become, remember to tread slow and easy. Don't blow it! Pretend this is the beginning; flirt with her, laugh with her, but most of all—woo her. And whatever you do, don't back her into a corner!*

He knew she was behind him; her presence soothed him like a spring day, and her smell was more potent than the rarest of wine. He turned slowly around to meet her widened eyes glistening with unshed tears that matched his own.

"I'm . . . I'm sorry," she whispered haltingly. "I shouldn't have said anything, because I know how raw your insides still are."

In that moment Reese wanted desperately to fold her tightly within the circle of his arms and wallow in her comforting sweetness. But he wouldn't allow himself to do it. He did not want her to think he was using his grief as a ploy to gain her trust.

But, goddammit, he was no saint! he reminded himself savagely. This was twice now he had ceased to take what she was offering. But he wasn't interested in just another temporary fling with her; he'd had that. He wanted her beside him every waking moment of every day. He didn't want a clandestine affair; he wanted a lifetime. But until she was ready to make the same commitment, he had to keep his distance. When she came to him it had to be for more than a physical hunger or because she felt sorry for him. No. It must be because she loved him, pure and simple. He could not settle for anything less.

He would just have to be content to stand like a statue with his belly coiled in a knot and watch as a lonely tear fell from the tip of her eyelashes and trickled slowly down her face.

"I'm the one who should be apologizing for becoming completely unglued and making you cry," he said softly. "But—"

"Shhh," Meryl demanded with extreme gentleness edging her voice. "It's all right. I understand . . . perhaps more than you know." Their faces were only inches apart, and suddenly the air around them began to crackle with an intimacy that had nothing to do with sympathy.

Meryl moved a fraction of an inch, just enough to give herself space to breathe. But it was enough to break the spell.

"If you're ready, we'll take a look at the pool now," Reese said thickly, taking her hand in his, but still he didn't move. Couldn't move. He found himself trapped by the almost tangible bond and the suppressed longing that coursed between them. He stroked her tender upturned palm with his thumb.

Her knees suddenly went weak as a feeling of warmth enveloped her. If she had ever doubted that the bridge had been crossed leading them from unpassionate sympathy into passionate desire, she was sure of it now. His rigid body telegraphed sexual messages that could be neither ignored nor denied. She waited breathlessly for him to sweep her into his arms and sip the moistness from her lips. Wasn't that what she wanted? One fling to purge him from her thoughts—a magic cure-all from Reese Corbett forever? Wasn't that, after all, the underlying urgency for agreeing to come here? She lowered her eyes and waited in floating anticipation.

"Let's go," Reese stressed, his voice low and grating. If he didn't get access to fresh air soon, he knew nothing short of a miracle would keep him from hauling her into his arms, and to hell with the consequences!

Meryl had difficulty in smothering the empty feeling of disappointment that washed through her at his sudden withdrawal. Somehow she managed to nod and mutely follow him through the patio door and outside. She tried in vain to calm her erratic heartbeat. Why had he turned away from her? Surely he sensed she would not have stopped him from touching her? She forced the burning sting behind her eyes to go away.

But even the night air caressing her face failed to calm her emotions; they were still elevated to a screaming pitch. The swimming pool was mystically lovely as the blue-green water shimmered in the bright moonlight, giving the entire area a haunting quality. The muted glow of lanterns stationed at various intervals lighted their path as they strolled leisurely around the oval-shaped pool. The rippling water looked terribly inviting and for an insane moment she was tempted to shed her clothes and dive in, positive it would temper the heat that burdened her body.

"Do you use the pool often?" she asked lightly, pausing at the edge of the shallow end, an awed expression on her face. "It's fabulous, really it is. It's what I'd imagined a miniature Garden of Eden would look like."

Her reaction to the pool delighted him. "I'm glad you like it," he said.

"And do you put it to good use?" she pressed, smiling.

"Every day, sometimes twice. It's heated, which means I can also swim in comfort in the dead of winter."

"It's not only unique, but so private as well."

"You probably didn't notice, but I don't really have any close neighbors. I'm one of the fortunate ones in River Oaks. My access acreage is loaded with trees and screens both sides of the house and the rear. But even if there weren't anyone around, with the fence it's impossible to see into the pool area."

Feeling the urge to sample the water, Meryl knelt down and swept her hand back and forth through it. It was cool and inviting to the touch. "It feels great," she said.

Reese eyed her with an indulgent smile, and when she stood up beside him once again, their eyes met and held. The way he looked at her made her bones turn to warm butter.

Never once taking his eyes off her, Reese lifted the hand that had been in the water and began to lick the rivulets of liquid clinging to her fingers, thinking she was ethereal as trapped moonlight and twice as beautiful.

"You taste delicious," he murmured huskily as his tongue continued to dart in and out between her fingers.

"I'm . . . I'm glad," she replied inanely, fighting off a wave of desire so intense it hardened her nipples and twisted in her stomach.

After a long moment Reese said tightly, "Let's walk."

Silence. Sensual, paralyzing silence raged between them as they meandered around the patio area. Meryl fought for control by concentrating on the whisper of rustling leaves in the treetops and the sound of crickets as they chirped about her. And the perfume in the air. The sweet odor of flowers flirted with her nose and heightened her senses to a disturbing intensity.

Although hot and humid, a typical South Texas evening, it was a night straight out of a magic storybook, she thought. It was made for lovers. She took a deep breath to ease the pressure within her, feeling as though she might explode any second now.

She was conscious of Reese's every movement as he matched hers step for step. Careful not to brush against him, she was nevertheless aware of the whipcord tightness of his body. She knew he was holding himself in check. His features had a pinched look, or better still, they reminded her of a dark thundercloud about to erupt. What had brought on this brooding mood?

She ached to touch him, to run her hands under his shirt and caress his damp skin, bury her head into the wiry hair that covered his chest, and smell the tangy scent of his sweat. *She craved to do all the things that were forbidden to her.*

Suddenly he stopped and turned to face her. "Are you by any chance in a mood to do something daring?" The spray of silver moonlight allowed her to see the grin splayed across his lips.

Meryl was astounded by the sudden change in his mood, but she wasn't about to put a damper on his enthusiasm, or at least she didn't think so.

"Depends on what you have in mind," she responded cautiously.

"A moonlight dip in the pool?"

She was quiet while her tongue swirled around her dry lips. "I . . . I don't have a bathing suit," she whispered, stating the obvious.

It was on the tip of Reese's tongue to tell her she didn't need one, but caution clamped the words in his throat. *Remember to woo her, gently, tenderly.* "I think I could probably come up with one." He strove to hide the disappointment behind his words.

"How do you know it will fit?"

"I don't."

"Well, then, what do you suggest?"

"I'll leave that up to you."

"Then let's forget it."

"What, the swim or the suit?"

Meryl turned her nails into the palms of her hands and dug deeply. "The suit."

The only identifiable sound in the heavy night air was Reese's sharp groan as Meryl closed her eyes and reassured herself that what she was doing was right. It was the *only* way to end her idiotic ramblings into the past. Even though she still didn't trust him and was positive she no longer loved him . . . may God forgive her, she still wanted him.

"Oh, Meryl," he breathed, hating himself for losing sight of his firm convictions of a moment ago. Just this once, he promised himself. Just this once. . . .

He leaned down and laid his lips onto the pliant curve of hers, feeling her hesitate instinctively when he pushed at her teeth with his tongue, and then she opened her lips so that he could invade her mouth more intimately. His hands wound their way through her thick silky curls, glorying in the soft feel and texture of them. Then one hand moved to her waist, arching her back so that she was pressed even harder against him, while his other hand roamed upward without hesitation, seeking the rounded swell of her breasts.

Meryl was yielding to intoxicating sensations that she had not experienced since the last time Reese held her in his arms. He was so sweet and real. Sweeter and more real than she had remembered. *Nothing had changed.* He still possessed the same body, the same raspy voice, the same tender mannerisms, and had lost none of his power to make her compliant and receptive.

She was divorced from reality when his long sensitive fingers began to fondle her breasts. Then urgently he reached around to the back of her dress and began to pull at the zipper. She felt the sultry breeze lick her naked skin as he disentangled himself from her and released the two buttons on her shoulder and watched as her dress became a flimsy swirl around her feet. Immediately and wordlessly, he held her arm while she gracefully shed her lacy undergarments. They too became a froth at her feet.

Making no apologies, Reese stepped back and feasted upon her exquisite loveliness. She was everything he remembered, and more. "You can't imagine how often I dreamed of this moment," he murmured, continuing to devour her smooth ivory-toned body as the moonlight bathed her in a translucent glow.

"Me too," she replied simply.

Holding her eyes with burning desire, Reese reached out and stroked the taut crest of one nipple, then the other.

Meryl's head began to swim and her senses began to reel as his talented fingers brought both breasts to burgeoning fullness, equaled only by the fiery flame that settled in the womanly part of her.

Momentarily he drew back and began to discard his own clothing with leisurely enjoyment, never once taking his eyes off her. Then without warning Meryl spun around and positioned herself at the edge of the pool, and much to his delight and fascination, she executed a perfectly controlled dive, surfacing at the shallow end. She whirled, kicked off, and began swimming a length, alternating between a flowing sidestroke and a perfect back crawl. There was nothing, he thought, in the least exhibitionistic about her swimming, just an apparent pleasure in the actual performance.

He shoved his clothes aside with his foot and made his way toward the deep end and smiled as she climbed onto the steps, scarcely winded.

"You're good," he said, his smile broadening into a grin. "Is swimming merely part of the training at your studios, or is it a favorite pastime?"

It dawned on Meryl with renewed sadness that they knew so very little about each other. "Both," she quipped, sweeping her hair away from her face and eyes. "Each summer I taught children and old people how to swim in classes held by the Red Cross. Now, of course, I often swim with my ladies at the studio."

"Did you grow up here in Big H.?"

"I've lived here all my life." She paused, tracing a pattern in the water with her fingers. "How about you?"

"Originally I'm from Tennessee. My parents and one brother still live there." He smiled. "But I'd always wanted to go to school at the University of Texas, so my parents agreed. From there it was on to medical school. Like father, like son." He smiled again. "Except that he's a general practitioner in a small town."

"Sounds like you really have a nice family," she said softly, unable to hide the strain of envy that tinged her voice.

"They're great. I'll take you to meet them soon."

She was quiet for a moment. "I . . . I don't . . ."

Realizing he was beginning to push, he interrupted gently with a change of subject. "Tell me about your family."

Her mouth turned downward. "My parents died in a plane crash, leaving us in the care of an old-maid aunt, my mother's sister."

"I'm sorry," he responded soberly.

She tossed her head back. "Don't be. Now that I look

back, it wasn't a bad life, really. There was money for our needs, and in her own way she was good to us." She paused, tired of talking about herself. "Aren't you coming in for a swim?"

"In a minute." His voice was low, seductive, as he took pleasure in the smooth flex of her thigh and stomach muscles while she stretched like a lazy cat on her back with her eyes closed, content to let the gentle ripple of the water caress her limbs.

After a moment of silence, she opened her eyes to find him still staring at her, his face a mirror of contradicting emotions. "Ready to take another turn?"

"All right," she whispered, returning his stare with equal fascination. He was as beautiful as ever, she thought. He reminded her of a Greek god standing proudly before her. She took in the rippling muscles, the crisp dark hair covering his upper body, and then brazenly lowered her gaze to the turgid strength of his manhood. *She couldn't stop thinking about touching him.* She lowered herself back into the deep water.

Reese followed, lowering himself over the side and disappearing underwater. As he swam across the bottom of the pool, seeing her legs kicking slowly just above him, he experienced an enormous, bursting elation—glad that she was here, so filled with expectation, anticipation. She was softening toward him; he was positive of it. Tonight was just the beginning of a long and satisfying relationship, he told himself. He loved her too much to doubt it.

Teasingly his hand snaked out and gently but firmly grabbed her ankle, wanting simply to touch her. He felt her squirm, trying in vain to get loose from his clutches, but he refused to let her go. Suddenly he tugged harder, pulling her underneath the water. She looked enchanting with burnished dark hair fanning in time to the movement of her body. Grinning, he finally released his hold.

Meryl made a face at him before treading up and getting her head above water. "You're a bully, Reese Corbett," she retorted, though a grin took the sting out of her words. However, she wisely put distance between them.

He gave her a leering grin in return. "I know," he whispered conspiringly, treading toward her, his intentions clear.

"Oh, no you don't!" She trod faster, using her backstroke in an effort to get away. "Stay away from me!" she screeched playfully, only to feel a hand clasp her around the waist while the fingers of his other one spread over her breasts.

It was too late. She was lost.

"Oh, God, Meryl," he groaned as he savored her silky skin.

She felt a pleasurable tightening in the pit of her stomach as she drifted closer to him, their lips meeting and locking. As he kissed her deeply, hungrily, her hand drifted downward, over and around his buttocks. They were hard and smooth, so satisfying under her hands. So real, and firm and alive.

This can't be happening, she thought wildly, feeling the hard thrust of his maleness between their bodies. Then she laughed exuberantly, lifting her mouth from his. She had never felt more alive and daring in her life. It was uncanny what this man could do to her body, her senses.

"Are you enjoying yourself?" he asked.

"It's great!" She frowned. "But I have a sneaky feeling I'm fast becoming a wrinkled prune."

They both laughed.

"I love you, free and easy like this." He hugged her spontaneously. "You're nuts, but it's catching."

"I've . . . I've never done anything like this before." She paused seriously. "Have you?"

"You're the only woman who's ever been in this pool. Does that answer your question?"

"Yes, and I'm glad."

He kissed her wet lips sweetly and then drew back. When he spoke, his voice was low and tense. "I want you." It was a simple statement, but it held a wealth of meaning.

"Now?"

"Yes, now."

"Here!"

"Yes, here."

Meryl had nothing to support herself with—her legs were suddenly threatening to give way. "I . . . I don't know. When I'm with you I don't seem to be able to control what I'm saying or doing."

"Wrap your legs around me," he instructed huskily, holding her underneath.

"Reese . . . ?"

"Shhh," he whispered. "Relax. I just want to be a part of you for a moment. It's been so long."

He was inside her before she realized it, full and throbbing. He was right, she thought, it had been so long. She held him against her as he closed his lips hotly around a nipple while he manipulated her buttocks with gentle skill.

It was over as quickly as it had begun. He disengaged himself, latched on to her hand, and pulled her after him out of the pool. "I . . . I hope you didn't mind. I . . . know it wasn't good for you." He paused. "But I honestly couldn't wait," he added by way of apology.

"I didn't mind," she said urgently, reaching for him.

He leaned over and scooped her up into his arms and made his way into the house, not stopping until he was in the bedroom.

Even the chill from the air conditioner went unnoticed as he laid his precious burden on the satin bedspread. The instant they lay side by side, Reese began to kiss her breasts, already wanting her again. He licked her stiffening nipples.

Then he moved his mouth to hers, his body, his whole being tingling with anticipation as though this were the first time he had ever kissed her. He began touching slowly, mouth to mouth, and then hard, holding her tight against him.

"Oh, Reese," she moaned, locking her arms around his neck, then moving down to sink her fingers into his back, thinking that surely she was close to heaven. "Don't . . . don't make me wait much longer."

He ran his hand down her body, coming to rest at that secret place between her thighs, his seeking fingers finding she was indeed ready for him. "I shan't, my darling, I shan't," he whispered into her mouth. His appetite for her was proving to be insatiable.

Her body, her limbs, felt light as air as he came down on her and slid deep with one fluid thrust, rocking in and out, filling her.

She heard his moan as she reached for his buttocks, hard as stone, and pulled him farther into her. Her body writhed frantically under him as he let his weight down on her. Together they descended into a long dark tunnel of pleasure, building spasms that went on and on as her breathing seemed to stop entirely. She then inhaled one long shuddering sigh before coming back to reality.

As he rolled on his side and lay facing her once again, he found her unbearably beautiful. He wanted to tell her he loved her, but thought how easily it might shatter the moment, so he said nothing. Instead he nuzzled the base of her throat and ran his fingers softly through her hair and repeated to himself, *I love you, I love you.* She was wild and hot and soft and he was crazy about her. He longed for time to stand still so they could remain joined together—without the world.

Meryl felt his lips grazing her throat, and her eyes fluttered open, still glazed with passion. She purred his name.

Suddenly he knew he must have a commitment from her. Now. He could not allow this evening to end without a promise of a future.

His tone bespoke urgency. "We have to talk," he said, crooking an elbow and propping his head on it.

She shook her head. "No . . . please, not now."

"Yes, now," he stressed. "We have plans to make. I love you, and I believe you love me. I want us to get married.

Tomorrow." He traced a finger down the softness of her cheek. "We'll have a good life," he mused. "Make up for lost time. We'll fill our home with love and the pitter-patter of tiny feet."

Meryl froze. She became stiff as a corpse in his arms, her blood turning to ice water. "No!" she screeched, jerking away from him and covering her ears at the same time.

Panic slapped Reese in the face. "What the hell . . . ?"

At that moment, Meryl could not have uttered another word even if her life depended on it. *What had she done? What had she done?* But she knew. God help her, she knew. She had betrayed not only herself and Morgana but Reese as well.

From the moment he had followed her home, he had made his intentions clear, and she had known from the beginning she could not accept them. What he had said to her just now had come from deep within—from his heart, not just from his loins. She was sure. This time he had been honest and forthright about loving her and wanting to marry her. She no longer doubted his intentions, in spite of what she'd told herself. She had been everything but honest.

She hadn't told him she was just using this encounter to prove to herself that what she felt for him was purely physical, nothing more, that she was married to her career. And that she had no intention of ever seeing him again.

And even if there were no Morgana, and no career in the way, she still could not—or would not—marry him, because there remained that one flaw to be reckoned with: she was not able to give him the one thing he desired the most—a child.

Before Reese realized her intentions, she rolled over to the opposite side of the bed, stood up and slipped into his robe.

Reese bolted off the bed, oblivious of his nakedness, and confronted her with blazing eyes. "Goddammit, what's wrong now?" he demanded, bone-chilling fear creeping up his body like a small death.

"It . . . it won't work," she whispered. Her head was spinning, her stomach churning. That was a weak explanation, totally wrong for a man like Reese Corbett. She was doing badly.

"Exactly what is that supposed to mean?" he asked with deadly calm.

She clasped her hands tightly together. "I've already told you."

"Tell me again," he demanded, stalking closer. His jaw was tight, making the cast of his chin hard and impenetrable.

She nursed her dry lips with her tongue. "I've already told you," she cried. "I don't want to be just a housewife ever again . . . and there's still Morgana," she added on a sob.

His eyes glittered dangerously. "Just tell me one thing, then: why the seduction scene tonight?" Sarcasm drove the words into her.

Meryl knew he was sure to hear her heart knocking against her rib cage. She was afraid to tell him the truth and afraid not to. But she knew she couldn't endure another scene like this one.

She avoided looking at him. "For two years you've . . . you've been like a demon inside of me." She drew a ragged breath. "I was convinced that by using you . . . I could . . . get . . . you out of my system. But . . . I . . ."

He stared at her in total disbelief—never, never expecting this. "You what?" He pivoted on his heel and went to stand by the window, his back to her. What she had just told him burned in his gut like acid. Then anger, raw, piercing anger, swept through him with a vengeance. He clenched his fists to keep from slamming them into the wall. She's right, he thought. All they did was hurt each other, and that was no damn good!

Meryl tried desperately to defend herself with words that strangled in her throat. She wanted to tell him her plan had backfired. That she not only still wanted him, but, oh, God, *she still loved him*. But tears jammed her throat, and she knew any further explanation would fall on deaf ears.

Suddenly he turned and confronted her. "You're right," he said, his face devoid of color and expression. He then walked over to his closet and jerked a shirt and jeans off a hanger and began to put them on. "This isn't going to work." There was an ugly tone to his words. "I'll get your clothes and then take you home in my car. I'll see that yours gets back to you in the morning." She thought it wise not to argue.

He was hurt. His pride was damaged. She hated herself for what she'd done to him and to herself. Even though she knew she still loved him, she also knew she could never have him. She'd had to do something to drive him away. Making him hate her was as good a way as any.

She stood rooted to the spot and watched him stomp out of the room.

The ride home was a nightmare in itself. She sat huddled in the corner, her heart showing signs of bursting. He kept his eyes glued to the road, his profile sad and set.

Once he'd seen her safely into the house, she secured the lock and made her way into the bedroom. Turning, she stared at the wall for a long time before crumpling dry-eyed to the bed.

It was over. Time had a way of repeating itself. She had driven him away for good this time. That's what she wanted, wasn't it? So why did she feel as if she'd just been cut open without benefit of anesthetic?

Chapter 9

AT FIVE O'CLOCK THE NEXT MORNING, MERYL AWOKE DISORIENT-
ed, with a blinding, throbbing headache. She lay in a prone
position, afraid to move for fear of bringing on another stab
of pain.

Twenty minutes later she was able to sit up, dangle her feet
off the side of the bed and focus her eyes. She was an
emotional wreck, and had no earthly idea what to do about it.
The terror was back—black, ugly and frightening. It had
begun the moment she realized she still loved Reese.

She wrapped her arms around herself tightly and wallowed
in her misery. What was she going to do? Going to work was
definitely out of the question, she told herself.

Then out of the blue a thought struck her. She would go to
Galveston, to the cabin. There she could lick her wounds in
private. Having made the decision, she got out of bed,
slapped on the minimal amount of makeup, slipped on a pair
of shorts, T-shirt and sandals, and she was ready. At the last
minute she remembered to call Nelda and tell her she was
dropping out of sight for a few days to rest. She also left the
same message with Morgana's answering service.

As she laid the phone back in its cradle, Nelda's hyper
voice was still ringing in her ear. "Well, it's about time you're
going to pamper your tired body," she had said. "You haven't
been acting like yourself at all lately. Is there something
you're not telling me?"

"No, everything's fine," she had responded, knowing she
was lying. For a moment she had been tempted to dump her
troubles on Nelda's capable shoulders. But she couldn't do

that. Her involvement with Reese was too private to discuss with anyone. It must remain her secret.

Approximately three hours later, Meryl pulled into the drive of the deserted beach house. She paid no attention to the stale air that greeted her nose as she stepped inside. She went immediately to the air-conditioning switch and flipped it to sixty-five degrees. Next she trotted into the kitchen and fixed herself a large glass of ice water and downed it as she looked out the window.

Even though it was summer, the middle of the tourist season, this stretch of the beach was deserted. There was only a scattering of cabins close to hers and most of them belonged to older couples, who had a tendency not to haunt the beach during the height of the season. She was glad of the privacy.

With a deep sigh, she made her way into the bedroom, stripped out of her clothes and crawled in between the sheets, praying that sleep would put her out of her misery.

A loud noise penetrated her befuddled senses and rousted her out of her dreamless sleep. As her eyes fluttered open, she first thought the sound had come from a string of firecrackers. But then she heard it again. This time there was no mistake. Someone was pounding on the door, determined to be heard.

Groaning, Meryl rolled over and searched for the clock on the bedside table, trying to orient her thoughts. Six o'clock! She couldn't believe it. She rolled off the bed very gingerly and made her way to the closet, where she latched on to a long robe and donned it over her nakedness. She couldn't imagine who could be at the door. Nelda wouldn't have told anyone her whereabouts unless it was important.

The insistent knocking was shaking the entire structure by the time she got to the door.

"Who's there?" she asked hesitantly before making any effort to detach the chain lock or open the door.

"It's Tucker, dammit. Open the door!" he demanded, rattling the doorknob harder.

Tucker? A frown creased Meryl's forehead as she released the chain and drew the door back toward her. She didn't have a chance to utter a word as Tucker swept past her like a tornado into the room.

He came straight to the point. "Have you completely lost your mind?" he ranted, his bushy eyebrows working up and down, clearly showing his fury. He was standing in the middle of the room as though holding court.

Meryl was appalled at his display of such a volatile anger. To her knowledge she had never known Tucker Hammond to lose his control like this. What had she done?

Not giving her a chance to ask any questions or defend herself in any way, her uninvited guest hammered on, "I'm afraid this stunt *was* the final kiss of death, if you'll pardon my mod choice of words."

Thoroughly fed up with his display of bad manners, to say nothing of his untimely visit, Meryl tossed her head back, ignoring the sharp pain that darted through her skull, and hissed through tight lips, "What's the meaning of this? If you can't stop raving long enough to tell me what's happened, then I have no recourse but to show you the door." She meant it, too. Her eyes were flashing fire as she stalked to the door and flung it open.

They glared at each other for a moment, each one hoping to call the other's bluff. But Tucker knew he was beaten by the mutinous look stamped across Meryl's face. He had seen it many times before, and he knew if he didn't calm down, he would indeed be asked to leave.

His attitude did an about-face. "I'm sorry," he said, his voice considerably more subdued and much more in keeping with the Tucker Hammond she knew.

"Apology accepted," Meryl clipped, "but only if you're ready to explain why you're here." She eyed him closely as she slowly walked over to the couch and sat down. "And please, no shouting, if you don't mind. My head feels like someone is pounding on it with a sledgehammer."

Tucker got the message, for he lost no time in sitting down

in the chair opposite Meryl, diving into his shirt pocket for his pipe.

By the time he had packed it with tobacco, Meryl was sitting on pins and needles, but she wasn't about to let him see her anxiety. She waited.

After drawing several long puffs on his pipe, he finally spoke, his eyes narrowed slits, making it almost impossible for Meryl to see them. "Why weren't you at the meeting this morning?" he asked tightly, a trail of moisture staining his upper lip.

Her features mushroomed into a perplexed frown. "Meeting? I . . . don't . . ."

With an agile quickness she wasn't aware he possessed, Tucker was up and looming over her before she could catch her breath. "Goddammit, Meryl, I swear you'd try the patience of a saint!" he snapped, his voice threatening to rise above the danger level again. "We, that means you and I," he vented sarcastically, "were supposed to have met with the bankers and sealed the deal for the television show." He swung around and tromped toward the window, all the while ranting to himself, but loud enough for Meryl to hear. "I don't believe this is happening! Dammit, I can't believe you just didn't show up."

Meryl sat stunned, feeling as though she had been doused in the face with ice water. Oh, God, no! she moaned silently, crouching over and burying her face in her hands. She couldn't believe it either. But the meeting had clearly slipped her mind. No wonder Tucker was furious, she thought. She didn't blame him.

A knot of uncertainty and dread weighed heavy in the bottom of her stomach. She had no one to blame for this oversight but herself. And Reese. Her obsession for him had cost her. Again. She had been so excited when Tucker's secretary had called last week, asking her to post the date on her calendar. Yet she hadn't taken the time to comply with that simple request, positive she would remember. *Oh, Meryl, how could you!*

She sensed Tucker was watching her, missing none of the despair that held her speechless and caused her shoulders to sag in weary defeat. She looked up at him through a gusher of tears.

"I'm . . . I'm sorry," she whispered, her chin wobbling like a severely chastised small child's. "It completely slipped my mind!" She groped for the box of tissues on the table, making an effort to dam the flow of salty tears.

Tucker stilled her hand, placing his laundered handkerchief there instead. Then in a softened tone and with the utmost patience he asked, "How could you have forgotten something so very important to you? To me?" He shook his head in bewilderment, but his tone did not change. "Are you sick? Or did something happen that caused you to come tearing off down here as though you were hiding from the world?"

Another long silence followed his questions as Meryl strove to get her mind back on track. He was so close to the truth. . . .

"I'm waiting," he said, a ragged edge to his tone.

Meryl could feel the blood rush to her already pounding temples as she shifted her eyes away from his face. She owed him an explanation, but she couldn't tell him the truth. "I was . . . upset and I had a sick headache," she explained, trying to delete the tremor that shook her voice. She took a deep breath. "Actually, there's been a combination of things preying on my mind. I've . . . I've been working too hard and too long hours." She hesitated again. "And there's a problem with . . . with Morgana, and I . . ."

"Oh, for God's sake, Meryl!" Tucker exploded. "When are you going to stop babying and playing nursemaid to your sister?"

He was frustrated again and made no effort to hide it. "It's high time you cut the apron strings and let her sink or swim on her own. Every time she asks you to do her a favor"—he paused in mid-sentence, pinning Meryl's eyes to his—"she did ask you, didn't she?" When Meryl nodded her head in the affirmative, he went on, disgust overriding his frustration.

"Well, this time her selfishness may have ruined you," he finished cruelly.

Blind, raw panic swept through Meryl and only sheer force of will kept her from screaming aloud. "What happened when I . . . I didn't show up?"

Tucker sat down beside her, his face ashen. "They have all but scratched the deal. They're seriously considering giving the money to that movie star, who, as you well know, has been snapping at your heels ever since this physical-fitness boom began."

"No! They can't do that to me. Not after I've worked as hard and counted on this for so long." Her voice rose with each word until it reached a high-pitched shriek. She was standing now, clutching her robe tighter about her.

"Now, take it easy," Tucker soothed, taking in the high color bathing her face.

"How can you say that," she cried, "when everything, and I mean everything, is crumbling around my feet? And what makes it worse, it's all my fault." Sobs racked her body. "Oh, God, I can't lose it all now, I just can't. Isn't there anything I can do?" She took a deep ragged breath in one last grim, raw-nerved effort to relax and get control of herself. *Damn you, Reese Corbett! Must I pay for loving you the rest of my life?*

"At the moment, no," Tucker told her bluntly.

"Are you sure?" Her eyes were pleading. "Couldn't you arrange another meeting? Something?" she asked desperately, the tears flowing freely down her cheeks.

For a moment Tucker's expression seemed to soften, but it was short-lived. The dark frown once again claimed his square features. "Now's not the time to fall apart," he said brusquely. "It's the time for action, and I have a plan in mind."

Tucker's rough words whipped her into shape. She even managed to dam up the gush of tears. In spite of herself, she experienced a flutter of hope. "What?" she asked, looking at him intently.

"I think I can persuade two of the men—the two that were reluctant to condemn you immediately—to take a tour of your studios, hopefully by the middle of next week, to show them exactly what they would be losing by not backing you. The other two men are leaving on vacation this weekend or I'd try to coerce them into coming too."

"I'll do whatever you say, whenever you say it. You're calling the shots," she said desperately.

"It's a shot, all right—a shot in the dark—but at the moment, it's all we have to count on."

"Do . . . you think there's a chance they'll reconsider?" Meryl asked, her heart thumping against her ribs.

Tucker heaved a sigh. "I honestly don't know. They won't make a definite decision for at least two weeks—maybe even longer." His eyes suddenly became hard as rocks. "If this plan backfires, we'll just have to find another way to put the pressure on them."

"How will I ever be able to thank—?" she began.

He waved his hand. "Don't thank me yet. We've just begun to fight—again."

Meryl rubbed the tight muscles in the back of her neck. "I'll be in my office early Monday morning getting ready for the tour."

Tucker stared at her for a long moment, then said, "I'll be in touch." He pivoted on his heel and started toward the door.

"Tucker."

He stopped and turned around, his eyebrows raised in question. "I'm saying thank you, whether you want me to or not."

He wrapped his fingers around the doorknob without taking his eyes off her. "I'm sure what I'm about to say is no longer necessary, but I'm going to say it anyway." He paused nervously, almost as though he didn't quite know how to tell her what was on his mind. Then he went on, "I just want to caution you that your dependability must never be in question again."

He hesitated. "Whatever's troubling you, if it's this thing with Morgana, or whatever, I suggest you stay here and come to terms with it, get it straightened out," he ordered. "And I also suggest you make up your mind what's really important to you." He hesitated again. "At this point, I'm not even sure you know yourself."

With those choice words, he opened the door and walked out without a backward glance.

Meryl existed in a state of limbo. She could not sleep, she could not eat, she could not do anything worthwhile or constructive. She did not know which dealt her the most misery—the pigeonholed television show or the realization that she still loved Reese.

And each time she would find herself on that dangerous slide into remembering what had driven her into this solitary confinement in the first place, she would rebel in panic. *No, no! I can't think, won't.*

On the morning of the third day after Tucker's departure, she decided that as soon as she jogged, she would pack, close up the cabin and return to Houston to work. She was accomplishing nothing by staying here.

Now was as good a time as any, she told herself, to face the fact that she had changed; her life had changed, and ignoring it would not make it go away. Reese. His name brought him, all of him, crowding in on her. She wanted to blame him for the costly error she'd made, and she did to an extent. Though she blamed herself more.

But Reese was gone. She had driven him away. Driven him, more than likely, back to Morgana. She must come to terms with that. She had to put it behind her and go on or risk losing not only her career but also her sanity.

Reese Corbett muttered an expletive and flung down his pen. "Come in," he said harshly to the persistent knock at his office door. Only good manners prevented him from scowling at his visitor.

Emory Cantrell sauntered into the room, a smile lurking around her lips. "What the hell's the matter with you, son? I haven't seen you smile in over a week now."

Reese's face lightened, but no answering smile was forthcoming. "It's been a tough one, Emory, in more ways than one," he admitted, his voice strained and low-keyed.

Knowing that he was welcome, Emory lowered his large frame into the chair across from Reese's desk, slouching comfortably. "Interested in a sympathetic ear?"

"Unfortunately, there's nothing that can be said or done to change my situation." Bitterness had crept once again into his voice as he looped his hands behind his head and leaned back in his swivel chair.

Emory's piercing green eyes shifted to the generous amount of papers, charts, and diagrams strewn across the desk. "Is it work or personal?" he probed delicately.

Reese grimaced as though in pain. "Both," he responded without hesitation.

"Well, your work I may be able to shed some light on, but the other . . ." He paused and scratched his chin. "It would be like the blind leading the blind."

Reese threw him a sharp glance. "What's that supposed to mean? Surely you and Janet aren't having trouble?"

Emory looked suddenly uncomfortable. "As a matter of fact, we are. However, I don't think it's anything we can't work out," he added hurriedly. "We've been married a long time, but all those days and nights I've devoted to my practice and research, away from home, have taken their toll on Janet. She accuses me of being married to my work and everything else can go hang." He smiled sadly. "Of course, I'd like to think she's exaggerating."

"I'm sorry, Emory. You know how I feel about you and Janet," Reese said sincerely, and then smiled, but it was hollow, never reaching his eyes. "I will have to admit, though, my sympathies do tend to lean toward Janet." He paused. "I know what it's like to love someone who's married to a career."

"I guess it must be tough. That's why this old dog's having to learn new tricks," Emory declared with a grimace. "It was either that or lose Jan, and as you well know, I wouldn't be worth a damn without her."

"I just wish my problem was as easily solved."

"It's Meryl again, isn't it?" Emory asked lightly, knowing he was treading on dangerous ground. Reese was one of the very few men he knew who was unable to hide his feelings. When something was troubling him, everyone knew it, except the patients. Around them he was his usual amiable self, never in the least short-tempered. They always received the very best of Reese Corbett. But his clinic and hospital staff didn't fare nearly as well. They had finally learned, though, to stay out of his way when he was in one of his "moods."

Emory had been so in hopes that Reese would find happiness with this lovely woman he was so obviously crazy about. After his ordeal with Kathy and losing his son, he deserved to be happy. But Emory was beginning to have his doubts that Meryl Stevens was the one who could bring him that happiness. He sighed inwardly.

Reese had told him that he had fallen in love with Meryl before Kathy ever let him go. And he had certainly gone through hell since then. Emory remembered when he had returned from that cabin long ago, and it wasn't a pleasant memory. Even though Reese was free now, there still seemed to be problems.

Finally Reese broke through the silence. "Yes, it's Meryl." There were both anger and sadness in his voice.

"She won't marry you, is that it?" Emory asked quietly.

"That's the furthest thing from her mind," Reese countered harshly. "It's a long story and I'm not about to burden you with my tale of woe. You've more than done your part by pulling me up when I've been lower than a snake's belly." He paused, his lips narrowing into a thin white line. "This is something I have to work out for myself."

"Well, I'll be around if you need me." Emory regarded him

quietly. "I hope for your sake you can get this all squared away. You've come a long way with your breakthrough in reconstructive surgery, and I'd hate to see you chuck it all now."

Reese eased himself out of the chair and crossed to the windows and looked out onto the loud hubbub of the Medical Center. His thoughts were in a turmoil, but his features gave nothing away as he turned and faced his friend again. He spoke distinctly. "Don't worry, I'm a long way from coming unglued at the seams," he lied.

"Well, if you don't mind taking advice from an old codger who's lived longer than you, I'd advise you not to give up. Not if you love her, that is."

"I'll remember that."

Emory threw him a confident smile before stepping over the threshold, then suddenly placed his hand against the doorjamb and swung around. "Oh, by the way," he said, his eyebrows raised, "What's the problem with the patient? Anything I can do to help?"

Reese shook his head. "No, not right now, maybe later. It's Wanda Adams, and she's a difficult case; one of my worst." He sighed. "She's scheduled for surgery the end of next week, and I still have several more X-rays I have to study."

"If you need me, just holler."

"Thanks, Emory . . . for everything."

Emory shrugged offhandedly. "Think nothing of it. I'll see you later."

Reese remained standing at the window, listening to the mad rush of traffic on Fannin Street twenty-four stories below him. Even this high, the noise carried; the shrill sound of an ambulance wheeling into the Hermann Hospital emergency entrance jarred through him, stringing his nerves tighter. There were sickness and death all around him, everywhere he turned. And most of the time he could cope with it, but not now.

Before Emory had come into his office, he had been on the

verge of calling it quits for the day. And he was still considering doing so. He might as well; he wasn't fit company for anyone.

He was miserable. And lonely. And he wanted Meryl. He felt totally thwarted, unable to think of a way to breach the wide gap between them, to get through to her. He couldn't force her to love him, though fool that he was, he was still clinging to the hope that she did. But she just didn't feel the urgency he felt. There were too many obstacles in the way for her to make a commitment.

She'd been opting for an out and he'd unwittingly supplied it. He'd made it too easy, when he never wanted it to end, he told himself, saddened immeasurably by the waste of it all.

It was somehow worse than two years ago when he'd lost her. Then he'd had Jason. But now he was left with only this incredibly gnawing emptiness. He didn't honestly think he could survive without her.

He just couldn't let her go; not yet.

She was closing the cabin door behind her when she turned and saw him. She stood nailed to the spot, every nerve in her body going haywire. What was *Reese* doing here?

Her heart hammered against her chest as she watched him unwind his gangly body from behind the wheel and make his way toward her, squinting against the glare of the hot sun. She blinked once, then twice, positive he was a mirage. But, no. He kept coming toward her, bigger than life.

He hesitated briefly at the foot of the steps and their eyes met. Meryl was not so rattled she failed to notice the new lines that dented the generous curve of his mouth, the unhappiness that gave his gray eyes a sharp edge.

"Can we talk?" he asked simply.

Meryl swallowed the lump that rose unbidden to her throat and turned and stepped back into the cabin, wordlessly giving him her answer.

Once inside, she couldn't sit; she was too high-strung. She

just stood in the center of the room and waited, her blood running hot one minute and cold the next. What was he doing here? she repeated in silent agony. Just when she had herself convinced it was over and that she must learn to live without him, he came roaring back into her life, reaping destruction like a spring storm. She began to tremble.

"I warned you that I wasn't going to give up," he said as though he had read her thoughts.

Those softly spoken words ripped through Meryl like a knife drawing blood in its wake. "How dare you come here and say that to me after what you've done!" she spat, her dark eyes flashing like hot coals.

Reese took an unconscious step backward, completely caught off guard by her vicious accusation. "Because I'm crazy!" he retaliated in kind. *And crazy in love with you*, he added to himself while trying to hang on to his simmering temper and wishing he hadn't come. Oh, God, he'd hoped she had longed for him as much as he had for her, that maybe there was still a chance . . .

Then it dawned on him exactly what she'd said. "What do you mean, what *I've* done?" he demanded, feeling as though he was floundering in the middle of the ocean without a life jacket. He hated being in that position.

Her tongue was still rabid. "Because of you—us—I blew my chance of ever getting my television show, that's what!" She knew she should curb her tongue. But she was angry, she was upset, she was worried, and she was using Reese as a scapegoat to bear the brunt of her own failure. She also knew she should not say another word, but she couldn't stop herself. "I've lost the most important thing in the world to me," she finished on a sob.

Reese was at a loss what to do, how to deal with her in this state. He had to quell the urge to turn her across his knee. "Why the hell are you blaming me?" He glared at her, his face rigid.

Meryl jammed her hands down into the pockets of her

shorts, recruiting fresh ammunition for her verbal attack. "If . . . if I hadn't let you make love to me, none of this would have happened."

Fury swept through Reese. "If I remember correctly, you seemed to enjoy it at the time," he sneered, anger contorting his features.

That was Meryl's undoing. She felt herself unraveling on the inside like a ball of twine. "Oh, Reese," she cried between gulps, "don't you see, this is no good. We're no good. Every time we're together, all we do is hurt each other."

Without stopping to weigh the consequences, Reese closed the gap between them and hauled her trembling body into his arms. He rocked her like a baby. "Meryl, my darling, don't you understand, I want to be hurt by you."

She pulled away and raised tear-filled eyes to his face. "How can you . . . you say that?" she whispered brokenly.

"Because I love you, that's how."

"Oh, Reese," she repeated, naked fear glazing the edges of her dark eyes, "what are we going to do?"

Chapter 10

REESE'S HOLD TIGHTENED. "I KNOW WHAT *I* WANT TO DO," HE said into the delicate fold of her ear. His voice was so low it was almost a whisper.

"What?" she whispered in return, her warm breath nipping his skin as her head nestled in the gentle crook of his neck. A shiver speared through him, leaving a hot flame in his loins. He drew back and looked down into her slightly flushed features with narrowed eyes.

"Make love to you," he responded tautly, his thumb probing lightly at the ticking pulse at the base of her throat.

Her heart gave an odd little jump, but she never broke out of the circle of his arms. Then, of their own accord, her fingers reached out and caressed his skin, and she felt his flesh tense beneath her feather-light touch.

"Are you going to stop me?" he asked thickly, his body trembling.

The tortured desperation of his plea penetrated the rampaging desire that stormed within her own body. Meryl shut her mind to everything except his consuming presence, wanting him, needing him above all else. Nothing had been settled. But she didn't care. Not now. All she cared about now was experiencing the powerful strength of Reese's body. She wanted to melt into him, become one with him.

While her thoughts were a caldron of seething emotions, his hands were playing over her body, searching, seeking, loving.

She could not deny him—anything.

At last she spoke. "No, I'm not going to stop you." She made no effort to control the shaky timbre of her voice.

He peered down at her, his eyes speaking volumes. He had won. This time. But that wasn't what was important. Time for tallying the scores in the win and loss columns would come later. She wanted him. The rest of the day and night would belong to her. And tomorrow? Well, tomorrow would just have to fend for itself.

It had been only a few days since he had touched her, but to Meryl it might as well have been an eternity. She watched with glowing anticipation while Reese readied the bed. He drew the bedspread back, folding it neatly at the foot of the bed, before crossing over and closing the drapes on both windows. The room instantly became shadowed and cool.

He turned and sauntered slowly toward her, his eyes snapping pictures to store in his memory of every delicious curve of her body. A smile gentled her lips as she stood waiting, her eyes wide and shimmering, her chocolate curls an unruly mass, her sloppy cut-off jeans molding her hips and derriere, leaving very little to the imagination. Patches of sweat broke out over his body as his eyes greedily sought the display of creamy bare skin between the waistband and the skimpy halter top that encased her full breasts and pebble-hard nipples. She looked adorable. And she was his. And he couldn't wait to lay his touch to every sweet inch of her.

Standing in front of her now, he reached out and traced a finger across a perfectly arched brow, down a cheek, and then across her lips, before slowly, intently joining his lips to hers. Caught in the web of sensuality that danced around them, she returned his kiss without fear or hesitation. He crushed her closer against the length of him, feeding hungrily on her mouth, rocking them both to their toes.

Reese was the first to pull away, freeing his hands to remove her scant clothing with studied slowness.

"We have all the time in the world," he murmured, his tone low and excited. "I want everything to be perfect."

"Me too," she answered huskily, her senses already spinning as though she were on a merry-go-round. She clutched at his shoulder for balance as his hands moved to her waist, heard the metallic whisper as he lowered the zipper on her jeans before giving in to the searing heat of his hands on her body as he tugged both the jeans and her panties down her trembling limbs.

With gentle persuasion he unsnapped her scanty top and thrust it aside. Instantly her uptilted breasts and ripe reddish-brown nipples were free, leaving them naked to his gaze.

He stood back slightly, his breathing heavy, his hands clasping her arms firmly, almost painfully, even as he held himself away from her.

"I need you so much," he whispered, his eyes searching her face in the dimness. "But my need will never overshadow my love for you. I—"

"Don't . . ." Meryl halted his flow of words with her lips, laying them against the parted moistness of his. "Don't . . . say anything," she whispered. "Just feel." She then flicked her tongue across his lips, making him forget everything except her delectable body strained against his. A groan of anguish escaped through his lips.

Knowing what it took to please him, Meryl let her hands stray to the buckle on his belt. From then on, it was only a matter of minutes and he was free of his clothes and standing in naked splendor before her, proud and beautiful.

Daring as she was deliberate, she lifted a hand and dipped it into the dark, silky curls that covered his wide chest and ran her eyes the length of his muscles and well-shaped hips, before dropping them lower. She caught her breath when she saw his erection jutting from beneath the dark triangle, her eyes marveling anew at the strength of it.

"Oh, Meryl," he groaned, half out of his mind with longing. "The way your eyes touch me as—"

"As though I can't wait to taste every inch of your skin," she murmured, her feelings expanding her heart to the bursting point.

"Nor I yours," he rasped.

The sheets were clean and smelled like a spring bouquet; lilacs, Meryl decided as she lay beside Reese, their erratic breathing the only identifiable sound in the room. But she was interested in nothing and no one but this man beside her. She reveled in him; she was exactly where she wanted to be, doing exactly what she wanted to do. Then suddenly, unpleasantly, she recalled an old Spanish proverb: "Take what you want, God said. Take it—and pay for it." But she wouldn't think about that now. Tomorrow would be soon enough.

The tip of Reese's tongue was a weapon of pleasure as he licked her breasts, bringing her back to reality, heavenly reality, with a jolt—a jolt of electric pleasure. She moaned and cradled his head as he continued his assault on her nipples, first one, then the other. By the time he had worked his magic on them, they glistened and were pouting proudly from the dew of his mouth.

But he did not stop there. He kept on going, putting his mouth to her navel, delving his tongue in the velvet center, flicking like a tiny whip in and out before moving to tease her hips and thighs, only then to return to her breasts. He then began running his tongue along the underside of their tender fullness until they each were bathed as generously as her nipples.

She was tantalized and tormented almost to the point of screaming by the skilled lash of his tongue and the fire of his lips. She tried to open her mouth to plead for mercy, but she couldn't speak, nor could she move. She was his captive. He made her body dance, flooding her whole being with heat and creating an unbearable burning sensation inside her, making her ache with longing.

While he continued his gentle wooing of her breasts, his hands traveled lightly over her stomach, then lower, skimming over her knees, the inside of her thighs. Her skin was soft as down, though firm, and he wallowed in the pleasure it was bringing him. He was on a high equal to nothing he'd ever experienced.

He wanted it to last a lifetime.

Meryl had never been so thoroughly possessed, as she was at this moment, by this lovable man. Granted, their past lovemaking had been wonderful and exciting, but never like this. In her wildest imagination she could never have conjured up the profound pleasure he was heaping on her. There was magic in his touch, as though he was reading her through her skin.

His hands, as they continued to caress her limbs, while his mouth suckled her nipples, felt like a silk scarf being drawn back and forth over her body, dragging her this way and that, awarding her with a weightless sensation.

She raised her hand and buried it deep into his thick hair, groping for a touch of reality. He released a nipple and looked into her glazed eyes.

"You're perfect," he murmured. "Incredibly perfect." He smiled at her, waiting for her to bring him closer, bring her lips to his.

His mouth tasted like sweet nectar. Dizzying. His tongue gently battled his way deep into hers. Warm, she inched him even closer, her mouth opening wider. They drank from each other, eagerly, purposefully, adoringly, while his hand slid the length of her unblemished stomach, coming to rest at the gate of her womanhood. Her legs drifted apart like a flower seeking the sun, leaving his hand free to touch, to find.

His fingers probed delicately, finding the sweetness of her, and rubbed gently. He lifted his mouth back to a breast as she began to move slowly, steadily against his hand. Sighing aloud, she gave in to the million shooting stars exploding within her.

Once she had stilled, she longed to bring him to the same delicious heights. She knelt above him, and her heart flipped over as she looked down at him. He was the perfect one. The whorls of hair staining his chest a dark color were thick and wiry, but gentle to the touch, his flat hard-toned belly and slim muscled thighs were a perfect backdrop for his impaling manhood joining the two. Yes, he was the perfect one, equal to none. And she could deny him nothing.

Her sure hand began to roam his body freely, wreaking havoc to his heart, no matter where they touched. She played him like a stringed instrument, leaving nothing unconquered by her hands and mouth. She brought his nipples to stonelike hardness before teasing his navel with her tongue, only then to concentrate on his manly pride.

"Oh, yes, my love . . . don't stop," he groaned as he gave in to the waves of exquisite agony that washed over him.

Soon reaching the edge of the abyss, Reese eased on top of her, fitting his body to her, and groaned, "I can't wait much longer. I want to be inside you."

"Yes . . . now . . . please," Meryl returned urgently, knowing she, too, was about to topple over the edge of the same abyss.

He kissed her suddenly, and the heat, the hunger, made them frantic. Their foreplay had lasted too long. She wrapped her arms and legs around him, taking all of him in one breath-stopping surge. Her moistness greeted and enveloped him as he began moving ever so slowly, then with increasing speed, until at last she felt his body quiver at the same time she gasped aloud, her insides lighted up like a thousand sparklers.

He rested atop her for a moment before rolling over on his side and pulling her gently with him. They lay side by side, legs lovingly entwined, him still a part of her, though passion was spent, gazing into each other's faces.

"I love you," he whispered into her mouth.

"And I love you," she answered, knowing it was useless to deny it.

"I love all of you," he countered.

She was incapable of controlling her mouth; it smiled without her permission. "And I love all of you," she echoed softly.

They slept, using each other's bodies for cover.

*   *   *

Meryl languorously stretched her limbs, but only after disentangling them from beneath Reese's warm body. She rolled over and looked at the clock and was amazed to see it was after nine o'clock. She scooted back over and treated herself to a free perusal of Reese. He was still sleeping soundly; she hated to disturb him. He looked years younger now, she thought with a severe tightening around her chest. So dear. A satisfied smile softened her features as she battled back the guilt nibbling at the edges of her happiness, wanting to destroy it. She wasn't ready to give him up. Not yet. Tomorrow was still hours away.

She snuggled against him and knew no more.

Meryl awakened a short time later to the erotic touch of Reese's tongue outlining her breast. She smiled, catching him off guard. He drew back and grinned boyishly. "Caught me in the act, huh?"

"That I did, that I did," she teased.

As though he had no control, his gaze drifted back to her breasts and lingered. "You have beautiful breasts," he stated matter-of-factly.

She went weak all over and her mouth went dry.

"Full and tender," he continued with hypnotizing slowness, the tips of his fingers passing like a breath of ecstasy over her hardening nipples. "They remind me of the juicy apples I used to pick off the trees and devour as a young kid."

She had difficulty swallowing, much less speaking. "I . . . I'm glad they please you," she stammered huskily.

He leaned down and kissed her deeply, roughly. Then he raised up with a grin and popped her playfully on her bare bottom. "Last one in the shower has to cook dinner." He bounded up and off the bed before she knew what was happening.

Meryl shrieked as she, too, plummeted off the bed. "Oh, no you don't!" She laughed, entering into the lighthearted banter. "You're taking unfair advantage," she added on another loud shriek as Reese was now crossing the threshold into the bathroom, his attractive laugh bouncing off the walls.

As Meryl came tearing in behind him, Reese was standing in front of the shower stall, his arms folded across his chest, a grin plastered to his lips, and staring lasciviously at her bouncing breasts. "What took you so long, my dear?"

She placed her hands on her hips in mock rage, but her chin jutted stubbornly. "Why, you . . . you pompous—" she began.

"Naughty, naughty," he interrupted, placing a finger against her lips, effectively silencing her. His eyes danced mischievously. "We don't have time for all that stuttering, woman. We have work to do here, and then it's off to the kitchen with you to slam the chow on the table."

Before she could heap further wrath on him, he grasped her hand firmly and yanked her under the stinging spray of the water.

They giggled uncontrollably as the water stung their eyes and pelted their bodies with tender force.

This was Meryl's first time ever to share the bathroom facilities with a man. Not once during her fifteen years of marriage had Elliot ever encouraged her to intrude on what he referred to as his private time, nor did he ever lead her to think he wanted to impose on hers.

Now as she and Reese stood laughing like two kids as they tried to keep the bar of soap from slipping out of their hands, she realized just how much she had missed. Then suddenly a feeling as sweet as warm honey flowed through her, because it was Reese she was sharing this intimacy with. It was another part of loving and being loved.

"Hey, wake up, sleeping beauty," Reese demanded in a deep, satisfied tone, nuzzling the side of her slippery neck while easing the soap in a rotating circle around her breasts.

She brought her mouth next to his and whispered, "Even if I was dreaming about you?"

Reese's eyebrows rose dramatically. "Well, in that case," he drawled thickly, "I guess it's all right."

Gracefully she lifted her arms around his neck, with an

eager passion that instantly aroused him. He molded his lips to hers and kissed her long and hard as the water continued to trickle over their bodies, soaking their hair and skin.

He shifted the soap from her breasts to her shoulders, lathering them thoroughly before moving down her back and to her buttocks. He stooped and washed her feet. Meryl giggled deliriously and held on to his shoulders as he soaped between her toes.

"Quit squirming, you little hussy," he reprimanded huskily, "and let me finish."

"I . . . I can't." She giggled again, feeling as she never had in her life. "That tickles."

"Well, then, let's see if this feels any better." But this time his voice had a different tone; it was deep and slightly strained. He then proceeded to travel up her body to the dark turf between her legs. He held her close as he discarded the bar of soap in favor of a sponge lying at his fingertips. He then passed the sponge, swollen with lather, between her thighs. He squeezed the liquid over her breasts and stomach in an unbroken stream. His fingers worked themselves into the tangle of wet hair and through her scalp. As his hands traveled her body, she shivered, turning, twisting, trembling, uttering broken moans of pleasure, while her loins moved rhythmically against him, bringing him to a throbbing stiffness.

Meryl dug her fingernails into his back as she sought desperately to keep her hold on reality, doing her best not to slide into the vortex of her own pleasure. But his hands were unwilling to release her as they teased, taunted, tormented her secret place until her bones felt as though they were disintegrating.

"Oh, please," she whimpered, "I need you . . . now!"

Effortlessly he lifted his hands and clamped them on either side of her waist and lowered her onto the heart of him. She opened herself, receiving him deeply into her with wanton abandonment, the warm water continuing to cascade down their anchored bodies.

Sharp moaning whimpers broke through her lips when the pressure increased within her, but her sounds were no match for Reese's roaring breath. She felt as though she were flying as a glorious pain racked her body, spasm following spasm. He, too, experienced the same wave of ecstatic pain as they rode the cloud of pleasure in perfect sequence.

Meryl, suddenly reminiscent of a rag doll, had to be carried into the bedroom. Reese laid his precious burden onto the rumpled sheets, where he immediately began to dry her limbs with a big fluffy towel. As he knelt over her and administered to her every need with sweet patience, she could read his heart through his eyes.

"Oh, Meryl, my precious love," he whispered, and dabbed gently at her breasts and carefully between her thighs, only to dry the most delicate place with his mouth.

As soon as he was dry, he lay down beside her, holding her close against him for a long sweet moment, only to have it suddenly shattered by a strange rumbling sound.

Scarlet-faced, Meryl moved and grabbed her stomach. Reese drew back and stared down at her with mock horror. Then laughter took over as he bracketed her face with his hands.

"Are you by any chance trying to tell me something?"

Meryl wrinkled her nose at him, her face still flushed with color. "If you mean am I starving to death, well, the answer is yes."

He grinned and tweaked the tip of her nose. "That's obvious, my love, if that loud gurgling sound I heard is any indication."

"Did anyone ever tell you that you're a menace to society?" she quipped, and punched him playfully in the stomach. Then, before he could retaliate, she twisted around, and in one bounce was off the bed. Leaning down, she reached for her robe that was strewn carelessly on the floor and put it on before casting her eyes back toward the bed and Reese. Even now, after many hours of arduous lovemaking, she felt her breath catch at the magnificence of his lean-hipped body. He was lying with his arms folded behind his head, watching her every action with possessive interest.

They smiled at each other for an intense moment and the world stood still.

"What do you want to eat?" she blurted out nervously, knowing the minute she'd said it what his answer would be. She was not disappointed.

"You," he said simply.

"Be serious," she scolded, unable to hide the quiver in her voice.

"I am serious."

"Reese!"

He merely grinned at her exasperation. "Oh, all right. I'll let you off the hook this time, you gorgeous wench," he conceded, "but only because you lost the bet and have to cook." His eyes danced merrily. "Otherwise you might not get off quite so easily."

She tossed her head back and sniffed airily, loving his good mood. "You're hopeless as well as insatiable," she taunted impishly before heading for the kitchen.

Reese lay still and listened to the clattering sounds of dishes as she made an effort to throw a quick meal together. Something inside him chanted as he imagined spending every day of the rest of his life with her, sharing, loving. After today he was confident he would be able to convince her to come to grips with her guilt over Morgana and consent to marry him. In fact, he felt damn sure of it.

"Need any help?" he called after a short span of silence prevailed from the kitchen.

"No, of course not," Meryl retorted. "I wouldn't dream of making you get up and work. Heaven forbid!"

Meryl smiled to herself as a round of hearty laughter reached her ears. Keeping her eyes on the skillet filled with bacon, she concentrated on Reese, thereby keeping other thoughts at bay, thoughts that weren't nearly as pleasant, such as regret, remorse, guilt. All those emotions she would have to contend with soon. But she was determined to squeeze every ounce of happiness out of this stolen time.

"It's lonesome in there without you," he whispered, stealing up behind her, circling her waist with his arms. "Mmmm, that smells good," he added, laughing softly while nibbling at her neck. "But then, it should; it's after twelve o'clock, and we still haven't eaten." He kept on nibbling.

His touch was all it took to relieve Meryl of her unhappy thoughts. It was like a heady breath of spring after a long, cold winter.

Catching him unaware, she twirled out of his arms with a grin and plunked a two-pronged fork into his hand. "We'll have none of that horseplay. If you trespass on my territory, you have to work."

Grinning, Reese played along with her, bowing from the waist and looking utterly ridiculous in nothing but a towel tied around his waist. "As you wish, madam."

Their shared laughter set the tone for the next few minutes as they hurriedly prepared the meal. While Reese saw to it that the bacon was fried to a crispy brown, Meryl fixed a condiment tray filled with juicy sliced tomatoes, lettuce, pickles and olives.

The freezer contained a package of french fries, which she handily dumped into the deep frier, and while they sizzled and bubbled in the hot grease, she mixed two glasses of iced tea. Thank goodness she had gone the day before to the small and only grocery store within miles or they would have been in big trouble, because up until then, the cupboards were bare.

Their endless chatter was the only thing that kept them from wolfing down their midnight snack. They discussed subjects they had never broached before: politics, mainly the state of the economy, his work and hers, though special care was taken by both not to mention the axed television show.

By the time their plates were empty and the kitchen spotless, Meryl's eyelids had begun to droop, more from exhaustion, she guessed, than from lack of sleep. Her body wasn't used to the long sexual marathons she had experienced since early afternoon. She yawned in weary contentment.

"It's back to bed for you," Reese exclaimed with a teasing grin, her state of exhaustion not having gone unnoticed by him. Before she could utter a word of protest, he scooped her up in his arms and carried her back to bed. After cuddling close to each other for warmth against the chill of the purring air conditioner, they fell into another dreamless sleep.

Meryl awoke just as the lazy fingers of dawn were painting the sky a bright gold. Without disturbing Reese, she slipped out of bed and made a quick dash for the bathroom before rushing back to bed and to Reese. He was sleeping as soundly as a newborn baby, his lower legs tangled up in the sheets. Tears welled behind her eyes as she remembered with a sharp pang that today she had to return home, back to reality, back to work. She had indulged herself long enough.

Reese stirred, claiming her full attention. She looked at him closely, noting the rise and fall of his chest, taking in the color riding his cheekbones. She lay unmoving beside him, becoming more attuned and more aroused by the warmth of his body. Suddenly she was determined to leave him with a memory he would never be able to erase. She would wake him up. But with a high. . . .

His eyes shot open, dazed with varying shades of passion, a soft hissing moan coming from his throat. "Oh, God, Meryl, please . . . oh, yes, yes!" He wound a hand in her rich curls as she bent over him, encouraging her, basking in the untold pleasure she was bringing him. But soon she had to stop. Her own appetite had returned full force, and she couldn't wait a moment longer to satisfy it.

She raised herself up and swung her leg over his hips, and using his shoulders to brace herself and holding him in place with her free hand, she eased down on him. Then, sliding up the length of his chest, she laid her lips against his and whispered, "Good morning, sleepyhead."

"You're wonderful! This is wonderful!" he whispered back, kneading the fullness of her breasts.

She felt him reach high inside her and watched his face shimmer with wonder as she clenched her muscles and began to move slowly.

"Marry me," he groaned.

She almost stopped moving. "You know I can't."

"Please."

"Don't do this. Not now," she pleaded.

"I love you."

"I love you too, but . . ."

"But what?" he asked thickly.

She continued rotating her hips.

"Just promise you'll think . . . think about it!"

"I . . . I promise."

"Oh, wonderful! Yes! I love what you just said. And what you're doing to me! I'm about to explode!"

"You don't want to?"

"Not unless you're ready."

"I'm ready! Oh . . . yes . . . Now!"

He welded her to him as an attack of sweet pain rocked her body. *What a delightful man you are,* she thought as his cry echoed hers as she rode the crest with him. So wonderful, so desirable, so tender for a man. So very tender.

Reese stood just inside the bathroom door a short time later and watched as Meryl put the finishing touches on her makeup. It was almost as though they were married, he thought, trying to garner the nerve to say what was on his mind.

"Did you . . . mean what you said?" he asked.

Meryl wanted to pretend she didn't know what he was referring to, but she couldn't. Although she had spoken those words in the throes of passion, she knew exactly what she'd said. But *why* she had said them, she didn't know. Could she plead temporary insanity and get away with it? she wondered.

It was ludicrous to even allow herself to think along those lines. Dangerous.

"Meryl?" His eyes were searching hers with disturbing intensity.

She stopped what she was doing and stared back at him under tear-fringed lashes, yet saying nothing.

Reese sighed. "If I promise to give you more time, not to press you, will you continue to think about it?" He wiped his hands on the legs of his pants. "I know there are still problems, but we can work them out. I know we can."

His plea, she knew, was spoken from the heart, and it plucked at the strings of her emotions, making her mind go around in dizzy circles. How could she let herself listen to him? Much less think there might be a chance. She felt heat at the base of her throat. *Oh, God, was she going crazy?*

Gut instinct warned Reese that he had said enough. He saw the play of emotions flicker across her face, and he longed to reach out to her, but he couldn't. She was on her own. He had done his part. He had planted the seed, his seed of love. Now all he could do was back off and give it time to nourish, to grow. And who knows, he told himself, with his love furnishing the needed sunlight, she might become his. He was willing to gamble the rest of his life on that hope.

"Reese, I—" she began, only to have her words aborted.

"Not now," he cut in gently. "Later. We'll talk later. Right now, I have something else in mind. Something crazy and outlandish."

"What?" she asked hesitantly, though intrigued in spite of herself, and relieved. Yes, relieved that she had gained a reprieve.

His eyes twinkled. "A day at Astroworld. How does that sound?"

"Are you serious?" She was astounded and it showed. "Aren't you a little old to be traipsing around an amusement park?"

He laughed, giving her a quick hug. "In answer to your first question, you bet, I'm serious. And I guess I'll always be a child at heart, in answer to your second question."

She frowned. "But I was planning to leave this morning, to go back to work." What she had facing her when she returned home was beginning to surge to the forefront of her mind, nudging her sharply back to reality.

"Same here," Reese replied easily, "but I'm going to forget it for another day." His lips curved endearingly. "Anyway, nobody works on the weekend."

Meryl hesitated for a moment and then threw up her hands in defeat. "Who am I to argue with logic like that?"

Reese insisted they stop for a leisurely breakfast, as it was too early for the park to open. Again they ate like they were ravenous, having worked up an appetite due to their strenuous early-morning activities. Once their empty plates had been whisked away by a smiling waitress, they lingered over coffee, chattering and laughing.

But hovering over them was an awareness that time was running out. Their return to the real world was imminent, and with it were decisions that would have to be made. Particularly one decision which could change the course of their lives forever, and it was not easy to push aside.

As Meryl drained the last of her coffee, she couldn't stop the wheels of her mind from grinding. She couldn't believe she was actually giving serious thought to Reese's proposal. But she was. Because at this moment she could not imagine giving him up—even for Morgana.

"You're doing it again." Reese reached across the table and hooked a thumb under her chin, forcing her head up.

Meryl returned his appraisal with questioning eyes as she tried to marshal her thoughts into order. "What . . . what am I doing?" she asked inanely.

"Shutting me out."

"Oh, well . . . I . . ."

He kissed her swiftly on the parted sweetness of her lips,

and then laughed. "Forget it! Let's go. We've got a lot of territory to cover."

And he was not exaggerating. For the next few hours, Meryl felt like she had been caught up in a whirlwind. With the hot summer sun beaming down on their heads, they joined the multitude of kids and adults dashing from one exhibit to another, one ride to another.

But for the most part, Meryl paid no heed to any of this; Reese dominated her every thought. They laughed wildly and clung to each other as they rode the roller coaster, the Ferris wheel, and even while they sat on a secluded bench and munched on hamburgers, cotton candy and ice cream. In their eagerness to sample it all, they were like two unsupervised children, alone in their charmed world.

Reese could not keep his hands off her, regardless of where they were or what they were doing. She was like an addiction he couldn't shake. And she basked in his adoration, neither looking nor acting her thirty-five years.

To Reese she looked younger than the majority of the teenage girls running around in droves. She was dressed in a pair of white shorts that exposed her long shapely legs, now tastefully colored by the sun, and a red V-neck shirt which lent a stark contrast to her dark hair and creamy skin. She was lovely and exciting. And she was his.

Now, as they stood in line to ride the Water Log, Reese draped his arm around her shoulders and pulled her close against his hard ribs. "Are you tired, hon?" he asked with a smile.

She peered up at him through her owl-shaped sunglasses, returning his smile. "Not really. How about you?"

"Me neither," he responded quickly. "But I'm afraid we may have to leave after this ride anyway." His eyes were bright with a touch of mischief. "From the looks of things, we'll be sopping wet."

"Mmmm, sounds to me like you're trying to chicken out," she teased, sneaking a hand under his shirt, which had worked loose from the waistband of his shorts, and began massaging his lower back.

He dipped his head. "If you don't stop that," he warned, "you can forget the ride and everything else—except being hauled back to the cabin and having your clothes torn off and being made love to until you beg me to stop," he said quietly, meaningfully, for her ears alone.

Lights began to pulse in her brain as she fought off the feeling of weakness that invaded her limbs. Underneath that teasing smile, she knew he was serious. His eyes were probing as a breathless tension snapped between them.

Meryl went limp on the inside. "I . . . I didn't want to get wet anyway," she whispered.

It took a moment for her words to register on Reese. His eyes widened, then narrowed, then lit up like a candle. Suddenly he gripped her arm, his touch burning her flesh. "What the hell are we still standing here for?" He gazed at her for another long, golden moment. "Let's go!"

As Reese's car raced down the freeway toward Galveston and the cabin, they were trapped in a web of aching warmth. Meryl sat next to him and kept her hand splayed across his firm upper leg, kneading the exposed flesh. She was hot, she mused as she felt her nipples become a budding crown and a tingling feeling settle in her most sensitive place.

She knew Reese was having the same difficulty maintaining his composure. A muscle in his jaw was working overtime and the hard swell of his arousal could not be ignored. Suddenly he shifted his position so that his arm circled her shoulder—he was careful not to touch her breast—allowing her to lean against him.

They hardly moved until Reese brought the car to a screeching halt in front of the cabin door.

They had just unlocked the door and stepped inside when the shrill sound of the phone jarred them out of their emotional stupor.

Before she thought, Meryl darted across the room and

lifted the receiver. "Hello," she said hesitantly, wishing suddenly that she hadn't answered it.

"Oh, thank God!" a voice sobbed on the other end of the line.

Meryl could almost taste the panic that threatened to strangle her. "Morgana, is that you?" She barely recognized her own voice.

"Yes, it's me!" Morgana wailed. "I'm so glad I found you. I've been calling all day."

Meryl sank into the nearest chair. "What's . . . what's wrong?" Her voice almost failed her.

"Oh, Meryl, I'm . . . I'm so upset." Tears were garbling her voice.

"Please, Morgana, try to calm down," Meryl pleaded, though she herself was trembling from head to toe. She dared not look at Reese. "I'm having trouble understanding you."

"Everything's gone wrong!" Morgana continued with rising hysteria. "My European tour ended up a disaster." She began sobbing again. "I . . . I was replaced by a young empty-headed bitch who didn't know her right foot from her left. And I can't find Reese." She gulped. "And I need him so much."

The bottom dropped out of Meryl's stomach. "I—"

Morgana cut in on a desperate note. "Do you by any chance know where he is?"

Chapter 11

MERYL LICKED HER PARCHED LIPS. OH, GOD, NO, SHE MOANED as her brain scrambled for something to say. *But what could she say?* She couldn't admit that, yes, she knew where Reese was, that he was waiting for her to get off the phone so they could make love. She swallowed, trying to control the hot saliva invading the inside of her mouth, making her jawbones ache.

"Meryl, are you still there?" Morgana whined.

Meryl stalled for more time, hating herself. "What . . . what makes you think I would know where he is?" Holding her breath, she cast a glance in Reese's direction; his face was dark and scowling.

A tremulous sigh filtered through the line. "It was stupid of me to even ask; I realize that now," Morgana said without spirit. "But I feel so lost without him, and I can hardly wait to thank him for the gorgeous red roses he sent me in Paris." She paused. "Nobody, and I mean nobody, seems to know where he is."

Roses. Reese sent Morgana roses! No, it couldn't be! "Where's Jay?" Meryl asked, groping frantically for something sane to say while trying to quiet her hammering pulse. She felt as though bullets were whizzing by her head, and no matter which way she turned, she would get hit.

"Jay! Why, he's the last person I want to see. He just doesn't understand me," Morgana whimpered. "We had a hellish fight, and I told him I never wanted to see him again and that I was going to get a new agent."

"Oh, Morgana, no!" Meryl cried. "How could you do that to him after all he's done for you?"

"Easily," she retorted. "But I don't want to talk about Jay. I *want* Reese. And now," she added petulantly.

"Oh, Morgana, I'm . . . sorry."

"Don't be. It's not your fault I can't find him and that the rug has been yanked out from under me. But if I don't find Reese soon, can I come down to the cabin? I want to see you, too," she said pitifully.

Meryl panicked. "No!" Then, realizing she was shouting, she forced herself to calm down and without any emotion added, "What I meant to say is that it's not necessary for you to come here. I was planning to come back today anyway." She paused and clutched at her stomach, feeling a bout of nausea coming on. "Why don't you meet me at my apartment about eight?"

Although Meryl tried, she couldn't ignore Reese's wild hand motions as he tried to keep her from giving in to Morgana. He was absolutely livid. And she was sick. Sick with guilt at having to deceive her sister once again and sick that her stolen time with Reese was over, never to be recaptured.

Morgana sighed. "Well, if I don't find Reese, I might do that, or I might decide instead to drown my sorrows in a Bloody Mary and go to bed. I'm exhausted. So if I don't see you tonight, we'll have lunch tomorrow. Okay?"

"Are you sure you'll be all right?" Meryl asked, wanting desperately to salvage her conscience.

"Don't worry, I'll be fine."

"Good-bye, then," Meryl whispered softly before literally dropping the receiver back on the hook.

She remained where she was, hunched over in the chair, still not looking at Reese. But she didn't have to; she knew his face would look like a dark thundercloud ready to burst.

When the silence reached a screaming pitch, Meryl cast a furtive glance at him out of the corner of her eye. At best, he was a blur, as her eyes were swimming with unshed tears.

The spell was broken. Morgana's phone call was like a blast out of a cannon; it had hurled them back to reality. A reality that forced her to accept that Reese had indeed sent her sister flowers. She wanted to lash out at him, to ask what kind of game he was playing. But she refused to sit here and accuse him like a nagging wife. After all, she had no right. But it hurt. . . .

It was almost as if she, Meryl, had been moving in a circle, only to find herself back at the center, having gone nowhere. Morgana needed her now more than ever. She could not bring her any more grief, no matter what the circumstances.

Meryl felt the couch cave in beside her, but still she said nothing. She was too busy keeping her lips from trembling and the tears from spilling down her face.

"We have to talk," Reese said, his voice strained, yet unyielding.

Meryl shook her head. "There's . . . there's nothing to talk about," she responded, a final ring to her voice.

Dark color swept up to his hairline. "I'm not about to let you do this to me again, or to us," he ground out, his voice rough with suppressed anger. "If you don't put an end to this nonsense, I'm going to."

Meryl snapped her head up and looked at him, her face drawn and very white. "What did you say?" she asked, knowing exactly what he'd said.

"You heard me, and I meant every word of it, too."

Alarm filled her. "If . . . if you so much as say one word to Morgana about us, I'll . . . never forgive you." Her teeth dug into her lower lip, drawing blood.

His expression was grave. "Never is a long time," he said quietly.

"I mean it, Reese," she responded, her voice riddled with the same deadly tone.

His patience evaporated. He sprang from the couch and loomed over her. "This is absurd and you know it. Morgana's blown everything out of proportion, and you know that, too," he added flatly, pushing back his hair with an impatient gesture. "She doesn't love me; she's not capable of loving anyone but herself. And you very well know that I don't love her!" He paused, breathing hard. "Oh, what the hell! I'm wasting my time; we've been over this all before, which makes me sound like a goddamned broken record."

"I . . . I know you don't . . . love her." *Why did you send her flowers?* "But that's not the . . . point."

"Not the point. Dammit, that's the *whole* point!"

She shook her head. "Oh, Reese, can't you understand, the fact that Morgana thinks she loves you is reason enough for me to back off."

Hot anger burned his insides. "For heaven's sake, Meryl, you're being unreasonable."

Meryl stared at him blankly as she wrestled with the conflicting emotions that stormed within her. "Reese, please, it's no use. You're the one who's being unreasonable." Her voice was brittle with pain. "How could we build a lifetime of happiness using Morgana as a stepping-stone? Answer me that."

A harsh expletive zipped through Reese's lips. "You want to know what I think?" he asked after a moment, his nostrils flaring.

Meryl drew a shuddering breath and shook her head.

"I think you're just using your sister as an excuse." There was an ugly underside to his voice. "I think when it comes right down to it, you're afraid." He paused and shook his head sadly. "But you can't see that, can you?"

"Because it's not true!" she defended hotly.

"Then prove it!" he countered. "Marry me."

"I . . . I can't," she cried. "Not now . . . maybe never! You're pushing me, backing me into a tight corner, and I can't stand it! Please, just leave me alone," Meryl ended on a sob, swiping angrily at the tears that were running down her face like a waterfall.

A silence deep as Grand Canyon fell between them as Reese stood deep in thought. He was at a loss as to how to deal with Meryl, to make her understand. Why wouldn't she listen to reason? Why couldn't he get through to her that he loved her and that she could trust him with her life if necessary. And that he had no intention of letting Morgana or anything else keep him from proving this to her.

He recognized that she was afraid—even if she didn't—at the same time striving to maintain her independence and prove she didn't need him or any other man in her life to make it complete. Her biggest fear, or so he thought, was not being able to make it to the top of her profession. She resented anything that interfered with that goal.

Perhaps he'd pushed her too hard, expected too much, too soon. She was still grappling with the past, afraid to turn it loose. He couldn't blame her. He had hurt her deeply; he knew that. And he had his own hang-ups and insecurities to overcome. For starters, he needed to learn to share her with her work and her sister. And for him that would be no easy task.

Somehow and from somewhere he had to dig up the strength to back off, to give her that precious time she thought she had to have. Oh, God, he didn't know how he was going to do it. But he had no choice, he knew. He couldn't stand to think about losing her. She was as much a part of him now as the blood that flowed through his veins. Without either he would surely die.

He listened a moment to the wind and the ocean and he knew they were trying to tell him not to be afraid, and to have faith, and to love as truly as he could. He would like to walk along the shoreline, smell the salt in the air, but depression fastened lead weights to his limbs. He felt suddenly empty, hollow and alone.

Finally he forced himself to move, taking a tentative step toward her hovering figure, and stopped. "We better be on our way," he said, his voice completely devoid of emotion.

"I . . . I know," she replied in a strangled tone, all the while grappling to recover from the blows that had been dealt her in rapid succession. Why, oh why, she lamented, had Morgana chosen now to call? Just when she had been so close to giving in to his gentle demands. Or had she just been kidding herself? Was she using Morgana as a scapegoat?

"Meryl . . ." he began, only to suddenly clamp his jaw shut, drawing his mouth in a taut white line.

But his quiet use of her name forced her back from the dark chasm of her thoughts. She turned and looked at him, watching silently as an inscrutable mask slipped over his face. He was hurting just as she was hurting, and there was nothing either of them could do about it.

Reese was the first to avert his gaze. "I'll take your bag to the car while you lock up," he muttered tersely, and then with heavy steps strode to the door, slamming it shut behind him.

Meryl remained glued to the chair, unable to move under the weight of a painful trembling that choked off her breathing and rendered her limbs useless.

The once securely tied strings of her life were slowly breaking, and she was powerless to do anything about it. . . .

The scorching summer days blended together, the same, never changing. And through them all, Meryl worked. She plunged body and soul into one project after another, as though demons were chasing her.

As promised, only a few days after her return from Galveston, Tucker brought the men to the studio for a guided tour. In spite of the clouded circumstances, they treated Meryl with polite courtesy and seemed impressed with her operation. After touring the three facilities, she presented each one with an autographed copy of her book, now number one on the New York *Times*'s best-seller list.

Following that visit, she pored over charts and books both at home and at the office, gathering information for her new book. Many times at three o'clock in the morning she would just be flicking off the light.

She made two local television appearances, which took time and preparation. She also spoke to several clubs' monthly luncheon meetings.

Then, two weeks later, she spent one entire morning

behind closed doors with Tucker and the entire group of men that she had stood up. It was an emotional meeting that drained her both mentally and physically, because she was determined to put her best foot forward, hoping once and for all to reverse their tarnished image of her. Whether or not she had accomplished her goal remained to be seen. Tucker seemed to think she had more than rectified the situation, that she had repaired any and all damage she had previously done. But she wasn't so sure. It was a "wait-and-see" proposition, and only time would tell.

During those busy days, she also spent time with Morgana, only to come away feeling more depressed and frustrated than before. The deceit she was harboring kept eating away at her.

To make matters worse, Morgana was determined to go through with plans to have her face-lift. Nothing Meryl said made any difference. She abhorred the thought of Morgana going through the pain of major surgery for vanity's sake alone. But ever since Morgana had come back from Europe and her unsuccessful modeling stint there, she rarely talked about anything else. Except Reese.

"He is being so patient and understanding with me," she had told Meryl. "Although I'm not with him nearly as much as I'd like, I still feel like the luckiest girl in the world to have found him. He continually showers me with flowers," she had added, her eyes warmly glazed.

Without fail, each time Morgana breathed his name, guilt and jealousy tore through Meryl's heart as swift and deep as a dagger. Although Morgana had not come out and said so, Meryl was positive that Reese was seeing Morgana outside office hours. *Why?* Meryl asked herself over and over, the old ache and its kindred anxiety once more wrestling within her. If he was trying to force her to make a decision by making her jealous, then he was certainly accomplishing what he set out to do.

Never a day passed that she didn't think about their stolen

time together at the beach. Her body ached all over with longing, just remembering the wild, tumbling, passionate lovemaking they had shared. And without fail her breasts would become heavy and swollen and a tight, aching feeling would develop between her thighs, making her wonder how she would be able to manage another day without him.

She was slowly but surely coming apart on the inside. Nothing seemed to help appease the constant hunger for his arms, his mouth, the feel of him inside her.

Today wrought no change. Not even groveling on the floor, teaching her instructors new advanced-level exercises, could oust him fom her mind. But she was determined to try. She planned to be so tired tonight she would sleep through a hurricane.

"Okay, ladies, one more and then we'll call it quits for the day and head for the sauna and the whirlpool. And that's an order," she said, breathing deeply in an effort to fight off the exhaustion that was worming its way into her limbs.

Completely ignoring the moans and groans that filtered through the air, she sat down on her mat and then lay flat on her back, turning her body sideways so that she could see her rather uneager participants.

"Watch me carefully," she commanded in a strong voice, "so there won't be any injuries to the lower back muscles. Now very slowly lift the right leg first, foot pointed toward your head, not in the air. Now raise your arms at the same time you're bringing your leg toward your head as far as you can. Then grab your calf muscles with your hands, pull and stretch and hold for a moment before returning to your original position. Let's do that four times with the right leg and then switch to the left one without resting."

She paused and threw them a weak smile. "Just be sure you keep your legs straight. No bending at the knee. Then I want you to bring both knees to your chest, press and relax." She smiled again. "That should feel good to your back. Any questions before we give it a quick run-through?"

Negative shakes of heads accompanying another round of low moans were Meryl's only answers.

For the next few minutes, with the stereo thumping a steady beat, Meryl took the small group through the exercise, watching each one through the wall-to-wall mirrors in front of her, making sure they weren't fudging on the exercise.

A short time later, satisfied with the workout, she took the class through a short relaxing cool-down before standing up and issuing orders.

"All right, ladies, put up your mats and head for the showers. I'll see you bright and early in the morning."

Once alone, Meryl turned and immediately shut off the massive stereo system before grabbing her hand towel lying on the table. Still too high-strung to sit down, she breathed slowly and deeply and dabbed at the perspiration clinging to her face, neck and arms.

She was glad Nelda was gone, she reflected bleakly as she slung the towel aside and gazed at the list of exercises that she had gone through the last hour. If Nelda had been here, she would have been harping constantly for Meryl to let one of the instructors teach the new exercises. But Meryl hadn't wanted anyone else to do it. She had explained to Nelda numerous times that she enjoyed working out with her clients as well as teaching her instructors. It not only kept her physically fit, it kept her abreast of what was going on in the studios.

Deciding that it was time for her to head for the shower as well, Meryl leaned down and yanked her yellow leg warmers off, stood up and with her fingers riffled through her damp curls. Then she raised her hands above her head, stretching every single muscle in her body one last time. God, but she was exhausted, she thought as she reached toward the ceiling, swaying gracefully.

After letting himself in the front door of Body Perfect and striding purposefully to the door leading into the exercise salon, Reese Corbett stopped short. He felt the air leave his lungs as he stood still and caught sight of the woman he sought. He was mesmerized by what he saw. He watched in fascination as Meryl lifted her arms high above her head and began moving from side to side. Every line of her beautiful body was visible through the tight-fitting shocking-yellow-and-purple sleeveless leotards and shiny yellow tights.

Desire rumbled through his insides as his eyes devoured her long shapely legs, trim thighs, the round, firm hips. It was all he could do to remain still, unmoving as he continued to feast on the narrow waist, the full upturned breasts.

Her beauty never failed to grip him. And though he knew every luscious curve of that body and each of its intimate secrets, he yearned desperately for more. He wanted *all* of her to be his for the taking, her sharp mind, her laughter, her sincerity and dedication. All of these attributes were as important to him as her body. She had truly become his obsession.

With this thought in mind, Reese began to walk slowly toward her.

Meryl sensed she was not alone before being conscious of someone behind her. For a moment she felt the hair on the back of her neck stand on end, and her heart almost stopped beating. She knew better than to be caught in the studio alone, she chastised herself frantically, still afraid to turn around. Then she remembered she wasn't alone—the girls were within shouting distance. She relaxed.

"Meryl." The voice that said her name was unbelievably familiar and her body began to tremble all over, partly from delayed reaction and partly from weakness that hearing his voice had evoked. She pressed her moist palm against her tights, striving for control, and slowly turned around.

Reese did not move; he just stood there and waited for her to make the next move. He was uncertain of her reaction, but he hadn't been able to stand not seeing her another day.

Meryl's tongue clung to the dry roof of her mouth as she

self-consciously reached up and pushed an errant curl off her forehead, thinking how awful she must look to him. Her makeup had long since disappeared, her clothes—if they could be classified as that—were hardly elegant. And such things were important when one was engaged in a psychological battle, she thought helplessly. He had her at a disadvantage, as he had from the beginning, not just because he had come upon her unexpectedly, but because she suddenly felt so vulnerable and raw.

He didn't look as though he was faring any better, Meryl noted, studying him closely. His face was drawn, as though he hadn't slept. There were dark circles under his eyes; he looked exhausted. But more than that, he looked haunted, sad.

Without waiting for an invitation, Reese closed the short distance between them and reached out and claimed her chin between his fingers, lifting her face, bringing her out of her misery. One look, one touch from this man, could make her bones completely dissolve.

"I'm sorry, I didn't mean to frighten you." Reese's voice was low and husky and unbelievably tender, disrupting her emotions, causing her heart to palpitate wildly.

"You . . . didn't, not really," she whispered huskily, not knowing how much longer she could resist the desire to turn her lips against his hand as he continued to stroke her chin.

"I missed you," he said thickly, his long finger flexing against the slender column of her throat.

"I missed you too." Her words were spoken on another ragged whisper.

With a deep moan Reese stepped back, raking restless fingers through his hair. He ached to hold her, to lay his lips against the moist softness of hers. But not here, not like this, he cautioned himself. He was aware they were not alone; he could hear the muted laughter as it tunneled its way through the thick walls.

Meryl heard it too. A ghost of a smile softened her lips. "It's my instructors. We just finished with a late exercise and dance session," she offered by way of explanation, hoping to break the tension that had a stranglehold on the air.

"Can we get out of here?" It was a low, husky plea.

Meryl searched her lips with her tongue. "Where . . . where did you have in mind?"

"You haven't eaten, have you?" he asked rather anxiously.

"No, no I haven't."

"How does Mexican food sound to you? Or would you rather have something else, since it's so hot?" He couldn't help but notice the beads of perspiration that still dotted her creamy skin.

"That . . . sounds fine to me." There was a waver in her voice. "Just give me a minute to shower."

His eyes were dark and penetrating. "I'll be waiting."

Meryl moved, as though she had suddenly sprouted wings, through the door and down the short hall to the room that housed the sauna, the whirlpool, and the shower stalls. To the left was a tastefully decorated large dressing room.

As Meryl glided past the hot gurgling whirlpool, she eyed it with longing but kept on going, knowing she wouldn't have time to dally there. Reese was waiting. Her heart lurched at the thought. How she had missed him.

Meryl hurried through her shower, not wanting to keep him waiting a moment longer than she had to. She intended making every second count. Suddenly she frowned, remembering. Remembering that tomorrow she was leaving on a week-long book tour. She groaned aloud as she vigorously rubbed her body with a fluffy towel. Oh, God, she wondered, how much longer could they keep seesawing back and forth, in and out of each other's lives? It was destroying them both.

Quickly she dried her hair until it clung to her head in soft shiny tendrils. And before donning a red-and-white scoop-necked T-shirt, opting not to wear a bra, and a pair of baggy red drawstring pants, she put on a minimum of makeup, slipped her feet in her open-toed sandals, and she was ready.

There was no need for words as she made her way back into the room. Reese's smile and warm eyes said it all. Meryl's heart upped its beat as they made their way, not speaking, not touching, out to the parking lot and into Reese's car. Before starting the engine, Reese faced her and let out a shaky breath, moving his hands slowly down her arm. Meryl's skin sang beneath his touch.

Then, as though in slow motion, Reese pulled her gently toward him, her body pliant and willing.

"I don't think I can function," he whispered close to her mouth, "until I do this." At first his mouth touched hers tentatively, as though he were handling a fragile object. But when she opened her mouth, his restraint crumbled. His tongue darted between his lips to stroke the moist contours of hers. It was a seductive, sensual onslaught on the senses, reviving embers of emotions that only his touch could do.

With a murmured protest, his hands left her throat to roam across the rounded fullness of her breasts. Even through her shirt, she could feel her nipples budding against his palm. Meryl had to control the impulse to jerk her top up so that she could feel his touch on her naked skin. This past week suddenly seemed like a lifetime.

"Meryl," he groaned, releasing her mouth to take a labored breath, and then with a supreme effort he moved away from her, placing his hands on the steering wheel. "If we don't stop this right now," he continued, "I'm not going to be able to get out of the car and into any restaurant." He smiled, albeit a brief one, but it nevertheless served to lighten the mood.

Meryl could feel a hot flush creep up her face at his bluntness, but then an answering smile found its way to her lips. "Well, in that case, I guess I'll have to be good," she responded impishly. "I'm about to starve to death, as I haven't eaten all day."

His eyes scanned her figure. "It looks as though you've missed several meals lately. Your bones were protruding in that snazzy little outfit you were wearing."

It was on the tip of her tongue to tell him that he was right, that she hadn't been eating or sleeping and that it was his fault for staying away so long. But she didn't. For one thing, she didn't want to admit verbally the power he exerted over her—now was not the time. Nor did she want to get into a heavy discussion. She just wanted to enjoy being with him. Tomorrow's trip was looming close on the horizon.

She threw him a sweet smile. "Well, I plan to make up for lost time tonight. I love Mexican food."

"I'll hold you to that," he said, staring at her a moment longer before abruptly turning and starting the engine. He was desperate to get moving; he didn't trust himself to keep his hands off her, not when she gave him that saucy smile and gazed at him with her big black eyes—as she was doing now.

It was only a matter of minutes until he was braking the powerful car in front of La Hacienda. Meryl had eaten here many times, but never with Reese. It was a stately old mansion that had been restored and turned into a restaurant. It offered small alcoves for intimate dining as well as several larger ones. One could feel at ease here regardless of dress.

To their disappointment, all the alcoves were filled, and rather than wait, they agreed to take a corner table in the main dining room.

"This is perfect," Meryl volunteered, cupping her chin in her hand and looking dreamily past Reese's shoulder through the huge window at the beautifully landscaped garden. Although twilight had descended into darkness, a full moon as perfect as a gemstone hung low in the sky, bathing the area in a soft glow.

"This place is a favorite of mine," Reese remarked casually, determined to keep the mood light. But he was going to be hard pressed just to make it through dinner. He had thought of nothing but making love to her since he had walked into her dance studio. She was like a fire raging out of control through his insides.

They were silent while a waiter filled their water glasses and set a basket of warm tortilla chips and two bowls of hot sauce in front of them. Studying the menu, they munched on the chips.

"I believe I'll have a large order of *nachos al carbón* and a margarita," Reese said after a moment. "What about you?"

"Mmmm." Meryl hesitated, chewing on her lower lip and deep in thought. "I think I'll have a taco salad and a glass of wine," she said, folding her menu and placing it at the edge of the table.

Reese smiled indulgently as he turned and gave their order to the hovering waiter. Once they were alone, he reached across the table and began idly playing with her fingers.

Meryl glanced around the restaurant while trying to calm her racing pulse.

"Hey, Meryl Stevens. Remember me?"

Meryl gave a start, then smiled with happiness. "Always," she said without hesitation.

His eyes narrowed into a lazy, measuring look. "I wish I dared believe that."

"It's true," she whispered, the erotic motion of his fingers causing her stomach to flutter.

"Oh, Meryl," he began, only to be interrupted by the waiter with their drinks. He withdrew his hand.

From that moment on, they managed to keep the conversation on light topics. Meryl told him about several funny incidents that had happened at the studio and he was laughing heartily by the time she finished.

Yet simmering underneath was a strong sexual current that neither could deny. And they were both aware it was only a matter of time before it would suck them under.

She was filled with love just being near him, felt warm just looking at his clean good looks. She had been ravenous when they ordered dinner, but now that it had arrived, she found she could swallow only a few bites.

"You didn't eat much," Reese said, covering her hand with his again and then lifting it and brushing it with his lips.

"Would you like something else? Coffee?" Although he had lowered her hand, it was still nestled warmly within his.

It was that intimate gesture that drew the attention of the man sitting in the alcove adjacent to their table. He could see them, but they could not see him. He had noticed what a striking couple they made and had rarely taken his eyes off them. At first he was shocked at seeing them together. Then his shock turned to curiosity. But as their meal progressed, and with it, each look, each gesture became more intimate, proving as nothing else could have that they were definitely more than acquaintances, his curiosity festered into hot, bubbling anger. His own food forgotten, he drank and watched, building a case, knowing that revenge when it came would taste ever so sweet.

Unaware they were being closely scrutinized, Meryl and Reese continued to exist only for each other.

"Sure you don't want coffee?" Reese asked again, unwilling to let go of her hand. His thumb was busy circling her palm slowly, erotically.

"No . . . no, thank you." She curled her fingers around his, suddenly embarrassed by her nipples as they pouted and began pushing against her shirt.

The change in her body was not lost on Reese. He searched deep for oxygen to speak. "Let's go," he demanded roughly.

The moment Reese ushered her through the front door of his River Oaks home and kicked it shut, they fell into each other's arms.

"I thought I would explode before I got out of that restaurant," he ground out tersely. "I can't ever remember being in so much damned torture."

"Me either," she whispered, clinging to him.

He held her tightly for several long, hard-breathing moments before taking her into the bedroom. There he entwined his hands in her hair and leaned down and seared her lips with his. Meryl swayed into him in a futile attempt to keep from collapsing, and he held her—and held her up—as she clung, melting. They were ablaze with desire as they stumbled backward across the room and fell breathless upon the bed.

Through a tangled mass of groping hands and uncontrolled breathing and low guttural moans, they managed to hastily rid themselves of their cumbersome clothing. It was at that precise moment they began to devour each other.

Meryl's breast thrusting upward, her nipples points of steel, her abdomen and thighs were flexed to receive the hard surge of his loins.

He came down on her, lunging forward, embedding himself within her. "I'm sorry," he whispered, kissing her lips, afraid he had hurt her.

"Shhh," she cried, starting to move against him. *"Reese!"* Her fingers sank into his back. "Don't move."

Her body surged to life under him, and without moving, he bore down, easing his weight onto her, watching her face change, going abstracted, as she moved faster and faster, slamming against him until her hands flew down to clutch him, holding him in place as she came, drawing at him inside, pulsing spasms that went on and on as their breathing seemed to stop entirely. Then she exhaled in one long, shuddering sigh and dropped slowly back to the bed.

He lay over her, his full weight still on her, knowing she wished it, finding her unbearably beautiful.

Later, so much later that she had lost all track of time, she lay curled up against him and reached up to touch his face, finding it wet. She sat up, leaning on her elbow to look at him, then dropped her head on his chest, hiding, distraught.

"I love you, Meryl." His voice was scratchy and raspy. "I was afraid that maybe it was over. Really over. I waited for a phone call, a knock on the door, and when neither materialized, I . . . I didn't know what to do."

"I'm coming apart too," she whispered. "I can't think straight anymore. Is that why you're crying? Because you're insides are as chopped up as mine? I . . . I can't stand to see you cry."

"Then marry me. Tomorrow." He mopped his eyes with the edge of the bedspread.

She shifted so that her head still lay on his chest, but she was able to see his face. Her fingers began to trail slowly across his jawline, wiping away the last traces of his tears, hearing a voice distant in her brain telling her: *Say yes. Tell him you'll marry him. Face it, you're only half a person without him. Give yourself. Tell him!*

"Yes and no," she said.

His hand closed fast around hers as he blinked twice, trying to clear the confusion that her words had stirred in his befuddled brain. He was afraid to hope. Yet . . .

"What kind of answer is that?"

Her heart turned over at the strangled uncertainty she heard in his voice. She smiled sweetly. "I'll marry you, only not tomorrow."

"Oh, Meryl, for God's sake, don't play any more games with me." His eyes were dazed with unexpected pain. "I can't take any more."

"Oh, Reese, my darling, it's not what you think," she cried. "I'm leaving in the morning on a promotional tour for my book. I was planning to tell you tonight."

She didn't move; she waited, scarcely daring to breathe, willing him to understand, anxious to hear what he'd say.

But he didn't have to say anything, she realized. She felt the tension when it eased from his body. Then he looked deep into her eyes. "I love you more than life itself," he whispered as he laid his lips against hers with gentle persuasion.

"And you take my breath away," she gasped, breaths mingling hotly before his lips bore down on hers, leaving her dizzy and yearning for more.

This time they could be gentle, easy, and relaxed with their lovemaking. The commitment was made; next they could leisurely enjoy their newfound happiness.

"I love you," she murmured as she lifted herself to him, pressing, trembling against him, moaning softly as he entered her. It was a long, leisurely, dreamy coupling. In time they drifted asleep in a haze of exhaustion and reconciliation.

It was well into the wee hours of the morning when they awakened. Reese rolled over and touched her, making sure she was real. He then lowered his mouth onto a nipple and gently brought it into full life, thinking it felt like raw silk against his tongue.

"Mmmm, that feels good," Meryl groaned, running her finger down the length of his back. "But we have to talk," she added unsteadily, "before I have to get up and pack."

Reese sighed and pulled away. "I know," he said simply, before leaning over the side of the bed and groping for the pack of cigarettes in his shirt pocket.

After lighting one and taking several puffs, he spoke again. "It's about Morgana, isn't it?" he asked in a strained voice.

Meryl's lips trembled. "We . . . we have to tell her."

Relief made him weak. "We'll do it together," he said, squeezing her cold hands, chafing new life into them.

"Oh, Reese," she cried, "we have to be careful. She's going through some rough times now, and I hate having to kick her in the teeth when she's already down."

"You really feel responsible for her, don't you?" he asked, not unkindly, but with a tired resignation. He sat up and turned his back.

She had to make him understand once and for all about her and Morgana. "Yes, I do," she said at last. "In spite of what you may think, Morgana's life hasn't been a bed of roses, if you'll allow me that cliché." She paused. "Oh, I know you think she's selfish and ambitious, and maybe she is. But because I love her, I can overlook her vices, knowing what has contributed to them. Like me, she's worked hard for what she's achieved and had to overcome insurmountable odds to do so."

She paused again. "Her ex-husband was a brute. He used her unmercifully as a punching bag. But very few people were aware of this; he was clever enough not to hit her in the face, which would have made it impossible for her to work. No, he just banged her around with body punches," she finished on an emotional note.

Reese wheeled around to face her. "Oh, Meryl, if you're trying to make me feel like a heel, you're doing a damn good job of it. But I—"

"I'm not," she assured him quickly. "That's not my intention at all. It's just that I wanted you to understand why I'm overprotective and can't stand the thought of bringing her any more pain."

Her face was clear to him as the moonlight washed the room a ghostly white. His eyes searched her soul. "You trust me, don't you?" he asked softly.

She nodded, unable to speak.

"Then don't worry, we'll find the words not to hurt her."

Meryl's eyes filled with tears. "I don't deserve . . ."

He leaned over and began nibbling at the underside of her breast, tantalizing it with feather-light kisses, effectively halting her flow of words. She melted on the inside.

"Will you promise we'll tell her the minute you get back home?"

She drew him close against her heart. "That's a promise I'll gladly make, my darling."

Chapter 12

THE LOUD BUZZ OF THE INTERCOM GRATED AGAINST REESE Corbett's taut nerves like fingernails against a chalk board. He cursed silently before pressing the lighted button.

"What is it, Susan?" he roared. "I gave explicit orders that I was not to be disturbed."

There was a moment of silence before a sweet but firm voice came back at him. "Now, Doctor, just calm down," Susan Menter, his longtime secretary and friend, advised calmly. "Remember, I know your bark is much worse than your bite. I've worked for you too long now."

"All right, Susan, you've made your point," Reese said wearily. "What do you want?"

"I took the liberty of sending down to the cafeteria and ordering an omelet and a cup of coffee for you."

"Susan, I *told* you I didn't want . . ." He broke off and then muttered to himself, "Oh, what the hell!" His power of concentration was already broken anyway—what little he'd had to begin with, he thought disgustedly—so he'd just as well indulge himself and Susan and take a break.

"Doctor, are you still there?"

"Bring it in," he muttered tersely, before releasing the button.

He stretched a moment before getting up and making his way to the window, rubbing his tense neck and shoulders. God, he was exhausted, but that was no excuse to growl at Susan or any of his other employees, he told himself. But the past three days had been hell. He missed Meryl, wanted her here with him, not traipsing around the streets of New York City.

Even though he had talked to her every night on the phone, it wasn't the same as having her with him in the flesh. Not only did he miss her, but a fear nagged at him constantly; he was afraid that while she was alone, with time to think, she would change her mind about marrying him.

Added to this worry was another, equally as pressing—his work. He had two severe cases of surgery scheduled for next week and both patients had health problems; this type of surgery was risky even for the healthy, so it was an awesome responsibility that kept him walking a tightrope.

That's why today of all days he didn't need any interruptions. He had come to the office at four o'clock this morning and had been hard at work since. However, he had not accomplished a third of what he had planned.

A soft knock on the door drew him out of his reverie. "Come on in," he responded with a tired sigh.

Susan Menter bustled through the door with a cheerful smile lighting her round face. She was a stoutly built woman, bordering on being overweight, in her early fifties, who had been working for Reese since he had gone into practice. With her wide smile and intelligent wit, she had become like a second mother to him, always hovering over him, making sure he took care of himself, as she was doing now.

"I know you could choke me for barging in on you like this," she retorted airily, "but in the long run you'll thank me." She placed the tray of food on his desk and watched as he crossed the room and sat back down.

A rueful smile curved his lips. "You remind me not only of my mother, but one of those sergeants in the army that I had to put up with."

"Huh!" She placed her hands on her hips like an unmovable object and watched him take a bite of the hot delicacy. "You can call me anything you like, but I know when enough is enough." Her eyes gentled with concern. "If you don't stop driving yourself like this, you're going to collapse."

Reese sighed between mouthfuls. "I know, and thank you for taking care of me, in spite of the fact that I growled like a bear with a sore paw." He sipped his coffee and smiled at her over the rim of the cup.

She rolled her eyes up in her head. "You ought to know by now, especially after all these years, that I don't let you intimidate me." Then her face softened as she took in the deep grooves around his eyes and the weary slant to his mouth. "Have you decided definitely that you can operate on the Cooper child?" she asked after her sharp eyes had watched him wolf down the omelet.

Reese frowned as he rubbed a hand over his forehead. "No, as a matter of fact, I haven't." He paused, glancing down at the rubble of X-ray prints and numerous sketches. "That's what I was trying to decide when you buzzed." He smiled, taking the rancor out of his words.

"Well, now that you've taken a break and eaten, I'll let you get back to work." She grinned as she made her way to the door. "And I promise, no more interruptions."

"I'll hold you to that," he murmured, his head once again buried in his work.

Reese lost track of time as he studied the problem, trying to figure out the number of skin grafts that would have to be done on the Cooper child in order to rework her tiny face.

He was so engrossed in what he was doing that at first the sound filtering through his door was only a mild annoyance. But when it grew louder, he threw his pencil down, a snarl curling his lips downward, and listened. What the hell was happening now? he groaned silently.

With each passing second the commotion in the outer office became louder; one shrill voice could be heard above the others.

Swallowing a savage oath, Reese bounded out of the chair, determined to find out what the hell was going on and put an end to it. He got no farther than the middle of the room when the door was flung open by a much different Susan Menter. Gone was the calm self-assurance. This time she appeared thoroughly harassed, with suppressed fury giving her face a pinched look. For a moment her large frame completely blocked out the other person following close on her heels.

Then Susan was literally shoved aside and Reese stood glued to the middle of the floor. *"Morgana!* What on earth?" His eyebrows were drawn together in a fierce frown.

"I'm sorry, Dr. Corbett," Susan apologized, her chest heaving, "but this woman came crashing in here—"

"I don't need you to speak for me," Morgana spat at Susan, her cheeks fiery red and her eyes shooting sparks.

"Why . . . you . . . you . . .," Susan spluttered, edging a step nearer Morgana.

Reese held up his hand, stalling her. He smiled reassuringly. "It's all right, Susan. I'll handle it. You just take care of the front."

Susan opened her mouth as though she wanted to argue, while her gaze ricocheted back and forth between Morgana's glaring stance and Reese's questioning coldness. Shaking her head, she finally pivoted and marched out of the room.

The second they were alone, Morgana turned on him once again. "How dare you do this to me?" she screamed, her scarlet lips curled back in a snarl.

Reese listened in stunned silence, barely able to absorb what she had said, so absurd did her question seem to him.

"Answer me, damn you!" Her voice was steadily rising, her control slipping.

Seeing the danger signals, Reese was jarred into instant action. "Morgana, keep your voice down and get hold of yourself," he demanded harshly, his own stiff control beginning to waver, but he forced his anger aside and tried another approach. "I don't know what brought this on, but coming in here, creating a scene, isn't the answer. If you'll just settle down, we'll talk."

"No! I will not get hold of myself, nor will I settle down," she shrieked, clenching and unclenching her fist, tears streaming down her face. "I'm not a child you can placate with your charms and lying lips. Not anymore, that is. I learned now what a low-down bas . . ." Suddenly she broke off and darted closer to Reese and raised her hand as though to strike him.

He saw the blow coming. His hand shot out and clamped around her arm like a vise, forestalling any further action on her part. "I wouldn't if I were you," he warned, his voice flat and deadly as a cobra.

Morgana twisted and jerked her arm out of his grasp, her eyes still naked with fury. "Don't you ever touch me again, you . . . you despicable creature," she spat hysterically.

It was all Reese could do to retain his composure. He had never felt more like belting a woman in the mouth than he did at this moment. But of course he could not. Would not. He could do the next-best thing, however, and get her out of his office before she added to the damage that had already been done. The outer office, he was positive, was listening to every word that was said. There was no way to ignore Morgana's loud, shrill voice. He was due to see patients shortly; he couldn't chance their being privy to this sideshow.

Reese's forbidding jawline took on a hardened twist. "I have about thirty mintues before I begin seeing patients," he said coldly, "which should just about give us time to get to the bottom of this matter. But not in my office." His tone was adamant. "Let's get out of here," he added abruptly.

"I'm not going anywhere with you!" Morgana balled her fists and shook them furiously. "You'll listen to what I have to say here and now."

He leapt forward, his gray eyes glittering with fury, his fingers snaking out and digging into her shoulder. "Stop it!" He shook her, quelling her to silence, but drawing no fear. She didn't so much as flinch. Yet this did not deter him. "You'll do as I say. This is my territory, and what I say goes. Understand?" His voice was menacingly low and tinged with violence.

Morgana lunged backward, then forward, trying frantically to break the stranglehold on her arm, but Reese just dug in deeper, aborting her attempt. Their eyes locked in silent warfare, Morgana's reeking of steely determination, Reese's of grim ruthlessness.

For countless seconds Morgana continued to battle him, standing as stiff as a rod, her shoulders squared, her head high. Then suddenly she relented, as though she knew she had lost this round. She spoke in a grating, contemptuous rasp.

"All right," she hissed, "let's go."

Eyes peered and mouths were agape as Morgana, her head still reared back, swept through the office, Reese directly behind her, his eyes glittering, colorless as ice chips.

Reese paused just long enough to whisper tersely to Susan, "I'll be back shortly."

By the time he rounded the corner, Morgana was way ahead of him, half-walking, half-running down the corridor. It didn't take Reese long to figure out she was heading for the doctors' parking area. He was right. When he shot through the swinging door into the harsh noon sunlight, Morgana had already cleared the steps and was jerking open the door of her car, which was in a no-parking zone.

"Dammit, Morgana," he shouted before he managed to catch up with her. "Wait! I can't leave!"

She paused and smiled slowly, bitterly, over the roof of the car. "What's the matter, afraid to be seen with me?" she taunted.

It should have occurred to him right then and there what was wrong. Both her words and her tone should have given him the clue. But for a moment, he was too stunned by her sneering words to think straight. Then it hit him. *Meryl!* Oh, God, no!

"Afraid my darling sister will find out and think that you're screwing around on her? *With me!*" she hissed before her harsh, mirthless laugh rang through the air.

Something inside Reese snapped, an explosive fury at whoever had told Morgana about him and Meryl before they got the chance to do so. Damn! Now what the hell was he going to do? And Meryl? He had to protect her at all costs. She would never forgive him if he didn't handle this with delicate care. But how?

The grinding down of gears jarred him out of his stupor, and not a moment too soon. Morgana was about to drive off without him. He had to stop her, make her understand. Sprinting forward, with the speed of lightning he jerked the door open on the passenger side and lunged inside, just as she hammered down on the accelerator.

It was a miracle that Reese was able to slam the door shut before they swooped away from the curb and sped out of the parking lot into the flow of traffic.

Morgana threw him a glance filled with loathing as she peeled around another corner, taking a side street.

"Dammit, will you slow down before you kill us both!" Reese exploded violently, struggling upright, attempting to maintain his balance.

"I thought you said you couldn't leave with me," Morgana retorted through tight lips, her eyes still glittering wildly.

A feeling of unease shot through Reese. He must have taken leave of his senses, he told himself furiously. Totally irrational, Morgana was in no condition to drive. But when she had told him she knew about him and Meryl, he had panicked and was desperate to try to reason with her. His gut instinct warned him that he had made a grave error.

"I thought we needed to talk," he responded at last, forcing a coolness in his voice, hoping to calm her.

"Is that so?" she replied, her tone clearly mocking. "Well, now that you mention it, maybe it would be interesting to hear how you lie your way out of this one." Then without warning she hurled the car around another curve, this time on two wheels, and slammed on the brakes.

Both moves careened Reese's shoulder against the door. "Damn!" he muttered harshly, his face a mask, tight and pale as he fought once more to regain his balance.

It was only after she had shut off the engine that Reese

noticed she had stopped in another unauthorized parking area, this time in Hermann Park. But he let it pass, just wanting to have his say and get the hell away from her. He'd bet anything that this was a side of Morgana that Meryl had never seen. Suddenly a vision of Meryl's lovely face swam before his eyes, making him aware again just how dangerous this situation was and how carefully it must be handled.

"Well?" Morgana demanded, turning to face him.

Reese's eyes softened as he took in her quivering lips. Oh, God, he prayed for the right words to keep from hurting her. "We . . . we were planning to tell you," he began hesitantly.

"When?" she clipped.

"As soon as Meryl returns from New York."

Her lips twisted unbecomingly. "How could you betray me like this? And with my own sister!" she spat. "I loved you and wanted to marry you, and I thought you felt the same way about me." She banged her hand against the steering wheel in sudden rage.

Reese sighed heavily. "No, Morgana, I had no idea you cared that much, nor did I ever indicate that I considered you anything other than a friend," he said gently.

"That's not true. You . . . you acted like you cared!"

"Of course I cared, but as a friend, not a lover."

Her expression was hostile. "I . . . I refuse to believe that."

Changing the subject, Reese asked lightly, "How did you find out that I was seeing"—he couldn't chance saying the word "love," not yet, still too risky—"Meryl?" He held his breath as he waited for the answer.

"That's none of your business," she lashed back at him. "What's important is that I was given a blow-by-blow account of all your little intimate maneuvers." Her voice was steadily rising again.

He didn't bother denying this. Instead he said, "I . . . we didn't intend for you to find out that way." He paused. "You see, I met your sister two years ago and fell—"

"What?" she gasped. "God, what a gullible fool I've been," she muttered more to herself than to Reese.

Reese chose his next words carefully, knowing he was treading on dangerous ground. "It's a long story," he replied cautiously. "I won't bore you with the details."

"Bore me," she demanded, sarcasm dripping from her voice.

Ignoring her outburst, Reese went on, "Although we fell in love, we couldn't marry. I . . . I wasn't free." He paused, hating this, hating himself, but knowing it had to be said, knowing that he had to be the buffer between the two sisters in order for him and Meryl to survive. "When I saw her again at your place, I knew I still loved her and wanted to marry her. But Meryl fought her feelings, fought me, because she couldn't stand the thought of hurting you."

"Spare me the gushy epitaph."

It took every ounce of willpower he had to sit there and take her verbal abuse, but he knew Meryl would never forgive him if he didn't try to reason with Morgana. He stayed. "It was only the day before she left for New York that she finally agreed to marry me." There, he'd said it. Now it was all out in the open.

"Marry you!" Morgana cried, tears beginning to stream down her face.

Reese knew then that he'd said it badly, said the wrong thing. But it was too late. "I'm sorry. I—"

"*Sorry!* Is that all you can say after making a fool of me and crushing my dreams?" she screamed, dropping her head against the steering wheel and sobbing.

Reese was mortified and at a loss as to what to do. He wanted to comfort her but didn't know how. He raised his hand and tentatively touched her shoulder, longing to put his fist through the bastard's face that had told her in such a brutal way.

The moment she felt his hand touch her, Morgana whirled around, her eyes wide and blinded with tears. "Stay away from me," she whispered. "I hate you. Do you hear me? I hate you both!"

Catching Reese off guard, she quickly turned the ignition switch, rammed the gear into drive and lunged the powerful car forward.

Trying to avoid being thrown through the windshield, Reese slammed his hand against the dashboard and turned furiously toward Morgana. "What the hell!" he thundered, before instant fear paralyzed him.

Directly in front of their path was a tall, spindly oak tree.

He stomped his feet into the floorboard as though he could stop the car for her. "Morgana, turn the wheel!" he shouted. His warning came too late.

The loud crunch of metal and Morgana's scream were the last sounds he remembered before a murky blackness overtook him.

New York. Meryl both loved and hated it. She loved it because it allowed her the opportunity of a lifetime: an appearance on a major morning news broadcast, enabling her to promote her book, *A Moment on Your Lips, Forever on Your Hips: A Beginner's Guide to Health and Nutrition*. She hated it because it took her away from Reese.

She had been here two days. And thoughts of Reese had filled her heart every minute. She yearned for this tour to end so she could return home to his waiting arms. The only dark spot on her bright horizon was having to tell Morgana, but it had to be done. She loved Reese too much to give him up. They would have a wonderful life together. She had planned it in her mind countless times; they would travel, exercise together, maybe even adopt a child if Reese wanted to. Of course, all of these things would have to be planned in and around their work schedules, but she was positive they could work it out. Yes, their marriage would have the best of everything, simply because it was founded on love.

It was with this warm thought wrapped around her heart

that Meryl stepped out of a cab in front of the television studio, practically into the arms of her agent, Heather Basham.

"Good morning," Meryl exclaimed, excitement making her breathless. "I hope I'm not late."

Heather grinned broadly as her slanted green eyes appraised Meryl. "Good morning to you, and no, you're not late. I'm just early. You look . . . Mmm." She paused, taking a step backward. "I guess the word I'm searching for is 'chic.'" She grinned again. "Or maybe a better word is 'perfect.'"

And she did. Meryl had chosen a black silk suit, simple yet elegantly cut. It complemented her dark hair and creamy complexion as no other color could have done. Her hair was swept away from her face, placing emphasis on her black eyes and the upward sweep of her thick smutty eyelashes and brows. Diamond studs in her ears and a diamond drop added the finishing touch.

Meryl linked an arm through Heather's and squeezed gently. "You definitely know how to feed a person's ego, my friend. I don't know what I would have done without you these past few days."

The moment Meryl had gotten off the plane, Heather had been there to meet her. She had taken her everywhere: shopping, sightseeing, to meetings with her publisher, and out to dinner. She had proved to be a good friend as well as a good agent.

"I wouldn't have missed showing you around for anything," Heather was saying, "and I certainly wouldn't have missed being a part of this television appearance."

Meryl was quiet for a moment as they made their way, still arm in arm, into the building. "I'm really nervous, you know, and if I thought about it too much, I'd go into a mild panic."

Heather rolled her eyes. "That's utter nonsense and you know it," she berated. "You'll knock 'em dead with that southern drawl and those big black eyes. And just wait till they hear all about you and the story behind your book."

Meryl's lips began to twitch. "Do you think I should tell the truth—I mean, actually say that my aunt used to say to me and my sister every time we started to eat a piece of candy or potatoes or anything high in fat content, and I quote: 'Remember, girls, a moment on your lips, forever on your hips'? You would've had to know her to really appreciate it. God love her!"

Both women laughed heartily as they waited for the elevator in the crowded lobby.

Meryl dabbed at her eyes with a tissue. "If I don't behave myself," she remarked, "I'm going to have to repair my makeup." Changing the subject, she asked, "What's taking that elevator so long?"

Heather looked up at Meryl from her five-foot frame and smiled. "Calm down, we have plenty of time."

Meryl sighed as she fingered the studs in her ears. "I guess you're right. But I'm anxious to get this over with because I'm nervous, and also because I'm ready to get back home to Reese."

"Of course you are," Heather soothed, just as the door of the elevator swished open. "Speaking of Reese," Heather continued as they stepped in and began going up, "am I going to get an invitation to my favorite author's wedding?"

Meryl raised her eyebrows. "Would you come?"

"In a New York minute," Heather quipped.

Meryl grinned as she reached out and tweaked a brown curl. "You're crazy, and I'll make sure your name is at the top of the guest list."

They remained silent while they stepped off the elevator and walked at a leisurely pace toward their destination, which Heather explained was at the end of the long corridor.

Suddenly Heather's face became troubled. "You're not by any chance planning to give up your writing once you get married, are you?"

Meryl looked shocked. "Heavens no!" she responded. Then hesitated for a moment. "Reese and I haven't talked about it, but he knows how much my career means to me. Of course," she added hastily, "he will always come first, but still . . ." Her voice trailed off.

"Well, that relieves my mind," Heather said, before adding brightly, "Here we are." She stopped and eyed Meryl closely, smiling her encouragement. "Ready?"

Meryl squared her shoulders and gave her a dazzling smile. "I'm ready. Let's go."

The next hour passed in a whirl for Meryl, but she knew she must have said and done the right things, because the interviewer and crew were extremely enthusiastic and complimentary.

It was only when she turned and saw Heather making her way hurriedly toward her that Meryl knew something was wrong. Heather's face was colorless and she was chewing on her lower lip.

With eyebrows drawn together in a frown, Meryl excused herself from the group and met Heather halfway. "What's wrong?" she asked. "You're as pale as a ghost."

"You have an emergency phone call."

Looking both surprised and puzzled, Meryl stammered, "Did . . . did they . . . they indicate who it is or what it's about?" Her eyes were on the phone as they worked their way toward it.

Heather's voice was guarded. "No, but I have a feeling it's bad news."

Meryl's steps floundered for a moment. *Reese.* Something had happened to Reese. Her legs suddenly picked up momentum as she jerked the receiver off the hook and lifted it to her ear. Her tongue felt twice its normal size as she breathed, "Hello."

"Meryl, is that you? Speak up, I can't hear."

Meryl went weak with relief. "Oh, Nelda," she cried, "I'm so glad it's you. I was afraid something was wrong."

Silence.

"There *is* something wrong," Nelda said at last, her voice heavy with dread.

In that moment Meryl felt as though the life were being

squeezed out of her heart. She felt faint, a blackness spinning before her eyes, an illness gripping her stomach. Her knees shook so she had to lean against the table to keep from falling.

"Meryl, honey, are you okay?"

It was a struggle just to breathe, but somehow she managed to get words through her raspy throat. "Tell . . . me . . . what happened?"

"I . . . there's been an accident. I'm . . . I'm at the hospital now. It's your sister . . . she's hurt badly."

Meryl's bloodless hands clung to the phone as she listened in stunned silence, barely able to absorb what Nelda was saying.

"Meryl?"

Searching for oxygen to speak, Meryl took deep gulping breaths. Finally she was able to eke out, "Was anyone else hurt?"

A deep sigh rattled through the line. "All I know is that your sister was upset about something and went storming into a Dr. Corbett's office and confronted him." Another sigh. "They left together in Morgana's car . . ." She broke off as if uncertain how to continue. "And ended up ramming into a tree. The doctor's all right, but Morgana . . . it's too soon to tell."

No! she mouthed, the word unable to pass through her frozen lips. Reese. Morgana. Together. In an accident. Her fault. Her body was swaying like liquid.

"Meryl . . . please come home on the next plane. Morgana needs you."

Somehow those three words—*Morgana needs you*—managed to jolt Meryl into action. Through cracked lips she whispered, "I'm . . . I'm leaving now."

She dropped the phone and bent double as dry sobs racked her body.

Nelda, her face grave with concern, stood waiting as Meryl stepped into the lobby at Houston's intercontinental airport.

Dropping her hand luggage down beside her, Meryl grasped Nelda's outstretched hand as scalding tears circled her eyes. "How . . . how's Mor . . . ?" Her voice cracked, cold fear rendering her speechless.

Nelda chafed Meryl's cold hands. "There's been no change for the worse, thank God," she said. "Morgana's still unconscious, but her vital signs are good."

"Let's get out of here," Meryl whispered abruptly.

Silently they made their way at a trot down the concourse and eventually out of the airport and into Nelda's waiting car.

As they were pulling out of the parking lot, Nelda braked suddenly. "Your luggage. We forgot your luggage!"

Meryl waved her forward with an impatient flick of her hand. "It doesn't matter. I thought about it, but decided I could send for it later. Right now, all I want to do is get to the hospital."

Nelda reached across the seat and gave her hand another comforting squeeze. "Morgana's going to pull through. I just know she is."

"And . . . the doctor?" Meryl whispered, still too distraught to speak rationally.

Nelda sighed. "From what I've been able to piece together, he has only a mild concussion and a few minor cuts and bruises."

"Oh, Nelda," Meryl cried, "I'm so thankful for that, but I'm . . . sorry . . . so sorry . . . I feel so guilty . . ." She paused and gulped back the tears. "So guilty about Morgana." She began ripping the tissue in her hand to shreds. "You . . . you don't understand, it's all my fault." She bit down on her lower lip to keep from crying out loud.

"Don't," Nelda scolded. "I may not understand what this is all about, but I do know it's not your fault."

Oh, but it is! Meryl screamed silently. Knowing the tight control on her emotions was beginning to slip, Meryl changed the subject. "Did the hospital call looking for me?" she asked, her voice sounding stronger.

"Yes, and I called you immediately. Then I went straight to the hospital, but of course I couldn't see Morgana, but I did talk to her agent, Jay Johnson, who by the way seemed in terrible shape." She paused. "He's the one who informed me of Dr. Corbett's condition."

"Thank God for you, my friend," Meryl responded unevenly.

"That's what friends are for. Why don't you lay your head back and rest. We'll be there shortly."

Although she complied with Nelda's request and flopped her weary head against the back of the seat, she couldn't stop her mind from turning and twisting. As soon as she closed her eyes, those nightmarish hours following Nelda's phone call began to circulate through her brain.

Heather had taken charge. She had forced Meryl to pull herself together and had whisked her off to the airport and onto the first available flight out of La Guardia.

As the plane had blazed its way through the blue sky, Meryl had found it difficult to breathe under the heavy weight of despair and fear—and guilt. Because she didn't know the details of what had actually happened or why, it was much harder to bear. But of one thing she was certain: Morgana had found out about her and Reese. Over and over she had visualized in her mind's eye the scene that had taken place in Reese's office.

It had nearly driven her crazy thinking about it, yet she hadn't been able to keep her mind off it. Nor had she been able to escape from the image of her lovely sister lying scarred and incapacitated in the hospital because of her selfishness, knowing that she had done what she had promised herself she wouldn't do—use Morgana as a stepping-stone to make her dreams come true and secure her own happiness.

She had walked up and down the aisle. She had cried silent tears. She had watched the hands on her watch crawl. And by the time the plane had landed, her heart had taken such a beating she doubted it would ever be the same again.

Now, as Nelda steered the car around the circular drive of the hospital and brought it to a stop, Meryl jerked her eyes open, leaned over and gave Nelda a fierce hug.

"Thanks again for everything," she said. "I'll call you later." She grabbed her purse and flight bag and was out the door.

It didn't take her long to reach the nurses' station on the intensive-care unit. Since she knew Reese was all right, her immediate concern was for Morgana. She would have to deal with Reese later; she knew that. But not now.

Her heart was racing out of control. What if she was too late? What if Morgana was dead? What if . . . ?

She swallowed her panic and forced herself to speak coherently. "I'm . . . I'm Meryl Stevens, Morgana Grimes's sister. How . . . how is she?"

The petite nurse's eyes were soft with sympathy. "I'm sorry, Mrs. Stevens, but there's been no change in her condition."

"May I please see her?" Meryl asked, her eyes shining with unshed tears.

The nurse inclined her head. "Follow me," she said softly.

Meryl's legs felt like jelly as she followed her into a large room consisting of small alcoves with individual beds. A small compact nurses' station took up the center.

Morgana's tiny room was the first one inside the door. Meryl smiled her thanks to the nurse before taking tentative steps farther into the room and closer to the bed.

She bit down hard on her lower lip to stifle her gasp. "Oh, God, no," she whispered aloud, the room beginning to swim before her eyes. Taking advantage of the chair sitting close to the bed, she fell into it, clinging to Morgana's lifeless hand.

Her sister's face was barely recognizable. Both eyes were black and blue and swollen. The left side of her cheek was bandaged, the other one puffy and red. Another bandage swathed her forehead. A bottle of glucose hung ominously from its silver stand, dripping sustenance into the still body.

Morgana lay unmoving, still as death itself. If Meryl hadn't seen the steady rise and fall of her chest, she would have sworn Morgana wasn't breathing.

Please, Morgana, forgive me. I didn't mean to bring you this pain. I'm so sorry, so very sorry, she cried silently as she laid her wet cheeks against Morgana's limp hand.

How long she sat there, she didn't know. She lost all sense of time. It wasn't until she felt a hand on her shoulder that she stirred. She looked up into the dazed eyes of Jay Johnson. He motioned for Meryl to follow him outside. She nodded her assent.

They were silent until they reached the deserted waiting room.

Then, to her surprise, Jay sat down in the nearest chair and began sobbing.

Meryl touched his shoulder as she lowered herself beside him. "Jay, what . . . ?"

"Oh, Meryl," he cried, looking at her from under bushy brows, "don't you see it's all my fault?"

Meryl's blood ran cold. "You . . . you mean you're the one who told Morgana?"

"With God as my witness, I didn't know she would go storming to his office and verbally attack him. I . . . I saw you and Dr. Corbett together at La Hacienda, and I wanted to get back at Morgana for ditching me because of *him*. But . . . but she went crazy, and nearly killed them both." He was sobbing profusely. "How will I ever make it up to her?"

Meryl couldn't say a word. She felt sick.

But Jay went on. "I tried to tell her he didn't love her, that he was playing her for a fool, but she just wouldn't listen. Oh, God, what am I going to do, Meryl?" he whined. "I . . . I love her so much, always have."

Meryl had had all she could stand. She jumped to her feet and glared down at Jay's hunched-over figure. "If you love her so much," she spat, "then quit feeling sorry for yourself and think about Morgana. If we all had been doing that, none of this would be happening. But right now, she needs our strength, not our weakness."

"Will *you* ever forgive me?"

She was quiet for a moment. "I don't know," she said. "I honestly don't know."

There was another moment of harsh silence before Meryl spoke again. "If you're going to be here awhile longer, I'm going home to shower and change clothes."

"I'll . . . I'll be here."

"Call me if there's any change," she ordered before moving toward the door.

Later, as Meryl walked out into the evening twilight, she had never felt more alone or frightened than she was at this moment. She would always remember this day as being one of the worst of her life.

Meryl had been home only thirty minutes and had done nothing but pace the floor the entire time, feeling with each passing second as though she were sitting on a time bomb about to explode. Suddenly she couldn't stand the thought of staying here alone another moment. She would go back to the hospital as soon as she repaired her makeup, she told herself.

She had just walked into the bedroom and switched on the light when the doorbell chimed.

"Damnation," she muttered, only to realize it was probably her luggage being delivered.

With a deep sigh she trudged to the door. "Who is it?" Her tone was cautious.

"Reese."

Fumbling to unlock the door, Meryl found it difficult to breathe. Her mouth was dry and the skin on her face strangely tight.

When she finally got the door open, she just stood there and stared at his dear face, assuring herself that he was indeed all right. She longed to throw herself into his arms and beg him never to let her go. But she steeled herself against the emotion that engulfed her. Her twin sister, an extension of herself, was lying in a hospital bed because of her love for this man. She must remember that and act accordingly.

Whereas she was holding herself in tight restraint, Reese certainly was not. He bounded across the threshold and grabbed her trembling body and clung to her as though he'd never let her go.

"Oh, God, I'm so sorry, so sorry," he said, his voice torn. "I'm here now; we'll see this tragedy through together," he added, filling his nostrils with the sweet scent of her.

For a moment Meryl was lost. She felt herself drowning in his strong protective covering as she dug her chin into his chest. She needed him and wanted him as she never had before.

Her mind ceased to function. Time ceased to exist. There was only the two of them and their excruciating need for each other as he blotted her lips with his in a kiss as deep and sweet as all eternity.

Meryl's knees buckled underneath her as his mouth continued to move silently, demandingly, over her lips, making her realize more than ever that all she wanted to do was stand here with his arms around her, giving her his strength to lean on. But it wasn't that simple anymore. Guilt and shame had changed her, changed the circumstances.

Suddenly she began to struggle, to push him away. "No," she groaned, breaking the kiss.

Reese looked down into her eyes, and his own had a passion and a promise in them that shook the very foundations of her being.

"Oh, Reese," she said in an agonized whisper, "we can't . . . we shouldn't. Not . . ." Her voice caught in her throat. She couldn't go on, because she didn't know herself what she was trying to say, except that maybe their love wasn't meant to be. There had been so many setbacks, so much anguish and pain. Pain that affected others as well. Loving him had cost so much and was still costing. And she wasn't sure she could continue to pay such a high price.

He stepped back and looked at her. She could see the

naked pain mirrored in his eyes. Yet she was torn and hurt and crippled with her own guilt and insecurity to such an extent that she couldn't think of anything else.

"I nearly had another wreck trying to get to you," he said softly. "I love you and want to absorb your pain." A pulse in his jaw throbbed revealingly. "I want us to be together."

A sadness weighed heavy inside her. "I know," she whispered, "but I . . . we can't." She spread her hands, her face contorted with grief. "Can't you understand that all I can think about or feel is guilt, and fright, and, yes, shame?" Tears seeped from beneath her clenched eyelids.

"Oh, God, Meryl, don't you think I feel the same way? I tried to reason with Morgana, to be as gentle as I could, but she wouldn't listen." His mouth was twisted with suffering. "But she *is* going to be all right. Just before I left to come here, I spoke with the doctor, and he assured me that she's beginning to rally. In fact the nurse was positive she saw Morgana's eyelids flutter open for a second. So you see, she's going to be all right. You've got to believe that."

"If I didn't, I don't think I could make it through another day," she said with frightening calm.

"Then let me help you." He drew a convulsive breath. "Don't shut me out."

An icy numbness had settled around her heart. "Please, Reese," she whispered, "just give me a little more time—I need to be alone."

"Don't, Meryl, don't do this . . ." There was a tender thread of pleading in his voice.

"Maybe . . . maybe when Morgana gets well I'll be able to think about us . . . to make a . . . decision."

Anger hardened his lean features. "No, Meryl, I won't buy that. Not anymore. You can use Morgana as your crutch for just so long."

A taut silence filled the room.

Meryl sucked in air but didn't allow herself to move. "How . . . how can you say that," she cried, "when . . . when Morgana's lying in that hospital because of us?"

His mouth thinned. "That's not true, and you know it. We have no control over what other people say and do. And how were we to know that someone would tell her before we could?" His eyes suddenly became rock hard. "I'd like to get my hands on the bastard who did tell her," he added roughly.

"It . . . it was Morgana's agent, Jay Johnson. He saw us at the Mexican restaurant. He's . . . he's been in love with her for a long time. When he saw his chance to get back at Morgana for hurting him, he grabbed it." A tortured moan slipped through her lips. "Don't you see, we have initiated so much pain, so much hurt—"

"No!" His voice was like a blade, piercing and edged with cold steel. "You'll never convince me that our love is wrong or tainted. Never!"

"Reese . . . please . . . don't." She could barely breathe for the hot throbbing ache that was growing within her. "You're . . . making it worse," she whispered, her mouth trembling.

Suddenly he closed his eyes against the hollow feeling of impending doom. "I have a feeling this conversation would be taking place even if Morgana wasn't ill," he said dully. "I was right all along. You are afraid." A note of despair hung on every word. "Afraid to trust, to commit yourself to me, to anyone. Afraid to live!"

He paused, and when she remained mute, he hammered on, "And I've also reached the conclusion that you value your goddamned independence and career above everything!"

Desperately she tried to defend herself with words that strangled in her throat. Oh, God, she thought, panic drilling her insides. Was he right, after all? *Was she afraid?* She shook inwardly. No! Of course she wasn't. He was wrong. She loved him, had never stopped loving him and wanted to spend the rest of her life with him. But first there was the unfinished business with Morgana to attend to.

Her hands curled tightly by her side as a seed of doubt crept through her. Maybe if she were honest with herself she would admit that one small part of what Reese had said was true.

Maybe she did have to prove to herself that she could reach the top in her profession. She had been a failure as a wife, and she didn't know if she could live with herself if she failed at her career as well.

That didn't mean, however, that she loved Reese any less. At this moment, she had never loved him more. But she needed more time. She had to make him understand.

Reese saw the tug-of-war across her features and felt a sudden chill, knowing that she was slipping away from him as easily as ashes disappearing in the wind.

He ignored the rising heat at the base of his throat, frantic to try one more time to hold her. "Oh, Meryl, don't you realize that love is not only very special but also very fragile, that it must be nurtured and fed, allowed to grow? If there is no hope, no return of love, it begins to wither and finally dies—not because it wants to, but because it has no choice." He paused, holding her gaze. "Do you understand what I'm trying to tell you?"

She breathed achingly, understanding what he meant. Yet she couldn't utter the words he longed to hear. For her, love was not that simple. Not anymore.

Her hesitation gave him the answer he sought. She saw him flinch visibly as hope faded from his features.

"All right, Meryl, you win. If you want to deny us a life together, I won't try to stop you." His mouth twisted sadly. "You've finally convinced me that we have no future," he said as he strode to the door, his shoulders locked in total defeat.

As the door slammed shut behind him, nothing could have prepared her for the swift and staggering pain that swept through her with destructive force, leaving her torn and bleeding on the inside.

Chapter 13

THE MUSIC BOUNCED OFF THE WALL OF THE STUDIO AS MERYL, wet with perspiration, practiced her new jazz dance another time. She was determined to work out the bugs before she introduced it to her advanced class. It was her deep concentration coupled with the loud beat that kept her from hearing her name being called.

It was only after the music came to an abrupt halt that Meryl jerked her head around, a surprised look on her face.

"Oh, hello, Tucker," she said, her breath coming in short spurts as she trotted over to where he stood. She immediately reached for her towel and began to mop her face. "What brings you here?"

Tucker was peering at her closely, looking as though he hadn't heard a word she'd said. "Have you looked in the mirror lately?" he asked bluntly.

Meryl was taken aback. "As a matter of fact, I have," she retorted. "Why?"

"Because you look like hell, that's why," he replied grimly.

"Thanks." Meryl's voice dripped with sarcasm. "You really know how to make a person feel good."

Color stained his ruddy complexion. "Sorry I had to be the one to tell you, but it's the truth. And I worried about you. It seems like ever since Morgana regained consciousness, you've been driving yourself too hard. You've lost weight, there are circles under your eyes that no amount of makeup can hide. You're either working like you're possessed or you're waiting on Morgana hand and—"

"Tucker! Will you please stop?" she cried, giving him a

bitter look. "I can't believe you came this far out of your way just to tell me how bad I look and that I'm working too hard." She was glaring at him now, her brows raised in question.

For a moment he appeared disconcerted, only to rebound quickly with these words: "Have you been sick?"

Meryl took several deep breaths and prayed for patience. "Yes, Tucker, I've been sick," she said with controlled exasperation. "Now, are you satisfied?"

His persistence proved to be relentless. "Only if it's the truth."

"Well, it's the truth," she admitted waspishly. "I've had a virus on and off for the last month. Or at least I think that's what it is."

"Have you seen a doctor?" he pressed.

She'd had enough. "No, Tucker, I haven't. What is this, anyway, Twenty Questions? If you don't intend to tell me why you're here, I'm going home and take a hot shower and go to bed." She reached up and ran the towel over her damp tousled curls.

Tucker's eyes softened as he reached out and traced a finger down her smudged cheek. "I came to see you for a distinct purpose," he said heavily, "but when I saw how ghastly you looked, I got scared." Meryl steeled herself not to flinch as he continued to caress her face. His fingers were soft like putty, whereas Reese's were callused, yet gentle . . . *Stop it!*

"You know how I feel about you," he added thickly. "I want to marry you."

She moved away, panic flaring up inside her. "Please, Tucker, I don't feel—"

"I know, you don't feel like discussing it now, and I can understand that, but soon I hope you'll give me an answer." He paused and suddenly grinned. "I'm hoping that what I'm about to tell you will help make up your mind."

Meryl blinked before knitting her brows together in a perplexed frown. "Tucker, you're talking in riddles, not making any sense," she wailed, wishing he'd just go away and leave her alone.

Suddenly he grabbed her and began twirling her around the floor, deep laughter rumbling in his chest.

Meryl was flabbergasted. Never had she known Tucker to behave in such an irrational manner; it was completely out of character for him.

On legs that were now as flexible as rubber, Meryl hung on and tried to keep up with his uncoordinated, loping gait.

"Tucker," she pleaded shortly, having reached her wits' end. "What on earth has come over you?" She smiled. "Have you by any chance inherited a million dollars?"

He stopped abruptly and pushed her to arm's length. His eyes were twinkling with excitement. "Nope, but I did clinch the television deal today."

Shock rendered Meryl speechless. She just stood there in a stupor and waited for the overwhelming sense of relief and excitement to wash over her, but it didn't. Instead she felt only a deep sense of gratitude that she would now have a new challenge to occupy her mind and body for the next few months, forcing her to concentrate on something other than her own never-ending heartache. But she couldn't let Tucker know this. She owed him too much to short-change him now.

Faking enthusiasm, she flung her arms around his neck and hugged him close before disentangling herself and stepping back. "I'm . . . I'm finding it hard to believe that after all this time, it's finally a reality. How did you finally manage to convince them that I was a more valuable commodity than a movie star?" she asked, motioning him to follow her into her office, where she could sit down before her legs completely failed her.

She was not only exhausted from dancing for two straight hours, but that familiar churning in her stomach was beginning to plague her once more. Maybe she should see a doctor after all, she thought. But she knew he'd just tell her to slow down and quit pushing herself so hard.

"I told you, when I want something badly enough, I leave no stone unturned until I get it," he was saying, jerking her back to the moment at hand. "Of course, having your book on every best-seller list in the country didn't hurt our case at all."

"Well," she said unevenly, "it looks as though you've pulled off a miracle. But I'm still finding it hard to believe."

He smiled. "Well, believe it, my dear. Production starts in a few weeks."

"I hope I'm ready."

"You'd better be. I expect you to be hard competition for the Richard Simmons show."

"Are you serious?"

"As serious as death and taxes," he shot back.

Meryl laughed. "That's about as serious as you can get."

"Are you up to going home, changing clothes and letting me take you out for a celebration dinner?" Tucker asked as they entered the quiet luxury of her office.

A touch of guilt pricked her conscience at having to disappoint him, but the thought of food made her turn green. "Would you be terribly upset if I opted for a rain check on the invitation?"

His crestfallen features gave her the answer as no words could have, but another sudden gurgle from her queasy stomach convinced her she was making the right decision. She winced noticeably.

"You really don't feel well, do you?" he asked, not missing her grimace of pain.

"No, I don't." She tried to smile. "But after I go home and take a hot bath and get some sleep, I'm sure I'll feel better."

Tucker stood up and pulled her up to stand beside him. He then leaned over and kissed her on the forehead. "Well, I won't keep you any longer. Take care," he whispered. "I'll call you tomorrow and we'll talk more then."

"Thanks again for everything," she said unsteadily as he walked out the door.

Meryl did exactly as she'd said. The moment she locked the door behind her, she began shedding her clothes and headed straight for the bath.

Once she was neck-deep in the hot, sudsy water, she leaned her head against the back of the tub and closed her eyes, giving in to the hopelessness that haunted her with maddening persistence.

Without Reese, her life was an endless aching void. When he had walked out of her house one month ago today, he had taken her soul with him. It was that simple.

She kept telling herself it was better this way—that she didn't need Reese and that he was better off without her. But that didn't work; she knew she was lying to herself.

As a result, she hadn't been able to function like a normal human being. Even learning that the funds were now available for production of her television show failed to mend the gaping hole in her heart or to ease her deep and abiding sense of guilt. She had found out that heartache and guilt were powerful emotions with the potential to destroy not only one's inner calm and one's health but also one's very life.

The only thing that kept her from falling apart altogether during the bleak and lonely days and nights without Reese was Morgana's improvement toward a full recovery. Although she was still too ill for any type of serious discussion, Meryl had spent as much time with her sister as the doctors allowed and was praying the day would soon come when she could beg Morgana's forgiveness.

Realizing the water was now tepid, she stood up, only to find that she was terribly dizzy. She clutched the towel rack, groping to maintain her balance. Only after taking several deep breaths did she venture a step farther. Damn, but this virus or nervous stomach or whatever was getting to be an aggravation she didn't need. This week, without fail, she vowed she would see a doctor for a thorough checkup.

A short time later, she crept between the sheets, hoping to drift into a dreamless sleep. However, by three o'clock she still hadn't gone to sleep, and she knew that indeed there was no rest for the weary.

* * *

At nine o'clock the following morning, Meryl tapped gently on the door of Morgana's hospital room. In response to the softly spoken "Come in," she pushed open the heavy door and walked in carrying a vase of freshly cut flowers.

"Good morning," Meryl quipped as she breezed over to the window ledge and deposited the vase among the multitude of others. "This place looks more like a florist's than a hospital room," she added, fiddling with the flowers, trying to ignore the tension that always followed her arrival.

"Meryl, we have to talk," Morgana announced quietly from behind.

New life pumped through Meryl's body; at last she was going to get the chance to speak her heart. "I . . . I know," she whispered, swinging around. Tears edged her thick lashes.

They stared at each other for a long moment, each fighting her own insecurities and private battles, while searching for words to heal the other's wounds.

Meryl was the first to move, taking a tentative step closer to Morgana's fragile-looking figure sitting up in the bed. Although her sister was better, she still had a long way to go, Meryl thought before she could be diagnosed as well. The right side of her face displayed a savage gash that would have to have extensive plastic surgery. But considering how badly she had been hurt, she had come a long way in a short span of time, and for that Meryl was deeply grateful.

Meryl made no effort to stem the tears that now poured down her face. "Oh, Morgana," she choked as her knee bumped the side of the bed, forcing her to stop.

No further words were necessary, for at that moment Morgana simply raised her trembling arms and held them out to Meryl.

With a jagged moan tearing through her lips, Meryl wilted onto the side of the bed and dived into Morgana's arms. It was hard to tell which was crying the hardest as they rocked back and forth, hanging on to each other for dear life.

"Oh, God, I'm so sorry, so sorry," Morgana began, sobs racking her thin body.

"No," Meryl countered, tears clogging her own throat, making it equally difficult to speak. "I'm . . . I'm the one who's sorry." She drew a shuddering breath and pulled away, realizing suddenly that this kind of emotional upheaval couldn't be good for Morgana.

Meryl smiled and wiped the honey-blond wisps of hair away from Morgana's face as she gently eased her head back among the pillows. "I . . . I should have told you that I—"

"Perhaps you should have," Morgana interrupted softly, "but nothing, absolutely nothing, excuses what I did." Her voice broke on a shrill note.

Meryl was concerned. "Please, don't," she pleaded. "It's not necessary. Don't you know that I understand, that I've always understood you?"

"I . . . I have to say this or I don't think I can continue to live with myself." Morgana paused, obviously struggling for composure. "Because . . . of my own selfishness, I nearly took the life of another person!" Her eyes were filled with self-condemnation and her lower lip trembled violently.

"But you didn't," Meryl reminded her gently. "So you must lay it to rest now or you'll never get well."

"Will you . . . you ever forgive me for what I did to you and Reese?" Morgana's voice was barely audible.

Meryl's face was covered in tears as she leaned over and hugged her sister once more. "Only if you'll forgive me for deceiving you." She made a helpless gesture. "If we'd been honest from the first, none of this would have happened," she added flatly.

A smile suddenly illuminated Morgana's pale face. "What do you say, then, we forgive and forget and try to pick up the pieces of our lives and go on?"

Meryl's heart soared with relief. "That's the best advice I've heard in a long time." She laughed as she reached in the pocket of her jacket for a tissue and began wiping her eyes.

But when she looked at Morgana again, her eyes were sober. "Are you in pain?" Meryl demanded anxiously.

Morgana smiled. "Yes, but not that kind of pain. I'm experiencing growing pains at thirty-five years old." She gave a tired sigh. "I've finally faced the fact that my modeling career is over. Even if Reese can glue Humpty Dumpty back together again, I'm still going to call it quits."

Meryl stood up jerkily and walked to the window and then turned back around, wearing a troubled look. "Don't you think you're rushing—"

Morgana shook her head adamantly. "Hear me out, please." She paused and licked her lips. "I guess what I should've said was that I don't want to model anymore. I've decided to marry Jay instead."

"What!"

Morgana chuckled. "You heard me," she quipped brightly, acting more like her old self. "Jay finally talked me into marrying him." Then her face became cloudy. "He really blames himself for . . ." Her voice faltered.

"You don't have to say any more," Meryl cut in. "I know he's sorry. And he, like the rest of us, had his reasons for doing what he did. I was rather hard on him that first night after I came back from New York. The first chance I get, I must apologize." She paused. "Do you love him?"

Morgana's gaze did not waver. "Yes, and I guess I always have," she responded soberly. "It seems everyone knew it but me." Then she was quiet for a long moment. "Meryl, I want you to know that I never loved Reese. I was just infatuated with his charm and good looks. But even more than that I saw him as a one-way ticket back to the top of my career. I thought he had the power to make me young and beautiful again."

Morgana paused with a sigh. "But when you do something for all the wrong reasons, it never turns out right. I've finally learned that loving and being loved is more important than being beautiful or obtaining material things."

She laughed suddenly, though it never reached her eyes.

"It took me long enough to figure that out, don't you think? And you want to know something else funny? The flowers that I assumed were from Reese were from my darling Jay. Talk about not being able to see beyond your nose . . ."

Meryl smiled sweetly. "Well, as long as you found it out, that's what's important. I know you'll be happy. Jay has loved you for a long time."

"When I get out of this bed, that's my top priority, to make him the most satisfied male around." Her grin was followed by a grimace. "Unfortunately, it'll be a while before I can set foot outside these sterile walls. Reese can't start my plastic surgery for at least another week."

Every time Reese's name was mentioned, it was like pouring alcohol on an oozing sore. Learning that he had never betrayed her by sending Morgana flowers or doing anything else underhanded deepened her remorse. She flinched against the hurt. But she fought to keep Morgana from seeing her inner feelings.

But Morgana knew. She had caught a glimpse of Meryl's white face and colorless lips.

A hushed silence fell over them.

At last Morgana broke it. "Meryl, I'd hate to think that it's over between you and Reese because . . . because of me. Please, tell me it's not?" she begged.

Meryl's shoulders curled in desperation as her mind searched for words to answer the question. She turned around slowly. "I . . . yes, it's over, but not . . . not because of you," she whispered, feeling as though her insides were in a shredding machine. And suddenly Meryl knew she spoke the truth.

"Then why?" Morgana pressed softly.

"Because . . . because of *me!*" Meryl sobbed. "I . . . I can't stand the thought of being a failure, of letting Reese down." She paused, trying to get hold of herself. "Of seeing that same disappointed look on his face that I saw on Stan's so many times, because I couldn't have a . . . baby."

"Oh, God, Meryl," Morgana whispered, "I didn't realize

that you were still harboring all that self-reproach, that fear."
Her eyes were wide and disturbed. "I thought I was the only
one of us with all those horrifying insecurities."

Meryl sniffed back the tears. "I didn't either, until . . .
Reese dug deep into the dark depths of my soul and pulled
them out in the harsh light and made me face them," she
admitted bitterly.

"Are . . . are you sure it's over?" Morgana's voice was
constricted. "Maybe, if you went to him . . . ?"

Pain. Unimaginable, indescribable pain. It threatened to
suck her under like a swift, brutal current; she struggled just
to stay afloat. "No!" she cried. "If you could have seen the
look on his face, you'd know that was out of the question.
"It's . . ." Just for a moment, her tenuous veneer cracked.
"It's . . . it's too late for us. There's been too much said and
done to ever bridge the gap." Her voice had disappeared into
a strangled whisper.

"What are you going to do?"

Meryl drew her dejected shoulders up to full height and
smiled through her tears, though her heart was breaking. But
she couldn't let Morgana know this or she herself would be
lost. Reese was her burden and she must bear it alone.

Still smiling, she walked toward the bed and looked down
at Morgana. "I don't want you to worry about me," she said.
"You concentrate instead on being happy with Jay and getting
well." She lifted Morgana's hand and patted it. "I'll be fine. I
haven't told you, but the money has come through to begin
production on my TV show, so you see, I have plenty to keep
me busy."

Morgana didn't appear convinced. "That's wonderful,
but . . ."

"There are no buts about it," Meryl whispered, leaning
over and grazing Morgana's cheeks with her lips. "I'm going
now. I love you, and I'll be fine. Remember, I'm a survivor."

Meryl slipped into her skirt and secured it with the
multicolor belt that blended with the iceberg blue of her

blouse and matching jacket. Thank God, the long-dreaded doctor's exam was over, she thought. Although she had vacillated for a week, she finally had made herself call for an appointment. During the last two hours, she had been prodded, poked, and stuck until she was worn out.

Through it all, Dr. Anderson had remained mute, merely nodding and grunting to himself at various times during the examination. Yet she wasn't worried, not really. The fact that the doctor had appeared calm and laid-back had curiously reassured her. It was nothing more than severe anemia or an intestinal bug that could be cured with a bottle of pills, she had told herself logically.

Now, as she crossed the hall into Dr. Anderson's office for the verdict, she was still relaxed and not the least bit concerned. Instead she felt relieved that it was over and that momentarily she could return to work.

Dr. Anderson joined her shortly and took a seat at his massive desk across from her. He opened her folder and smiled at the same time.

"I'm going to fuss at you, young lady," he said sternly, though his smile and twinkling eyes took the slight edge off his words. He reached for his glasses, and after fitting them to his rather large nose, scanned her chart briefly. When he looked up, his white brows were drawn together in a frown. "You've neglected your body terribly; you are severely anemic. Added to that, you have acquired a slight kidney infection, which, under the circumstances, isn't good." He paused, giving his diagnosis time to soak in.

Meryl frowned, not at all sure she understood. What did "under the circumstances" mean? she wondered with a sudden attack of anxiety rushing through her. To her un-trained ears, it sounded ominous.

"Are you . . . you telling me that I'm ill—really ill, I mean?" she asked. Her tone was a hodgepodge of fright and concern.

Dr. Anderson's smile ruptured into a full-fledged grin as he reared back in his chair, changing his position. "Not unless you consider being pregnant a critical illness."

Meryl sat dumbfounded as strange lights began to flash through her brain. For a moment she thought she might faint. She blinked and then blinked again, fighting the urge to give in to the blackness that was taunting her, begging her to succumb to its healing oblivion.

"No!" she squeaked out at last, staring at the doctor as though he were an alien from a foreign planet.

"Yes," he countered calmly.

"Are . . . are you sure?" she whispered, her eyes glazed with disbelief. "Isn't there a chance you might have made a mistake?" She felt herself clawing through thin air, but she couldn't believe . . . No . . . Impossible . . . He *had* to be wrong. Doctors were human. Weren't they? They made mistakes like everyone else. Didn't they?

His next words smashed that thought to smithereens. He smiled patiently. "I'm sure," he said in a tone that sanctioned no argument. But he did smile again and looked as though he was enjoying humoring her. "Not only is your uterus enlarged, but your breasts are swollen and extremely tender. However, if you need further convincing, the results of the tests will be available tomorrow." He paused and stared into her pale face strangely. "Didn't the fact that you'd missed a monthly period along with the bouts of nausea give you a clue or at least make you suspect?"

Meryl remained in a stupor, even though she heard every word he said. They were echoing endlessly through her brain. Clues? Suspect? How could she have suspected anything out of the ordinary when she was positive she could never have a child? Oh, God, that was the last thing that would have crossed her mind. Cancer, yes! Pregnant, no! She still couldn't quite comprehend it.

"Are you all right?" Dr. Anderson inquired, jerking her away from her turbulent thoughts.

Her tongue circled her dry lips. "I'm . . . I'm fine," she whispered. But she wasn't fine. Now that warm blood was beginning to replace the ice water in her veins, she felt as though she had been kicked in the teeth.

Dear God, she cried silently, why now? Hadn't she driven Reese away because she hadn't been able to give him a child? And now that she had finally managed to destroy his love, she found out she was carrying his child. Oh, God, the irony of it all.

Suddenly, blind panic surged through her. She gripped the chair arms with her hands until they were bloodless, wanting to disappear, to go away and be alone. To think. . . .

"Mrs. Stevens, my medical eye tells me that you're far from being all right," Dr. Anderson said at length. "Why don't you lie down for a while before you drive home?"

Meryl forced herself to relax. "No . . . that's not necessary. It's just that I wasn't expecting this," she murmured inanely.

Dr. Anderson sighed. "Obviously this news doesn't have you jumping with joy." Concern made his voice rough. "Why don't I write you a prescription to take care of the kidney problem today, and then in a few days you come back to see me and we'll continue our discussion." He smiled reassuringly. "There's still plenty of time to decide what you want to do."

Somehow Meryl managed to make it to the parking garage and into her car without making a fool of herself. But the second she slammed the door shut, she slumped against the seat, flopped her back against the velour upholstery and let the tears flow. Deep sobs racked her body as she tried in vain to come to grips with the situation. Reese. Oh, Reese, her heart cried. What was she going to do? It had never occurred to her that missing her monthly period wasn't due to fatigue and nerves. She had never dreamed she was going to have a baby.

A baby. Flesh of her flesh. And after all this time. Suddenly her heart began to sing as the tears turned to joy. It was a miracle, that's what it was—a miracle. She cleared the tears from her eyes and dropped her gaze to her flat stomach and stared at it for a long time before placing her hand there, giving in to the happiness that coursed through her.

But then, just as quickly, her happiness gave way to another emotion equally potent: terror—electrifying terror. For it suddenly dawned on her that she was *alone*. There was no Reese to share in this awesome responsibility. Then, on the heels of that thought came another, equally disturbing: her career. The blood began to pound in her head like a hammer. *What would become of her television show?*

It was only a matter of weeks before she was to begin production for the show. How could she prepare for it and do the strenuous exercises required and look her very best when she was pregnant? And this television project was to have been her ultimate show of success—proof that she had made it to the top.

In that bleak moment she felt despair as she never had before. Where did she go from here? She turned and stared wildly out the window, listening to the rapid thumping of her heart. But she did have a choice, after all. Hadn't the doctor told her there was still time? With the flick of a surgeon's knife, it could be over. No one would be the wiser. And her career would still be intact. Could she do it?

Tears saturated her pale features as she sat like a wooden statue. No, of course she couldn't do it. Even if she never saw Reese again, and even if it meant the end of her career forever, she could never purposely destroy their child, the seed of their love.

But then, her career didn't matter, not really. It was only a tiny dot of importance compared to the miracle growing within her and her deep and abiding love for Reese. Love was the only key that could unlock the door to happiness. Reese had tried to tell her, only she hadn't been listening. But then, she hadn't known she was possessed of a miracle, either. That alone would have made all the difference in the world. Involuntarily she felt her heart leap with unexpected hope.

Was there a chance she could salvage the mess she had

made of her life? Would Reese be willing to listen? Dare she take the chance? *Dare she hope?*

Suddenly she desperately needed to talk to someone. Morgana. Morgana would help her. Help her make the most important decision of her life.

As soon as the elevator door swished shut behind Meryl on the fifth floor, she made a beeline for the ladies' lounge. She wasn't about to go into Morgana's room looking like she had been on a crying jag. Even though she had, she was afraid of frightening her sister with her disheveled appearance.

But she soon gave up the effort. The ravages of confusion and distress were too deeply engraved to cover up. Besides, she had something much more important to worry about, she told herself as she scurried out the door and down the hall.

Without knocking, she pushed against the heavy door and barged in. The door had barely closed behind her before she froze in her tracks, her wide hopeful eyes colliding with a pair of cool velvet ones.

Although she heard Morgana's high-pitched voice chattering at high speed, she wasn't aware of anything at that exact moment, except Reese. And his big, overpowering body.

Suddenly the atmosphere was charged with emotion as Meryl filled her eyes and heart with the sight and smell of her beloved. It had been so long. Six weeks! It seemed like a lifetime. Somehow he seemed different. Was his face thinner than she remembered? And were his eyes sunk deeper into his head? And didn't his clothes hang on him rather loosely? Or were her eyes playing tricks on her?

She had a sense of *déjà vu* as Reese was regarding her now with hostile eyes.

She felt a constricting pain inside her.

"Meryl," he clipped, nodding slightly.

The single word epitomized the fear that had gnawed at her from the moment she had crashed through the door and seen him standing there. There was no compassion in his voice, no liking either. She gazed at him unsteadily, striving to maintain her composure.

"Hel . . . hello, Reese," she stammered, twisting the strap of her purse between her fingers.

Meryl's greeting was met with a smoldering silence as his eyes remained fastened on her face.

For one long exquisite moment Reese indulged himself, letting his eyes drink in her beauty, carving deep into his memory: the gleaming dark hair, capping her head in silky disarray; the large dark eyes, starkly clear; the translucent glow of her skin; the rounded swell of her breast.

Then a feeling of anger and deep sadness filled him as he remembered she would never be his. Words spoken what seemed now like aeons ago came back to haunt him. He had told her that after a time, love can simply burn itself out if it has no response to nourish it. He groaned inwardly, mocking himself. His love hadn't worn out, hadn't even dimmed. Damn, it was still there, making his heart hurt, his throat hurt and his eyes hurt with the need to weep, to shout, to scream his agony at her refusal of that love.

Suddenly Morgana broke the enduring silence, looking frantically between the two of them.

"Oh, Meryl, I was just telling Reese that the money for your television show had come through and that you were on your way to becoming a star." She laughed nervously, trying to cover the awkwardness of the situation.

Oh, God, Morgana, no! Meryl cried silently, knowing that as far as Reese was concerned, those words had signed her death warrant. She watched in horror as scathing contempt flooded his features.

"Congratulations," he said. "I'm glad you finally got what you wanted."

Meryl somehow managed to hold up under the lick his cutting words dealt her as she saw the hope and dreams of a reconciliation crumble in a heap around her feet. She should have known better, she told herself miserably. How could she have been so conceited as to think that he would come running back to her after she had put her twin, her career and her pride before him? He no longer wanted her. And she didn't blame him. Her legs sagged as pain ran like a menacing stimulant through her veins.

"I . . . I . . ." She found to her dismay that she couldn't go on. But it didn't matter. Reese was no longer there to hear her.

The abrupt click of the door was the only sound to rival the hollow silence.

For a heart-stopping moment, Meryl was too bereft to move.

"Oh, Meryl, oh, God, what have I done?" Morgana wailed. "I'm so sorry. I . . . I thought it would help if I . . ." She began crying softly.

Trying to see through her own blinding tears, Meryl turned to face her. "It's . . . it's all right," she whispered. "You . . . you didn't know. If it hadn't happened now, it would have later." Her voice caught on a sob as she looked beyond Morgana.

"I . . . don't understand," Morgana said.

"There's nothing to understand," Meryl whispered. "It's just that for a moment, I had visions of capturing a rainbow."

Moments later, as Meryl rode the elevator to the parking garage, she closed her eyes against the dizziness that overpowered her. What now? she asked herself. But then a surprising calm settled over her as she answered her own question.

She would pick up the pieces of her life one more time and go on. Hadn't she told Morgana she was a survivor? Well, that she was. What she and Reese had shared was over—and yet would last a lifetime. She was carrying a special part of him within her. She could be content with that. Couldn't she?

It was only after she was halfway home that she remembered she hadn't told Morgana about the baby.

"What the hell do you mean, you're not going to do the show!" Tucker snarled as he stalked around Meryl's den like an animal on the prowl, his hand tightly fisted around a glass of Scotch.

Meryl snagged her lower lip between her teeth to keep it from trembling and remained silent. She had dreaded this conversation for two weeks, but she had not been able to postpone it any longer. As it was, Tucker was one of the last to hear the news. She had told her sister last week, and following much laughter and tears of joy, Morgana had told Jay. Of course, there was Nelda. The list went on. She knew if she waited much longer, Tucker would find out from another source. She couldn't chance that. It was her place to tell him.

But how did one go about telling the man who had done so much for her and who wanted to marry her that she was pregnant with another man's child? Because of this, his plans for her future had gone down the drain. And she hadn't even told him about the baby.

"Tucker, will you please sit down?" Meryl pleaded, her nerves frayed to the breaking point.

He paused in his pacing and threw her a cold look. "Sit down," he hissed. "That's the last thing I want to do. What I really have in mind is the urge to wring your delicate neck for doing this to me."

Meryl felt herself grow pale under the cruel lash of his tongue. But she took his abuse, knowing she deserved it. *Oh, God, would a time ever come when her love for Reese wouldn't hurt someone?* she cried in silent anguish. She had delayed telling him long enough.

"I . . . I can explain," she began, forcing herself to meet his granite glare.

"Explain!" he exploded, before downing the remainder of his drink in one gulp. "I don't want to hear any goddamned excuses. I just want you to honor your end of the bargain, that's all."

"I can't!" she cried, his antagonism goading her into shouting back at him. Inhaling a deep breath, she plunged forth, "I'm pregnant, Tucker." There, she'd said it. She'd delivered the bombshell.

She didn't move a muscle as she waited for his reaction.

A savage oath flew from his lips as he stared at her as though she had two heads, his mouth gaping open. "Pregnant! But . . . but . . . how?" he stammered incoherently, shaking his head.

A tiny smile flickered on Meryl's lips in response to his poorly phrased question, but then it quickly disappeared when she saw the shock turn into fury.

"Whose is it?" he demanded, his nostrils quivering in his blood-red face.

Meryl's eyes sparked suddenly. "Mine," she said emphatically, her arms making a protective covering over her stomach.

"Meryl!" he warned. "Stop playing games with me. How do you think *I* feel, especially when I didn't even know you were seeing anyone, much less screwing around. And why the hell didn't you take precautions so you wouldn't get trapped? I want answers and I want them now."

Meryl turned her head, wincing against the blow, but taking it nevertheless. "It's a long story," she said wearily, "and I refuse to give you all the gory details of my demise," she added with bitter humor.

"You mean to tell me you're going to see this madness through—alone!" His tone was an icy sneer.

"I'm . . . sorry," she whispered, feeling her insides turn to mush, "but I can't tell you whose baby it is. Anyway, it's not important."

Her sarcasm was wasted on him. "I'll be damned if I'm going to stand by and watch you tear yourself and your life to pieces without trying to stop you."

"Oh, Tucker, don't you realize there's nothing you can do to change my mind?"

"I don't know about that," he retaliated sharply. "You owe me Meryl, whether you want to admit it or not. You don't know what all I had to do to get those men to reconsider putting up the money for you. I don't intend to back down now."

"You have no choice."

"Oh, yes I do."

"What?"

"You could have an abortion."

For a moment, shock robbed Meryl of her speaking voice. Then suddenly bloodcurdling anger raged through her with potent force. It was one thing for her to consider destroying her child, but for someone else to do so was out of the question.

She jumped up, fury twisting her features, but it was the cold composure of her eyes that did the damage. "Don't you ever say anything like that to me again," she said fiercely. "As far as I'm concerned, you can take that television show and do what you damn well please with it. I'm through with it and through with you. I've taken all of your abuse I'm going to. Now, get out of my house."

Tucker knew he had gone too far this time. He looked like a man with a rope around his neck, headed for the gallows.

"Oh, Meryl, I'm sorry. I didn't mean that. Please forgive me," he begged. "It's just that I had so many plans . . ."

Tucker was suddenly a broken man, and in spite of what he had said and done to her, she wanted to forgive him. There was already enough pain in her life without adding to the list.

"Oh, Tucker, I'm sorry too." She pressed her palms to her hot cheeks. "I'm like you, I had plans that just didn't work out," she said achingly.

A heavy silence filled the room, permeated only by the thudding of Meryl's heart.

"I'm sorry," he said again, rubbing his forehead with a gesture of weary dejection.

The pain was nearly intolerable as she whispered, "My relationship with . . . with the baby's father . . . is over. It just didn't work out. It's over," she repeated.

"Just like that?"

"Just like that."

"Are you sure?"

"Yes."

"And you don't intend to tell him about the baby?"

Meryl's heart lurched. Had she decided definitely not to tell Reese about the child of his loins, which he had wanted so desperately? Oh, God, she wanted to tell him, longed to tell him, but she was scared. Scared he would try to take the baby away from her.

"No, I don't intend to tell him about the baby."

"Then marry me."

Her head popped back, her expression stunned. "You . . . you mean you'd marry me knowing that I'm carrying another man's child?"

"If that's the only way I can have you," he muttered bitterly.

Hot tears burned her eyes. "Oh, Tucker, you have no idea how much your proposal means to me or how sorry I am that I've hurt you. But . . . I can't marry you; it wouldn't be fair."

Tucker released his breath on a ragged note. "All right, Meryl. If that's what you want, I won't argue with you. But I don't have to like it."

Meryl closed her eyes and then opened them again, trying to speak, but she couldn't get past the lump in her throat.

"What will you do?" he asked at length.

Meryl's quivering lips fell into a smile. "The same as always," she whispered. "I have my book to finish and three health studios to oversee." She paused and glanced down softly at her stomach. "And a baby to get ready for."

Tucker looked at her for a long moment. "If you change your mind, you know where to find me," he said.

"I know," she said tremulously.

She remained where she was long after he had gone, thinking about what he had said. But she knew she would never go to him. She could never settle for second best.

Chapter 14

As THE COOL GENTLE BREEZES OF OCTOBER SWEPT AWAY THE stifling heat of September, Meryl's body began to blossom with the early signs of motherhood. Physically she had never felt better, her days drifting into a steady pattern.

She went to the studio each day, where she was hovered over by Nelda, whose hawk eyes made sure she lifted nothing heavier than a pencil. Nelda worried needlessly, because Meryl realized that the days were gone when she could dance and exercise for hours until she nearly dropped from exhaustion. The baby's welfare was uppermost in her mind. To compensate, she took long afternoon walks, following long hours of sitting, researching and writing on her new book.

Even Tucker, to her surprise, kept in touch, becoming a staunch friend and ally. Once again it seemed he had pulled off the miraculous by convincing the corporate powers to table the production of the television show until after the baby was born. But Meryl had made no promises.

She spent time with Morgana, finding that her and Jay's happiness helped soothe her troubled heart. Three weeks following Morgana's release from the hospital, they married. It was a happy time for all, and Meryl plunged in and did her part to make the small but plush wedding a success.

However, as soon as the wedding was behind Morgana, she concentrated on taking Meryl under her wing. But Morgana's "mothering" was not always to Meryl's liking. She begged Meryl to tell Reese about the baby—as the baby's father, he had a right to know.

Meryl was not fooled. She could see through her sister. She knew Morgana was secretly hoping that in the event she went to Reese about the baby, they would get back together.

Knowing that wasn't possible, Meryl continued to turn a deaf ear to her sister's pleading, raw fear still overriding her conscience.

But throughout the lazy days and nights, thoughts of Reese could not be avoided. At the most unwelcome times, he would invade her heart, forcing her to remember his smile, the feel of his tender hands on her body, his gentle teasing, to have those images fade away, leaving in their place a feeling of emptiness and pain.

The mornings were the hardest. When she awoke, lying alone in her bed, she ached for him to be near her. Her longing for him fluttered like a trapped bird within her, its wings beating frantically. It was only when she spread her hands over her stomach, knowing she would always have part of him, that the ache lessened and she could breathe again.

And yet, as the magical days blended one into the other, and her condition became more obvious, she could no longer ignore the growing danger of her silent deceit. Today was one of those days. She had felt the baby move for the first time that morning, sending a thrill of joy coursing through her, but along with that incredible feeling came the harsh reminder that she was depriving Reese of the thing he wanted most in life—another child.

Now, as she stepped out of the bath, guilt hung over her head like a dark cloud. Quickly toweling her body, she began rubbing her protruding stomach with lotion, only to suddenly still her hands as she felt another gentle flutter. It was then that she knew. Knew she had to tell Reese about the baby.

"Oh, God," she cried aloud as she sank down on the side of the tub, a spasm of pain tearing through her. She had no choice. Even if in the distant future it meant a fight to keep her child, she knew she had to share her secret. It was the ultimate sacrifice, but she would make it.

Having made that soul-shattering decision, she felt tired, washed out. Slipping on her robe, she padded into the den and sat down on the couch with the intention of resting only a moment before fixing herself a bite to eat.

A short time later, Meryl jerked upright with a start. What had aroused her? Was it the loud bang of a car door? With an exasperated exclamation, she glanced at her watch. Seeing that it was after eight o'clock, she got up and went to the entry hall, flipped on the outside light and peered through the drape on the door.

At first Meryl thought she was dreaming. She quickly turned her back to the door and flattened herself flush against the wall. Her breath came in rapid pants as she forced air through her constricted lungs. *Reese!* It was him. She wasn't dreaming. Didn't the insistent clamor of the doorbell prove that?

She longed to jerk open the door and fling herself into his arms. But suddenly, spine-tingling fear ran through her veins like ice water. She lowered her eyes to the rounded swell of her belly, making sure it was adequately disguised by the full flowing robe. Oh, God, it was one thing to tell herself she had to confront Reese about the baby, but another to have him show up on her doorstep unexpectedly.

Yet wasn't his coming to her advantage? she asked herself, relief replacing her fear. It meant only one thing, didn't it? Dare she hope he was here because he still loved her? Wanted her back? It had to be. Suddenly her limbs began to tremble as though she had been struck with palsy. She was barely able to unbolt the door.

"Meryl, I know you're there." His voice was muffled, competing with the simultaneous rattle of the doorknob. "Please, open the door."

The sound of his familiar voice drove her into instant action. She unjammed the lock and yanked open the door in one fluid movement.

Meryl stood transfixed, searching his face with a wild hunger, waiting breathlessly for him to sweep her in his arms and tell her everything was all right, that he had forgiven her.

For an endless moment their eyes met with bruising force as weeks of pent-up hunger surged untamed and free.

Then suddenly the light faded from his eyes as he swept past her, not stopping until he reached the middle of the den. "Hello, Meryl. You're looking well," he said, his voice heavy with sarcasm.

Instinctively clutching at her chest in an effort to control her pounding heart, Meryl wordlessly shut the door and took a tentative step toward him, only to halt abruptly.

Something was wrong! She saw it in the narrowed slit of his eyes, in the rigid set of his shoulders, heard it in the low-pitched timbre of his voice. He reminded her of a coiled snake ready to strike. *Was she the prey?*

"Reese . . ." She broke off, fighting the hot bile that rose to the back of her throat as she stood paralyzed and watched as he suddenly closed the distance between them. His features were a contorted jumble of pain, fury and hurt. He stopped within inches of her trembling body, and before she realized his intentions, a hand snaked out and uncoiled the sash of her robe, baring her naked flesh to his burning gaze.

Meryl whimpered at the same moment Reese's harsh intake of air split the hushed silence.

He stood rooted to the spot, unable to take his eyes off the alluring fullness of her creamy breasts, the rounded swell of her stomach. To think, he cried silently, his child, the seed of his loins, lay harbored within her silken web, and she hadn't even told him. *Well, Meryl Stevens, you finally got your pound of flesh.*

Seeing his expression suddenly change from breathtaking desire to cold hostility, a strangled cry erupted from Meryl's lips as she stepped back, suddenly afraid—afraid for herself and her baby. *The baby!* Oh, God, no! He knew!

"How could you? How could you do this to me?" he spat, once more towering over her as though he would like nothing better than to wring her lovely neck.

She pushed the words through tight, stiff lips. "Who . . . who told you?"

"Goddammit!" he roared. "Is that all you have to say'

Meryl squeezed her eyes shut and prayed she woul faint. "Please," she strangled out, "I . . . was going to tell you."

"When?" he demanded fiercely.

"Soon," she whispered, battling against the tears crow her voice. "Tomorrow." She shook her head at his disbel ing contenance. "Or as soon . . . as I could get up courage. You've got to believe me." The defensive w spilled from her lips as tears drenched her face, her pleading with him to understand.

Reese's lips twisted. "If only I could believe that . . ."

"Don't hate me," she whispered, her eyes filled anguish. Then with a stifled sob she whirled around, unabl bear the pain in his eyes.

"Meryl!"

His tormented use of her name was like an abrasive car suddenly giving her the courage to tell him the truth, gut-wrenching truth.

Slowly she turned back around, clawing for air as she sv back the dark curtain of hair, and half-blinded by tears half-wild with grief, gazed at him, unflinching. "I . . . I afraid."

"Oh, Meryl, *why?*"

Her chin began to shake. "I . . . I didn't think I could have a child. My . . . my husband never forgave me for flaw." She ignored the strangled moan that erupted f deep within him. "I knew you wanted another child so ba and I couldn't bear the thought of disappointing or . . . or seeing your love turn to hate."

Her voice had dropped to a mere whisper as she tasted hot tears that cascaded down her face. "And when I fo out I was pregnant, I . . . I was afraid you'd want the baby and . . . not me."

She bent her head and gave in to the sobs that raked slender body. It was no use, she told herself, pain slashing heart to ribbons. He would never forgive her.

Reese made a terrible sound, one that tore right through her as he closed the gap between them and flung his arms around her, seizing her with all his might, holding her crushed against his chest.

"Oh, Meryl, Meryl," he groaned, "how could you have thought such a thing? Don't you know that if we never had a child, it would have made no difference in my feelings for you?" He eased away from her and with trembling fingers gently lifted her face. "I love you more than life itself, and baby or no baby will never change that, my darling."

"And I love you," she cried, her tears mingling with his as she melted into him, murmuring his name again and again. "So sorry, I'm so sorry."

"Shhh," he murmured against her lips. "No more tears, no more apologies."

"Oh, my love," she said huskily, her mouth greedily finding his, responding to his aching hunger, reveling in his closeness, his own growing need. They clung together, his arms like steel traps around her as they drank from each other's mouths, life-giving serum. She loved the feel of his body, the flesh-and-blood reality of his comfort and compassion. Love as huge and tender as the man, she thought, basking in the warmth of his forgiveness.

Reese pulled back slightly, struggling for breath. "Oh, God, I want you," he whispered, his eyes searching her face in the dimness. "But I'm afraid . . . the baby?" he finished, concerned.

"It's all right . . . I promise. Just love me!" she moaned, reaching wildly for his belt, knowing she had never wanted him so badly.

"Oh, yes!" he sobbed, tearing his clothes from his body.

Caught up in her urgency and his own need, they collapsed as one onto the couch. It was as though they had never been apart as her body fitted itself to the hot demanding thrust of his. His heartbeat was like a small hammer at her breast, and his arms a haven. And even to the last, he was, as always, gentle, loving, when there was no more control, no more separation, only the madness, the flow that carried her to the peak of ecstasy and beyond. . . .

"So this is what your bedroom looks like," Reese said, laughter crinkling the edges of his lips.

Meryl laughed in return, gouging him playfully in the side with her fist. "You couldn't have been too interested in it; it took you long enough to get here." Her eyes were twinkling saucily. And she had never felt happier or more at peace as they lay entwined in the middle of her king-size bed, sated from hours of lovemaking.

He leaned over and circled a rose-tipped nipple with his lips. Ignoring her gasp, he drawled, "Well, you'll have to admit we were having too good a time to move." He shifted slightly and began favoring the other nipple with the same sweet stroke of his tongue.

She sighed and wiggled closer to him, his tender ministrations making her want him again. "I agree, but this is so much more comfortable."

His eyes darkened momentarily. "I didn't hurt . . . ?"

She smiled and shook her head. "No . . . silly, I'm fine." Her eyes dipped to his hand, now spread lovingly over her belly. "And our baby is fine too," she added softly, gazing at him through misty eyes.

"Oh, Meryl," he groaned before molding his lips to hers in a searing kiss. "I'll always be grateful to Morgana."

"Morgana! You mean my sister told you about the baby?" Her expression was incredulous.

He smiled at her astonishment and tapped her on the lips. "Close your mouth," he teased. Then added on a serious note, "Thank God, she did. The day she came to my office, I couldn't have been feeling any lower. As far as I was concerned, my life was over. Without you it meant nothing. Then Morgana told me about the baby, and I was ecstatic. I wanted to shout the good news from the top of the nearest building." He paused, drawing crazy patterns over her breasts and her stomach with a lazy, unerring finger.

Meryl twitched, having difficulty keeping her mind on what he was saying. When he touched her like that, she felt as though her bones were dissolving.

"But when I didn't hear from you, I began to think that maybe Morgana had been mistaken, that you weren't pregnant after all. Then, the longer I thought about it, the madder I got. Finally I couldn't stand it any longer. I had to come to you. If nothing else, to see for myself that you were indeed carrying my child."

"Oh, Reese, do you think that's why Morgana told you?"

"Yes, and I also think it was her way of making amends for hurting us."

Meryl nodded her head in amazement. "And I guess she also figured I'd never have the courage to go to you."

She reached up and locked her arms around his neck, holding him close. "We have so much to thank Morgana for, don't we?"

"I'll always be eternally grateful to her," he said thickly, and laid his lips against the parted sweetness of hers for a timeless moment. Then, raising his head and propping it on his hand, he smiled. "Let's get married tomorrow."

"Well, I guess that's soon enough," she teased, delving her fingers into the nest of hair on his chest before traveling lower to caress his stomach, searching, probing, tantalizing . . .

"If you don't stop that, you wanton hussy," he groaned, "I won't be able to finish what I have to say." But he was not without fault; his own eyes were resting covertly on her breasts and pouting nipples. He swallowed hard. "And what I have to say is damned important, too."

"Go ahead, I'm listening," she said innocently, her hands continuing their questing journey.

He sucked in his breath, but went on, "About your . . . job." For a moment her hands stilled, and she waited, without breathing, for his next words. "I want you to continue with it, if that's what you want. Throughout these months of suffering, I made a vow to myself that if I ever got you back, I'd never be selfish again. I would gladly share you with your work and with your sister." He took a deep shuddering breath. "Whatever makes you happy will make me happy too."

She lifted shimmering eyes to his as her hand came to settle around the iron-hard strength of him. His breath was coming now in short rasps. "My happiness lies with you and our baby," she said softly. "My work will never interfere with either." Suddenly she went loose on the inside as his hand found her hip and he began to ease himself slowly inside her warm moistness. "I've . . . I've finally gotten my priorities straight, my darling," she added, her head bobbing backward like a heavy flower on a weak stem as he penetrated her fully.

"Oh, Meryl, I love you," he rasped, rolling over and taking her with him, rising fully into the tight, heated center of her body. She opened her mouth softly over his, drawing his tongue into her mouth, running her tongue around it lazily.

His gentle hands wrapped around her thighs, holding her, drinking her in, the motion of her body hypnotic.

"You're wonderful," she whispered, quickening her pace.

"So . . . are you," he ground out, going with her rhythm, feeling her heat spread over him like a blanket.

"Sweet man," she sighed at last, going limp against his neck, "I forgot to add that I love you with all my heart."

He held her against him for a long sweet moment. "Oh, my darling," he whispered, "don't you know, you *are* my heart."

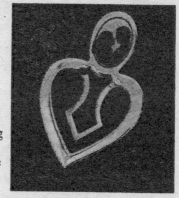

Silhouette
Intimate Moments

more romance, more excitement

—————— $2.25 each ——————

#1 ☐ DREAMS OF EVENING
Kristin James

#2 ☐ ONCE MORE WITH
FEELING
Nora Roberts

#3 ☐ EMERALDS IN THE DARK
Beverly Bird

#4 ☐ SWEETHEART CONTRACT
Pat Wallace

#5 ☐ WIND SONG
Parris Afton Bonds

#6 ☐ ISLAND HERITAGE
Monica Barrie

#7 ☐ A DISTANT CASTLE
Sue Ellen Cole

#8 ☐ LOVE EVERLASTING
Möeth Allison

#9 ☐ SERPENT IN PARADISE
Stephanie James

#10 ☐ A SEASON OF RAINBOWS
Jennifer West

#11 ☐ UNTIL THE END OF TIME
June Trevor

#12 ☐ TONIGHT AND ALWAYS
Nora Roberts

#13 ☐ EDGE OF LOVE
Anna James

#14 ☐ RECKLESS SURRENDER
Jeanne Stephens

#15 ☐ SHADOW DANCE
Lorraine Sellers

#16 ☐ THE PROMISE OF
SUMMER
Barbara Faith

#17 ☐ THE AMBER SKY
Kristin James

#18 ☐ THE DANVERS TOUCH
Elizabeth Lowell

#19 ☐ ANOTHER KIND OF LOVE
Mary Lynn Baxter

#20 ☐ THE GENTLE WINDS
Monica Barrie

#21 ☐ RAVEN'S PREY
Stephanie James

#22 ☐ AGAINST THE RULES
Linda Howard

#23 ☐ THE FIRES OF WINTER
Beverly Bird

#24 ☐ FANTASIES
Pamela Wallace

#25 ☐ THIS MAGIC MOMENT
Nora Roberts

#26 ☐ OLD LOVE, NEW LOVE
Jane Clare

#27 ☐ DIANA'S FOLLY
Jillian Blake

#28 ☐ WALTZ IN SCARLET
Muriel Bradley

#29 ☐ A SECRET SPLENDOR
Erin St. Claire

#30 ☐ RACE AGAINST THE
WIND
Sue Ellen Cole

#31 ☐ STAR SPANGLED DAYS
Jennifer West

#32 ☐ DANGEROUS PARADISE
Joanna Kenyon

#33 ☐ ENDINGS AND
BEGINNINGS
Nora Roberts

#34 ☐ LOVER IN THE ROUGH
Elizabeth Lowell

#35 ☐ MOMENTS HARSH,
MOMENTS GENTLE
Joan Hohl

#36 ☐ DESIGNS
Lynda Trent

#37 ☐ INTERESTED PARTIES
Brooke Hastings

#38 ☐ MEMORIES
Jeanne Stephens

#39 ☐ DARK SIDE OF THE
MOON
Lisa Jackson

Silhouette
Intimate Moments

more romance, more excitement

#40 ☐ A TIME TO SING
Kathryn Belmont

#41 ☐ WIDOW WOMAN
Parris Afton Bonds

#42 ☐ HER OWN RULES
Anna James

#43 ☐ RUSSIAN ROULETTE
Möeth Allison

#44 ☐ LOVE ME BEFORE DAWN
Lindsay McKenna

#45 ☐ MORNING STAR
Kristen James

#46 ☐ CRYSTAL BLUE DESIRE
Monica Barrie

#47 ☐ WIND WHISPERS
Barbara Faith

#48 ☐ CRY FOR THE MOON
Pamela Wallace

#49 ☐ A MATTER OF CHOICE
Nora Roberts

#50 ☐ FORGOTTEN PROMISES
April Thorne

#51 ☐ ALTERNATE
ARRANGEMENTS
Kathryn Thiels

#52 ☐ MEMORIES THAT LINGER
Mary Lynn Baxter

Silhouette Intimate Moments

Coming Next Month

Objections Overruled by Pat Wallace

Kaiti and Tor had once been husband and wife but the time hadn't been right for their love. Now they were together once more—as opposing lawyers in a murder trial. Kaiti knew she could save her client but could she defend her heart against Tor?

Seize The Moment by Ann Major

Threats on her life drove top model Andrea Ford to Mexico, only to find that love had failed her. There she met courageous painter Race Jordan, but did she dare try to find *real* love—and safety—with the brother of the man who had betrayed her?

Power Play by Eve Gladstone

By day Annie and Peter were consultants who fought on opposite sides of the political fence. Peter still worked for the man who had shattered Annie's dreams, but that didn't prevent their after-hours battle for their hearts.

An Old-Fashioned Love by Amanda York

Gwen Halliday was a southern belle dressed in crinolines and Cade Landry was wearing a Union uniform when the Civil War was fought again. But when the game of make-believe was over it was clear that the love of the soldier for his southern lady was no fantasy.